Fleur McDonald has lived and worked on farms for much of her life. After growing up in the small town of Orroroo in South Australia, she went jillarooing, eventually co-owning an 8000-acre property in regional Western Australia.

Fleur likes to write about strong women overcoming adversity, drawing inspiration from her own experiences in rural Australia. She is the bestselling author of *Red Dust*, *Blue Skies*, *Purple Roads*, *Silver Clouds*, *Crimson Dawn*, *Emerald Springs* and *Indigo Storm*. She lives in Esperance with her partner Garry, her two children and a Jack Russell terrier.

FLEUR McDONALD

Sapphire Falls

ARENA
ALLEN&UNWIN

This edition published in 2017
First published in 2016

Arena Books, an imprint of
Allen & Unwin
83 Alexander Street
Crows Nest NSW 2065
Australia
Phone: (61 2) 8425 0100
Email: info@allenandunwin.com
Web: www.allenandunwin.com

Cataloguing-in-Publication details are available
from the National Library of Australia
www.trove.nla.gov.au

ISBN 978 1 76063 096 6

Set by Post Pre-press Group, Australia
Printed and bound in Australia by Pegasus Media & Logistics
20 19 18 17 16 15 14 13 12

The paper in this book is FSC® certified. FSC® promotes environmentally responsible, socially beneficial and economically viable management of the world's forests.

To my beautiful, gentle soul, Garry.
Thank you for your understanding, your calmness
amid my chaos, and for the way you love me.

Prologue

Charlie could feel the mist settle on his shoulders. It was coming directly from the nearby creek and it sent a chill down his spine. As he held onto the back of the ute to pull himself up, his fingers touched the cold dew and immediately his hands were wet.

He glanced out into the darkness. There wasn't much to see—the sky was covered with thick, grey clouds that had dumped an inch of rain earlier in the day. It was hard to make out even the outline of the shed, let alone the road.

Maybe this wasn't such a good idea.

He slotted the spotlight into the frame, which was bolted to the railing on the top of his ute, and tightened it, before flicking the switch to make sure it was connected.

Instantly, the yard was flooded with a brilliant white light and Charlie squinted against the glare before quickly turning it off again.

Raucous laughter rang out and he could hear the footfalls

of his two companions. One of them must have tripped because he heard a scatter of stones, then an expletive.

'Oi! Turn it back on again!' Eddie yelled. 'We're not bats, you know.'

'Can't see in the dark,' the other confirmed in a loud voice.

Charlie tried, but this time nothing happened. There was a silence followed by the sound of splashing water. 'Ah, shit. I've just walked into a dirty great puddle. Turn the bloody light on would you, Charlie?'

'Sorry, mate,' he answered, getting down from the tray of the ute. 'Terminals must have come loose. The light isn't switching on. Stay put.'

He didn't expect they would stay in one spot. He could hear them walking towards him. The clinking noise Eddie made as he walked gave them away: the .303 bullets he kept in his pocket always made that jangling noise.

Reaching for the button on his headlight, he pushed it and was rewarded as a bright glow showed him the way to the engine. He wiggled the alligator clips to get a better connection and light once again flooded the yard, chasing away the late-night darkness. It was close to ten pm.

'There we go,' Geoff said as both he and Eddie stopped next to Charlie. 'Right to go?'

Charlie looked up at them and reversed out from underneath the bonnet. Both were holding rifles tucked under their arms, their eyes shaded by hats, even though it was dark. Driza-Bones flapped around their ankles. It was almost like they wore a uniform.

'I don't know, fellas,' he said, scratching his head. 'Reckon it's a bit wet and slippery, don't you?' It was a half-hearted question, for even though he felt apprehensive, he was keen to get this bastard of a wild dog.

The mongrel thing had been stalking sheep within a fifty-kilometre radius for the past three months and all the farmers within the area had lost sheep as a result of its attacks.

'I'll drive,' Geoff said, ignoring his hesitation.

Charlie sighed and an extra cold blast of wind blew across the yard. Cold fronts were unusual at this time of year, but this one had swept across the peninsula and over the ranges, bringing icy temperatures and chilly winds. Like a forewarning of the winter.

Still, the coolness gave him more opportunities to cuddle his wife. That's where he'd much rather be at the moment. Snuggled up to Fiona inside, next to the roaring fire. Repeating last night's lovemaking. He felt himself begin to harden as he remembered the desire in her eyes flickering in the firelight. The way she had trailed her lips down his chest, and over his arms and stomach. The way her blonde hair had fluttered across his skin.

He shook his head to clear it. He needed to concentrate on what had to be done tonight. 'We'll pick up Leigh on the way,' he finally said as he swung himself up onto the back of the ute. 'His meeting finished early.'

ഗ

Half an hour later, Charlie was standing between Leigh and Eddie, looking through the sites of his gun and trying to work out if the glowing red eyes belonged to a fox or a wild dog. He was pretty sure it was a fox.

He tapped lightly on the cabin roof to indicate he had a clear shot and for Geoff to stop.

Eddie shifted the spotlight briefly and Charlie lost the eyes. He drew in a measured breath as the light picked them up again.

Squinting slightly, he squeezed the trigger. A deafening shot rang out, quickly followed by the thump of a bullet hitting a body. Leigh thumped his arm in a congratulatory gesture and Eddie let out a whoop.

'One less of the bastards,' he said excitedly.

'Bloody good shot!' Geoff stuck his head out the window as he called up to them.

Charlie inserted another bullet into the barrel and clicked it shut. 'Check him out, ay?' he called back, grabbing hold of the rail as Geoff launched forward, quickly picking up speed.

Suddenly Charlie couldn't make sense of the noise—a scraping sound, the ripping of metal. All too quickly he realised he was falling . . . slamming against Leigh.

He reached out for the railing of the ute but the force of the tipping vehicle snatched it away.

Letting out a yell, he propelled himself forward, desperate to hold on to something, to steady himself from going over the side.

The ute teetered on two wheels before landing heavily on its side.

A flash of fire and a gunshot.

A sickening thud echoed through the night.

Charlie felt something warm squirt all over him.

'What the fuck!' he screamed in panic as Eddie fell heavily onto him. Charlie smacked into Leigh and together they tumbled from the ute, landing in a heap on top of one another.

He heard the *oomph* of air leave one of his mates, but he couldn't be sure who it was.

Everything was a mass of screams and shouts. Loud engine and then lights. Slamming doors, as Geoff attempted to get out of the ute.

Charlie tried to get up, but he was pinned to the ground by . . . Eddie? Was it Eddie? He couldn't see!

'Fuck. Oh my God, are you serious? Eddie? Eddie!'

Charlie knew from Geoff's high-pitched scream that something was seriously wrong.

There was the flash of a spotlight in his eyes and then the weight was lifted from his body.

'Call an ambulance!' cried Geoff.

Now he was free, Charlie shot to his feet and looked around. He needed to get his bearings—he needed to know what was wrong.

Eddie was lying on the ground, Geoff and Leigh bent over him.

Charlie felt for his mobile phone. His pocket was empty.

'Shit.' He looked around, hoping to see it. His brain kicked into gear and he ran to the ute. Reaching inside, he grabbed the mic and called: 'Help! Can anyone hear me? We need an ambulance.'

All Charlie could hear was silence punctuated by the low static from the radio and panicked voices coming from behind him. 'Anyone? We need help!'

Leigh appeared at his shoulder. 'Get through?'

'Nothing. Where's your phone? I've lost mine.' He jiggled up and down on the spot, desperate to do something.

Leigh reached inside his jacket pocket and looked down at the screen in his headlight.

'No range. I'll run back to your house for help. Help Geoff.'

Shedding his heavy jacket, Leigh started to run, stumbling over the rocks. He was swallowed up by darkness.

Rapidly, Charlie moved towards Eddie and Geoff.

'My turn,' Charlie edged Geoff out of the way and placed his hands on Eddie's upper body, applying pressure to his chest and feeling the blood, warm on his hands. He tried not to vomit.

It seemed like an eternity before he heard the ambulance sirens. Heard the comforting tones of the paramedics. Then a blanket was placed around his shoulders and someone asked if he was hurt.

He was shaking badly, but he didn't think he was. Charlie couldn't form the words to answer them.

Two other paramedics loaded Eddie into the back of the ambulance and drove quickly away.

As if from underwater, Charlie heard the sirens start and saw the flashing lights illuminate the paddock.

In the distance he thought he heard the wild dog howl.

Chapter 1

Three months later . . .

Fiona Forrest sat next to her dead husband's coffin, staring at it dully. Music played softly in the background and she could smell the roses that filled two urns on stands nearby.

The church felt exactly like she did. Cold and empty.

Her hands gripped the handles of the casket, hanging on for dear life. In an hour she would have to leave Charlie and let his parents and everyone else have their moment to grieve for him. It made her want to rip open the lid and demand that he come back.

Demand that he get up out of there and come back to her. To hug her, to love her. To be there for the rest of his family and friends. For her!

How dare he leave her like this? How could he be such a coward?

Rage coursed through her like a wave of hot lava.

But how could she think like that? she berated herself. Of all people, she, Charlie's wife, had known how *desperate* he'd felt. How he'd *fought* to cope with the guilt that had been gnawing away at him. The horror had kept playing over and over and over in his head; it didn't matter if his eyes were open or shut, Fiona knew that memories of that night would never leave him, the moment when he'd been told Eddie couldn't be saved and that it had been his gun that had fired the fatal shot.

She could only hope that his tormented mind was now at peace.

'Charlie,' she whispered, resting her hand on the lid of the casket. Fiona knew she had been powerless to help him, but she would have given anything to have been able to ease his pain!

It had made her feel so *helpless*.

Fiona felt a hand on her shoulder. She pulled her head to the side to release her long blonde hair from Leigh's touch but her blue eyes continued to stare at the coffin.

Briefly she wondered why she couldn't cry. She hadn't yet. Not even in that hideous moment when Leigh had knocked on her door, tears coursing down his cheeks, his chest heaving.

Of course, the minute she'd seen him, Fiona had known what had happened. She'd almost been expecting it.

All she could do was open her mouth and say, 'No.' So quietly she wasn't sure Leigh had heard her above his own sobs.

Of course, her low plea hadn't changed anything. She'd made Leigh take her to where he'd found Charlie.

'No, Fee,' he'd implored. 'You don't need to see.'

He hadn't understood that she *did*. Of course she had to see her Charlie. How else could she believe he had really gone, had really left her?

Now that sight was something she would have to live with, the same way Charlie had been besieged by his own memories and thoughts.

In a weird, roundabout way, with all that had happened, now it was she who was left with the horror, not Charlie.

The hand left her shoulder and Leigh squatted down next to her.

She turned slightly and out of the corner of her eye saw his familiar bearded face and vivid blue eyes. He was staring at her, full of sympathy. Fiona didn't say anything or acknowledge him. They were both grieving and she thought they could take comfort in each other's presence without words.

'I'm sorry, Fee,' Leigh finally said, his voice a strangled whisper.

'What for?' she asked, tearing her eyes away from Charlie's resting place.

'I don't know,' he shrugged. 'Got to say something—' He broke off.

'No, you don't. There's nothing to say. Just be here.'

Fiona saw he was swallowing hard so as not to cry.

Her eyes flew back to Charlie's coffin of their own accord. She heard Leigh clear his throat and take a deep breath.

It would be over soon, this horrible, horrible day, and they would be able to start moving on. She never thought she'd have to say that at thirty-two. Move on. From her husband's death. She was a widow.

A widow.

'I keep thinking I'm going to get a text from him, tell us we've made a mistake and he's coming back.'

Fiona turned back to Leigh. 'What?'

'You know, those funny one-liner texts that would have us laughing for hours? "*Thought you could get rid of me? Try again!*" Just him being . . .' His voice faded away. He brought out a handkerchief and wiped his nose.

'Being Charlie,' Fiona finished for him.

Leigh cleared his throat again, nodding. 'Being Charlie. That's it.'

Swallowing, she knew she couldn't say anything, that there were too many raw emotions. Too much anger, sadness and despair rolled into one.

'I'll help you, I promise, Fee. I'll help with the farm. We all will.'

'No!' The word burst from her and she stood up to face him. She ignored his look of surprise. 'Not now, Leigh. Not today. I know your intentions are good, but just not today. Let me bury my husband. The bloody farm will look after itself for a few days.' She turned and walked away.

ᔓ

Twirling the glass of wine between her fingers, Fiona stared into the fire. It was all she seemed to do since Charlie's death—stare.

What a hell of a day, she thought as the flames danced around the few thin logs she'd thrown on. The wood box was nearly empty. *I must tell Charlie we need to cut some more* . . . The thought fizzled as quickly as it had appeared and an awful hollow feeling spread through her.

'Do you need anything, love?' her mother asked, sticking her head into the lounge room.

'No thanks, Mum,' she managed to answer, trying to ignore her feelings. *Just Charlie.*

'Jo's just sent a text to say she's nearly here.'

'Okay.'

'William and Felicity are devastated they couldn't be here for you. They sent me another text this afternoon, after the funeral, to see how you were.'

'It's too far to fly back from the US, Mum. I understand that.'

'Your husband has just committed suicide and your brother should be here for you,' Carly huffed.

Fiona clenched her jaw, desperate to yell at her. It didn't matter that her brother and sister-in-law weren't with her. It didn't matter that Jo was almost here. Couldn't her mum see that? All that mattered was that her beautiful man, her Charlie, was gone. Unbidden, an image of Charlie lying in the coffin came to her. Just before the funeral director had closed the lid of Charlie's coffin, Fiona had taken one last look at him. When she'd touched him, the iciness of his hands had shocked her. For some silly reason, she thought he'd still be warm—he looked like he should be. She blinked.

Instead she said, 'Funnily enough, Mum, I'm aware of the situation.'

The all too familiar queasy sensation started in her stomach again. It seemed to get worse during times of great pressure, but it had been ever present since the accident, often making her vomit.

Carly kept hovering at the door and Fiona expected her to say something like 'Chin up', but thankfully she didn't. She just sighed and after a while left the room.

Fiona drew her legs up and hugged them to her chest. Then she rested her chin against her knees and looked about.

The room was full of flowers and hampers. Charlie's sister, who lived interstate, had sent a huge bouquet with a sympathy card. Jo had placed them on the mantelpiece. Fiona thought how empty the gesture was—Charlie hadn't spoken to his sister in years. A repercussion of the family rift that Fiona had never understood. It had been the same with Charlie's parents at the funeral. They had been polite and distant. His mother didn't even shed a tear. How incredibly sad that a son could die without his parents seeming to care. She felt they were there to keep up appearances and nothing else.

The rest of the community were devastated, that was clear. There had been a constant stream of visitors bringing food, and offers of help.

In spite of the flowers and cards, however, the room was still the same as it had been before.

But how could it be? It didn't feel the same.

Still, there was the *Stock Journal* lying beside Charlie's chair, where he had been flicking through it last. Fiona knew he hadn't been reading it—he hadn't been able to concentrate. He'd just been going through the motions.

The red shag rug that covered the grotty carpet was still the same and the pictures that hung on the wall hadn't moved. How would she feel when something *did* change and she couldn't tell him about it or show him? If a sheep in the paddock died, or if she sent off a truckload of lambs. As the crops grew a bit more since he had last seen them . . . All of that was going to happen.

The last two weeks seemed so surreal. Until the accident,

they had both been so happy. Satisfied in every way. Charlie was her best friend and she was his.

They had done everything together since they had first met six years ago. An unexpected flat tyre on the highway between Adelaide and Port Wakefield had seen Charlie stop to help her.

Fiona had been standoffish with him as he'd changed it for her; she wasn't sure how else to be. She'd been grateful for his help, but he was a complete stranger and it had made her extremely nervous on one level, despite how nice and trustworthy he'd seemed. Who still did that these days? Most people were too wary of strangers to offer random assistance. The backpacker murders had seen to that.

On the other hand, she'd been oddly attracted to the sparkle in his brown eyes, and his big smile. She'd pretended not to watch the muscles in his arms flex while he pumped the jack and tightened the nuts. He was tall—he'd towered over her by a good foot—and beefy. He was strong and dependable. Fiona could just tell.

She'd never been one to take risks, so when he'd shyly asked for her phone number she'd felt a little scared and refused. But she'd given him her name and told him if he tried hard enough he should be able to find her.

And he had.

She thought back to Leigh's words at the funeral, anger beginning to creep over her. *Being Charlie.*

Well, to her, 'Being Charlie' seemed pretty bloody selfish at the moment. How could he have done this to her? To all of them?

She wished the boys had never gone chasing the wild dog. Still, her wishing couldn't change anything.

Fiona still didn't quite understand what had happened but she was sure the police were working on it.

Geoff had told her the ute had hit a huge rut, then a pile of stones, and flung them all sideways. Because it was wet and slippery, it had kept sliding, despite his best efforts, until finally it had tipped over. Somehow, in the confusion, Charlie's gun had discharged, hitting Eddie in the chest as they had tumbled together to the ground. From then on nothing had been the same.

It wasn't only Charlie who had changed. All of them had. Survivor's guilt, the counsellor had called it. The three men had gone to a therapist for help. Together at first, then one by one. Leigh had only recently stopped, but Geoff was still going.

It obviously hadn't helped Charlie. He'd been too kind, too gentle to be able to deal with taking another man's life, even if it had been an accident.

'I would have helped him,' Fiona muttered against her jeans. 'I wanted to *help* him.'

She closed her eyes but then made herself open them as a vision of Charlie in their car came to her. He'd looked like he was sleeping. Beside him had been a bottle of scotch. It was half empty and the glass, which he must have dropped into his lap as he'd fallen into unconsciousness, still had some liquid left in it.

Picking up her wineglass and the bottle, she went into her bedroom and lay on the bed.

Her mother had suggested she sleep in one of the spare rooms with her, in case Fiona hadn't wanted to be in the bedroom she'd shared with Charlie. But Fiona couldn't bear to be away from him. She could still smell his scent on the sheets. See the dent where his head had lain on the pillow.

Yesterday, when she'd looked closely, she'd even found some of his hair on it.

Taking another sip of wine, she grabbed the pillow, hugged it to her and picked up the photo, which was sitting on her bedside table. She had slept with her arms wrapped around it every night since Charlie had killed himself, pretending it was him.

Jo, her best friend, had taken it at the Christmas drinks party their little community had held. Charlie had his arm around her shoulders, looking down at her. She'd been laughing up at him. It was her favourite photo of them—even more so than their wedding photos. Jo had somehow managed to catch a moment of pure love between them and it was obvious to everyone who saw it.

They were so different to each other in looks and it really stood out in photos. Fiona was so slight, Charlie so solid. She remembered saying to him that there was so much of him to love and how much she adored that.

She put the photo down and looked at the condolence book on the bedside table. The funeral director had handed it to her as she left the wake earlier in the day. Pulling it to her, she opened the book and saw lines and lines of different handwriting.

As she started to read, her breath caught in her throat. She'd known Charlie was popular in their small community, but these words showed just how popular.

We will mourn Charlie's passing, right alongside you. He was a truly special man. Gail and Dan Tupper.

We know we can't make your pain ease, Fiona, but we are right here if you need anything. Kate and Paul Carter.

One of life's gentlemen. Sylvia Jones had large, scrawly writing.

Will always remember his loud laugh and huge smile. Mark Simmons, their stock agent. *Please call me if there is anything I can do.*

Top bloke. Shit of a way to go. We'll miss ya, big fella. The Footy Club boys.

Preg-scanning on Charona won't be the same. Let me know if I can help out in anyway. Rob Cameron.

The Footy Club boys had formed a guard of honour as the coffin had been taken out to the hearse. Mark, Leigh and Geoff, along with Charlie's Uncle Raymond, had been the pallbearers. The four of them had been so kind and gentle with her.

Seeing Rob's comment, she smiled. It had particular meaning. The local vet had arrived early in the morning for a day of preg-scanning. Mark was due later in the day to have a look at the dry ewes who would be sold. The ewes had been running really well and everything seemed to be going smoothly . . . But the yards were dusty and no one had seen the gate separating the two mobs come open.

By the time they'd worked out what was going on, the three hundred ewes were boxed up and they had to start all over again.

Rob had smiled in a good-humoured way and not even charged for the extra scanning. Charlie hadn't been so happy—in fact he'd been downright angry. A silly, simple mistake like that was enough to test any man's patience. Especially since it had been his decision not to mark the dry ewes.

By the end of the day, when Mark had arrived, there was a pen of empty ewes; the pregnant ones were back in the paddock. Charlie decided it was time for a drink and no one contradicted him. A few beers later, between Rob and Mark they'd jostled him out of his bad mood and they were all laughing about the muck-up.

The door creaked open and Fiona looked up, hoping it wasn't Carly again.

'Hi there,' Jo said with a small smile. 'I brought more wine.' She held up a bottle.

'I'm not sure I should drink any more,' Fiona answered, waving at her empty glass. 'I've given it a fairly good hammering and I've been so sick in the mornings. It makes me feel awful.'

'Doesn't the oblivion help?' Jo came over and sat on the edge of the bed. 'Reckon you're probably entitled to a bit of that. For a while anyway.'

'To a point, but it's all still there the next day, isn't it? Doesn't go away. The only time I don't have to think about it is when I'm asleep.'

Jo put down the bottle.

'I've got to be honest, I don't know what to say or do, Fee.' She sighed as she put her arm around Fiona.

Fiona leaned her head against her friend's shoulder. 'Neither do I.'

Chapter 2

Fiona knew Jo was knocking on the bathroom door, but she couldn't get off the floor to answer it.

Another wave of nausea hit her and she vomited into the toilet bowl.

Groaning, she let her head fall forward and blindly felt for the toilet paper to wipe her mouth.

'Are you alright?' Jo called through the door.

'No. I think I'm going to die,' Fiona mumbled. Her eyes still shut, she pushed her hair back from her forehead. She was fed up with this! She'd felt queasy for a while now, all day, every day. Fiona had put it down to being so worried about Charlie, and the extra wine she'd been drinking. Once he'd died, things had got so much worse and the nausea had too. She tried to remember how much she'd had to drink last night. Three glasses? Four? Was that enough to make her this sick?

'Unlock the door!'

Fiona tried to move and was rewarded when she managed to stand up and reach the lock.

Jo burst in and Fiona could see her mother hovering in the background. She didn't have time to say anything before another wave of sickness hit her and she was forced to turn back to the toilet and vomit bile.

'I didn't think I had that much to drink last night,' she gasped, eyes watering, finally voicing what she'd been thinking.

'This isn't alcohol,' Carly said knowingly from the passageway. 'Have you got a headache?'

'No.'

'Stress, anxiety,' her mother said in a firm voice. 'The body reacts strangely to trauma. You've had a bit of it.'

'Exactly.' Jo agreed with Carly in a tone that didn't invite argument. 'Come on, we need to get you to the doctor.'

'I need to stay near the toilet.'

'We've got a bucket. Come on. Into the car with you.'

Moments later, Fiona managed to stagger to the car at the front door and climb into the back seat. 'I want to die.'

Carly glanced at her in the rear-vision mirror, the dread plain in her eyes. 'That is not even funny, Fiona. Whatever the reason for you feeling like this, we'll get to the bottom of it. You won't have to feel like this for long.'

Fiona closed her eyes as Jo put the car into gear and drove towards Booleroo Centre.

'My daughter needs to see the doctor,' Carly said as they walked into the surgery.

She was feeling so ill that Fiona almost didn't catch the enquiring looks from the other patients. Clutching the bucket, she tried to make herself as inconspicuous as possible.

'We're fully booked,' Janey, the receptionist, responded. 'Would tomorrow be okay?'

'No,' Carly said in a flat tone that invited no argument. 'No, tomorrow won't do. If you don't get her in to see Scott next, I'll personally go into his office and demand it.'

Janey stared at Carly, her jaw working overtime.

Jo pushed her way to the front. 'She really needs to see Scott,' she added in a quieter tone. 'She's in a bad way and after everything she's been through . . .'

The waiting room was so quiet, they could hear the murmur of voices and a short laugh from Scott coming through the door.

The receptionist sniffed and looked at the computer screen. 'Mrs Reynolds, do you mind if Mrs Forrest slips in before you? I *hope* it won't take long.' The sarcasm in her voice left Fiona momentarily bewildered. Why was this woman being so awful?

'Of course not. Let her go in. I don't mind.' The elderly lady pushed her glasses back up her nose and peered at Fiona.

She wanted the floor to swallow her up, but she was racked by another wave of nausea. Holding up the bucket, she rushed outside and bent over, dry retching.

'Fiona!'

Barely able to move, she looked over and saw Scott standing in the doorway. He walked over to her and helped her back into his office.

ᔕ

Fiona stared at the doctor, not believing what he had just said.

'You can't be serious?'

Scott smiled ruefully. 'I am. See for yourself.'

She reached out and took the stick he was pointing in her direction.

Two blue lines.

Two. Blue. Lines.

She started to shake and her hands flew to her stomach. Her mouth opened but nothing came out, then the tears started. Just like that. After weeks of being so completely frozen, tears began rolling down her cheeks.

'He didn't know,' she whispered as she closed her eyes. 'How unbearably cruel.'

'I really believe that nature has a way of giving us what we need, when we need it, Fiona. This baby is going to be a blessing for you and all those who love you. Something else to think about.'

'I don't want to think about anything else!' she cried. She got up and crossed the room, unable to stay still. 'I want to think about him all the time. I *need* to.'

Scott let her talk.

'What if I forget something about him? Something really important? Like the colour of his eyes or the way his voice sounded?' Her breath caught and she angrily brushed away tears again. Finally, she sat down, exhausted by her outburst. By this whole sorry business.

She looked down at her hands and twisted her rings. 'Do you think he knows?' she asked softly.

'Oh, Fee, who knows?' Scott sighed, the look in his eyes kind but sad. 'Doesn't it depend on what you believe?' He paused. 'You won't forget him,' he said with conviction. He gently took Fiona's hands in his. 'You won't. You've got too many reasons to remember everything. Think about what you can tell this little one when he or she's a bit older. Maybe write things down as they come to you. Keeping a diary is a good kind of therapy.

'But you won't ever forget the important things—they're in here.' He tapped his chest. 'Look, I just know this pregnancy is a good thing. It's going to be hard, traumatic and sad and joyful all rolled up into one, but this baby? It's a beautiful thing.' Scott turned businesslike. 'Now, you need to get an ultrasound so we can check your due date. I'd like you to start taking folic acid and you'll need to make another appointment. One of the things we keep an eye on during pregnancy is blood pressure and weight. I'll get you to come in once a month or so, okay?'

Fiona nodded.

'I also want you to go to the hospital—I'll ring them and organise it. We need to get some fluids into you by drip, but you can head home as soon as you've had a couple of bags. You're pretty dehydrated. We'll have to keep an eye on the morning sickness. Sounds like you've had it quite bad.'

'I thought it was the wine,' Fiona said, looking at the floor. Dread seeped through her. What if, after everything, the baby was born with a disability she'd caused?

'Wine?'

'A coping mechanism,' she answered, embarrassed. 'Will it have hurt the baby?'

'Not surprising, I'm sure you've needed something to help you forget at times. Look, until now, you've not known. At this early stage, it shouldn't. It's binge and prolonged drinking throughout a pregnancy that cause problems. We can do some tests if you're concerned, but I certainly would advise you to stop now.'

Fiona nodded, ducking her head to hide the flush that stained her cheeks. Having to drink to cope, then being found out like this, made her feel so weak.

'I'll get the nurses to take some bloods, too. Okay, then.' He stood and held the door open for her. 'Remember, Fee, this will be a good thing. Hang in there.'

ග

As she walked out into the waiting room, Fiona decided Scott was wrong. There was no way a baby could be a good thing. She was by herself.

She was grieving; had a farm to run. Charlie needed to be here for this.

They hadn't even intended to have a baby yet. How it had happened, she couldn't be certain, although now that she thought about it, she was pretty sure it had happened the night before the accident. The night in front of the fire.

Charlie had suggested they wait another year. The marriage would have been five years old then, and he had been hoping everything would be financially secure. The crop this year was going to be a burster, he'd told her, although Fiona knew there was no way he could confidently say that. There were too many months to go before harvest. Anything could happen in that time. A hail storm, a drought, a locust plague—the list went on.

It was the sheep that were going to make them the money, Fiona had teased more than once. He was the cropping man and she the sheep lady. Or rather, he *had been* the cropping man, she corrected herself on a wave of melancholy. They had always had competitions about which enterprise was the better one, which would make the most money, even though they knew that both were integral to their operation. It had been a long-standing joke between them.

With growing wistfulness, she began to comprehend that there was a piece of Charlie growing within her. And just like Scott had said, there were a million different emotions running through her. She hoped it was a boy. Maybe he would look and act like Charlie. She imagined a little boy wearing her favourite expression of her husband's. His brow crinkling as he looked at her.

Charlie's brown eyes staring solemnly at her. An old soul in a young body.

She gasped as a shaft of pain pierced her heart. Grief hit her like a tidal wave. Charlie would never know his own son.

She put her hand up against the wall to steady herself as her vision blurred, her heart beating so fast it was hard to catch her breath.

'Fee?' Scott had opened his door to fetch the next patient and quickly grabbed her before she fell. He got her back inside his office and sat her in the chair.

'Breathe slowly,' he instructed. 'In,' he stretched the word. 'Ouuuuttt. In, ouuuutttt. That's right.'

Slowly her vision started to clear and her heart began to slow.

'Sorry,' she mumbled.

'That's a panic attack,' Scott said, ignoring her apology. 'Have you had one before?'

'No, I don't think so.'

'I don't find this at all unusual after everything you've been through.' He paused. 'Look, Fee, I can't give you any medication to help with this type of problem because you're pregnant and, honestly, talking and working through your emotions is the best way to deal with grief, not tablets. I'll give you the number of the psychologist who visits here monthly. Go and see her—you'll be surprised at how effective it is.' He pulled out a piece of paper and wrote on it. 'Talking is important,' Scott repeated. 'She can give you some strategies to deal with all the emotions you're feeling right now. You've got so much going on.'

He looked at her with compassionate eyes, and at the sound of his sympathetic tone, Fiona felt herself well up again. She tried to shake it off. She would be strong for Charlie. For this new life growing inside her.

There was no other choice; this was how it was going to be.

Fiona accepted the piece of paper he held out. Scott helped her up and escorted her into the waiting room, where Jo and Carly were waiting. She could feel people staring at her, watching her every move. She imagined them gossiping about her later. Telling their friends what they'd seen. She could almost hear the conversations in her head—God, she'd heard similar ones in the deli and at the hairdressers. It made her want to scream.

'Let's get out of here,' she said to her mother. Jo and Carly closed in around her.

'What did the doctor say?' Carly asked as soon as they were settled in the car.

Fiona hesitated. She wasn't sure she was ready to share her news yet. Not with all these emotions running around inside her.

'Fee?'

Jo was leaning over the passenger seat and looking at her intently. In that instant Fiona knew there was no point in hiding anything. They would work it out very quickly. Plus, she needed to go to the hospital.

Looking out the window, she saw heavy grey clouds gathered on the tops of the hills that surrounded the town. Like cotton wool, they lay across the peaks, hiding the trees that grew there. Raindrops started to ping on the roof of the car and run down the windows. She wished Charlie was there to see it. He had always loved the rain.

'I'm pregnant,' she said.

Carly inhaled sharply and covered her mouth.

Jo sat upright and became very still, staring at her, before reaching out and holding Fiona's hands in hers.

'I don't know what to say.'

Fiona gave her a watery smile. 'Didn't we have this conversation last night? Me either.' She looked across at Carly. 'You're going to be a grandma, Mum.'

Clearly overwhelmed with emotion, Carly just stared at her daughter in the rear-view mirror. Fiona wasn't sure whether to take that as a good or a bad sign.

The rain became heavier and it wouldn't have mattered if anyone in the car was speaking or not; they wouldn't have been able to hear.

Finally, Carly put the keys in the ignition and drove them all to the hospital.

ᘓ

Fiona slipped out of the house and made a beeline for the rain gauge to measure how much had fallen in the hours they'd been out.

It had been getting a bit dry in the last few weeks and the crops needed the moisture. Ten millimetres would be just about perfect.

She snuggled further into her jacket against the bitter winds that were blowing from the south. The dark clouds above were scurrying, doing their best to keep up with the wind, while the sun was hovering on top of the hills, about to set. Shadowy clouds crossing the sky made it seem darker than usual for that time of the evening.

The gum trees she and Charlie had planted together along the driveway were bending over, leaves streaming from their branches.

Sick of her hair whipping across her face, she pulled it back into a ponytail and fastened it with a hair band she kept on her wrist.

Looking across the land, scenes from her life kept flashing before her. Everywhere she looked she could see Charlie.

He was in the machinery shed, grinning from underneath the tractor as he greased it. He was in the ute, out in the paddock or walking across the crops as they pushed their way through the soil; on his hands and knees, checking the precious seedlings for insects or diseases. He was there in the sheep yards, pushing his hat back and wiping sweat away from his brow, teasing her.

Oh and then . . . That time in the shearing shed. Fiona pressed her hands hard into her chest to try to stop her heart from physically hurting.

They'd just finished crutching lambs to send to the abattoirs and Taylor Swift came on the radio. Moving in time to 'Style', Charlie had given her an impromptu striptease, before pulling her into his arms and whispering: '*You and me, babe, I promise you, we won't go out of style. It'll always be us.*'

They had tumbled onto some empty wool packs and made love as the sun was sinking below the horizon, the lambs' hooves clicking on the grating and the tin roof creaking above them.

So many memories. So many good times. And now he was gone.

She wanted to cry but something didn't let her. Numbness? Detachment? Disbelief? Absolutely. And more.

With shaking hands she pulled off the rain-gauge lid and reached inside. There was a perfect ten millimetres of water.

She raised her face heavenward and let the gentle spit of rain, which had just started, fall on her. 'Thank you,' she whispered, needing to believe that Charlie had sent it.

Turning away, she ran towards the house, not wanting to be outside after dark. She found she was getting scared at night without Charlie lying alongside her in bed.

As the rain started again, in earnest, her foot hit the verandah and she raced inside, stopping only to throw one more glance across the land.

Now, she had to check every room and convince herself there was no one else in the house—her over-active imagination, she knew, but she couldn't help herself.

Satisfied she was on her own, she dragged a chair across the front door and jammed it under the handle. That security would have to suffice until she could find someone to put some locks on the door.

Chapter 3

'Push 'em up, push 'em up!' Fiona yelled to the dog at the front of the race. 'Get in there!'

Obediently, Meita jumped over the yard railing and plunged in among the lambs and under their bellies. Fiona could hear her muffled barks as she made her way towards the end of the race, making them pack up against one another. A few minutes later she appeared from under the last lamb, her tongue hanging out, the grin on her face wide.

'Speak up,' Fiona commanded, holding on tight to the gate and pushing it against the rump of the last lamb. 'Hey! Hey, get in there!' She let the gate rest against her thighs and used her hands to twist the stub of its tail. After a heavy shove, she chained the gate shut.

'Good girl, Meita,' she said, bending down to pat the dog, who now sat at her feet. 'Good to go, Mark!' She gave the thumbs-up sign to the stock agent standing at the front of the race.

He opened the gate into the weighing crate and the first lamb ran in. Fiona watched with relief as she saw Mark run a blue rattle mark down its back, let it out, then repeat it on the next lamb.

She looked around and nodded to herself. It was a lovely time of year—the country was green and even the yards, which were covered in small purple stones, were a pleasure to work in—there wasn't any dust. Although she was always careful where she put her feet—the stones had caused her to roll her ankle on more than one occasion.

Charona was in the southern Flinders Ranges area, sandwiched between Booleroo Centre and Melrose. The country was undulating and deep creeks ran around the bases of hills as well as through them. From where she stood in the yards, she could see the tree-covered mountain of Mount Remarkable. In a good rainfall year, when you were close enough to the creeks, you could hear the trickle of little waterfalls as they ran over the moss-covered rocks around the thick gum-tree trunks. Every waterfall Fiona saw she called Sapphire Falls—it sounded strange, she knew, but it didn't matter if it was only an inch or two feet high. It was still a waterfall and she loved it. This country could be so dry and harsh. A waterfall made her feel like she was on holidays, somewhere lush and tropical. As a kid, she'd spent hours on the edges of Rocky River, floating leaves and sticks down it. She'd always thought the sun on the water had looked like diamonds sparkling, but diamonds were clear. The water there was blue. Like sapphires.

During summer, it wasn't anywhere near as pleasant. Days of forty degrees in a row and shimmering heat mirages over dry and dusty country with no feed. She was sure this country grew stones. When they hand-picked them every year, they never seemed to get them all. She'd lost count of the number of times she and Charlie had had to clear the paddocks of stones before seeding season. But that was part of living in this country and she loved it regardless.

Now, however, casting her eye over the lambs, she smiled. They were good—as good as the ones she and Charlie had ever produced. Heaving herself over the rail, she walked towards the front, pushing the lambs as she went.

Her slowly growing belly brushed on the rails.

'Sorry, Mark, I'm a bit slow!'

'You look like you're doing pretty well to me,' he answered. 'What are they averaging?'

They talked figures for a while, but the noise from the lambs separated from their mothers, in addition to the clanging of the gates and the barking from Meita, made it almost impossible to hear.

To Fiona, the monotony of the pushing, weighing and letting out was soothing. She'd done this thousands of times and here, in the yards, surrounded by the ewes, lambs and her dog, she felt calm and peaceful. Even though her heart still ached and fear rolled around in her stomach every time she thought about the bank.

Despite all of this, how could she not enjoy the sun shining after so many grey days? She'd begun to hate the dark, overcast days with a passion. It didn't matter that they brought life-giving rain and the promise of a bumper season. The darkness of them mirrored her mood.

When the sun shone, it lifted her. The glistening raindrops on green grass, which shimmered in the sunlight, made her happy. As did watching the sheep graze on the hilly paddocks. The green grass screamed of positive things.

The gently undulating country, dotted with gum trees and crisscrossed with minor creeks, had been her home since she had left the small country town of Laura and moved to Charona with Charlie.

In one way it had been hard to leave her mum; in another it had been easy. After all, Carly had been her rock ever since her dad had walked out on them when she was thirteen. It had been their mum who had held the family together, working two jobs so she could keep both William and Fiona at boarding school. It had come at a cost though—her once sweet, tender mother had become overbearing and brittle. Frightened of losing her children as well as her husband, she began to force herself into their lives and business. She hadn't been at all happy when Fiona had announced her intention to move to Charona with Charlie.

Fiona stood fast, though, despite her mother's vocal reservations, and gave up her receptionist job at the Laura council office to be with Charlie. It hadn't been a hardship—she hadn't really enjoyed the job and, as much as she loved Carly, she loved Charlie too.

Before Charlie, all she'd ever done on the land was drive through it to get to other towns. The land, she'd discovered, was a living, breathing being and she had fallen in love with it, the stock and the lifestyle almost straightaway.

She learnt quickly, and it hadn't been long before she came to understand the breeding of prime lambs and could run the sheep program with only a little help.

It was Charlie who had renamed his farm Charona—a mixture of their names—and it was Charlie who had encouraged her to be involved. He had wanted someone who would work alongside him and be his partner in every way.

Now, these were the things that Fiona knew she needed to keep her going. Especially considering the bank had just told her they were going to freeze the business bank account. Charlie had left a will, giving everything to Fiona. But Wayne Fontana, the bank manager, had rung that morning, very apologetic. Something out of his control, he'd told her. Thank goodness it was a close-knit community and he'd told her what the next step would be. That wouldn't have happened in a city, she was sure. Maybe it shouldn't have even here! But it had and she was grateful for his insight.

'Transfer as much money from your overdraft as you need for the next couple of months,' he'd told her. 'Put it in another bank account and you'll still be able to operate. It's not frozen yet, so do it as quickly as you can.'

She'd done just that, worrying she hadn't taken enough out, then she'd rung Mark to come and weigh these lambs. If she could sell a few hundred, that would give her extra breathing space until probate was issued. She needed the money because it was going to be tight. The money side of things was new to her—Charlie had done all the budgets—so she was relying on help from the bank manager and knowledge from Mark.

Charlie had inherited the farm from his grandparents, Stephen and Bessie, who passed over their own son. That was a skeleton in the closet and not one Fiona knew a lot about. She was sure his parents wouldn't tell her about it now. The little time Fiona had spent with them hadn't left her with an urge to see them again. Ronda and Don were mean and self-centred.

Ronda, unfriendly and cold. Don, loud and obnoxious,

happy to cut his son down at any turn. Their open animosity towards Charlie had made Fiona angry and she had said as much to Ronda over a Christmas roast lunch five years ago. That had been the last time Charlie and Fiona had seen them.

Both had been so glad when Charlie's parents decided to leave the district and move to Victoria, after buying a small block in the mountains. There would be no visits from Charlie's parents unless they invited them. Fiona often wondered how they could have produced such a gentle and sweet-natured boy.

She lifted her face towards the sky, feeling the warmth of the sun on her skin, and she was almost happy. Almost. Some of the sorrow and shock melted into the rhythmic sound of gates opening and closing, of lambs bleating, and work. Her mind was kept busy doing something she loved.

As the yards began to empty out, it became quieter and easier to talk.

'So how are you going, Fee?' Mark asked as he ran the blue marker down the back of another lamb, indicating it was ready for sale.

Fiona gave a tight-lipped smile. 'I'm doing okay,' she replied in a practised tone.

'Right.'

'Well, the bank rang today and said they were going to freeze my bank account, I'm tired, I'm sad and I still feel sick most mornings, but it's just in passing. Nowhere near as bad as it was. And out here, doing what we're doing, I can almost forget.' She crossed her arms and frowned.

'Morning sickness is a bastard,' Mark agreed. 'Debby really suffered, too.'

Fiona ran her hands over her stomach. 'I just feel fat and stretched. Hate to think what I'm going to feel like in five months' time, when it's time to pop.' She paused. 'Do you know, the funny thing is that I haven't got any spatial awareness now? My stomach seems to bump into everything, even when I think I'm far enough away from it!'

Mark let out a laugh. 'Don't think you're on your own there.' He paused as he patted his large stomach. 'What's this about the bank?'

Swallowing the lump that appeared in her throat without warning, she nodded and told him what the bank manager had said.

'Wayne is a good bloke. He'll be keeping an eye on you,' Mark reassured her. 'We're all watching out for you, you know.' He let the last lamb through the gate. 'It's been a hell of a time—not only for you, but for Geoff and Leigh as well. The ripple effect of this has been huge, and you've all suffered in different ways.'

Fiona inhaled sharply. 'Everything considered, I don't think I'm doing too badly. Four months and one week preggers.' She looked towards the mob of sheep that were milling around, trying to find scraps of green grass in the compound. There was never much in the yards because at this time of year, when there were so many ewes and lambs coming through, it didn't get the chance to grow. The sheep nipped it off too quickly.

'Everything else? I don't really have a choice, do I? I have to get on with life. I have this little one to think of. Just got to keep going. It's the evenings that are the worst. I feel pretty empty then and, for some stupid reason, I've started to get scared when it's dark. The house creaks and groans a lot—sometimes I think there's someone prowling around.' She let out a laugh. 'Silly, really. There's never anyone there—just my imagination. It would be so easy to fix. Get some locks on the doors. Must get around to that.' She tried to brush it off.

Fiona wouldn't tell him about the nights she sobbed so hard she fell into an exhausted sleep, or the early mornings when she sat by the window and just looked out across the land. Or the times when she sat for hours at the computer, willing her mind to think about anything but the last image she had of Charlie. Sometimes the time spent at the keyboard was put to good use. She would research the best drench or new husbandry techniques for getting ewes in lamb.

Most of the time, her brother, Will, was on the other end of the computer, sending her funny little pick-me-up messages or a smiley face when she least expected it. Carly had been so annoyed that Will hadn't come back for the funeral, but he had certainly made his presence felt in so many other ways. In fact, they'd become closer in the last few weeks, even though they hadn't spoken face-to-face.

Fiona paused, trying to work out how to word the question that had been going around in her head for weeks now.

'Um, Mark? You know Ian Tonkin?' She bent down and started to undo the wire holding the equipment in place.

'You know I do,' he replied, pressing a few buttons on the readout of the scales. 'Right, three hundred and twelve ready to go, out of four-fifty.' He wrote it down in his notebook, before adding the average weight.

'They're solid lambs,' she said confidently.

Mark snapped the notebook shut and leaned against the crate. 'So why are you asking about Ian Tonkin?' he asked. 'You thinking of selling the farm?'

Fiona stared out across the paddocks, trying to formulate her words. 'No,' she said slowly. 'I don't want to sell.' She turned back to him. 'But for some reason he thinks I do. He's been visiting and ringing at least once a week since Charlie's funeral. *Very* persistent.'

Mark pursed his lips. 'Doesn't sound like him.'

'And what's really weird is that a couple of people in town asked me who I was selling to—like I'd already signed a contract or something. Geoff was one of them.'

'You haven't given any indication that you want to sell to anyone?'

She shook her head. 'In a weak moment I think I might have said to Jo or Leigh—I can't remember which—that I didn't know how I was going to cope and maybe I should sell, but I never really meant it.'

In reality, it wasn't just Ian Tonkin who was encouraging her to sell. Her mum was pestering her about it as well. It seemed there were very few people who thought she could cope with a farm and a baby. Selling was the only option, apparently.

She would prove them wrong.

After all, the one thing she'd realised since Charlie had died was that every single person had an opinion on what she should do now she was a widow. 'I don't want to sell, Mark,' she said earnestly. 'Charlie and I have worked too hard for me to let it all go just because he isn't here. We have . . .' She touched her neck, her face reddening. 'Ah, we *had* too many dreams. I can't take this little one's heritage away until he or she works out if they want to farm. That wouldn't be fair.'

He nodded. 'So have you told Ian that?'

She fiddled with her wedding rings. 'Yeah, I have. But he still keeps ringing.'

'Want me to have a word?' He started to unscrew the readout from the stand. His face was impassive, but Fiona knew him well enough to realise there was a lot running around in his mind at the moment.

'I was just wondering if you knew if he had an order or something. If there was a reason he was so insistent.'

Mark stopped and Fiona could see him thinking about the question. He'd been their stock agent ever since Charlie had taken over Charona. Mark had been new in town when Charlie was struggling to find his feet with the farm. He had helped Charlie by giving him confidence in his own ability, talking through marketing options and explaining the markets. They'd had a business relationship for over eight years before Charlie died, and even though Mark was twenty years older than both Charlie and Fiona, they'd always got along well and had a lot of respect for each other. He would be honest and upfront with her.

'I don't know of anything off the top of my head, Fee.' He frowned. 'I reckon I'd've heard something. He knows I'm your stocky. We work out of the same office and he'd normally talk to me first. He's not usually so insistent. And he's had a few sales lately, so it's not like he's on Hard Luck Avenue.'

'Really? Who's sold? Strange time of the year to be selling, we're halfway through a season.' Fiona straightened at the thought.

'They're not settling until February next year. They're mostly older blokes who don't have anyone coming up behind them to take over. Henry Fairway and Craig Duttors are two of them.'

Fiona cocked her head in interest. 'They're next door to each other,' she said. 'Same buyer?'

'Yep.'

'Anyone local?'

Mark grinned. 'Nosy!' he teased.

'Not at all! Just curious to know what's going on in my community.' She threw him a quick smile. 'You never know, I might show everyone that I've got what it takes and buy more land!' She gave Mark a cheeky smile.

'That'd be cause for some conversation, for sure,' he answered with a laugh. 'Anyway, it's a company doing the buying. Ian said they've got cropping land in New South Wales and Victoria. They want to get into stock to spread out their risk. There's been a couple of bad years over there. They're called BJL Holdings.'

A couple of galahs flew overhead and Fiona could hear the swish of their wings. They would be enjoying the day of sunshine, too.

'Neither of them is that far from here. What? Fifteen kilometres away?'

'Yeah, something like that. I think it made sense to both of them. Henry is there by himself and hasn't got any kids. He's nearly eighty! Got to admit, though, I never thought money would've made a difference to him when it came to selling, but it must've. No other reason to sell.' Mark walked to his car and put the readout in the back. 'I thought we'd have to carry him off that place in a box.'

Instantly, Fiona saw Charlie's coffin in her mind's eye.

'Oh shit.' Mark must have seen the look on her face. 'Sorry, Fee. That was thoughtless of me.'

She gave a half-shrug. 'It happens. Don't worry about it. I had old Mrs Nolan come up the other day and ask,'—she made quotation marks with her fingers—*"How are you, dear? Coping okay since that man of yours topped himself? Silly bugger, wasn't he?"'*

Shock passed over Mark's face. 'I really hope you're joking.'

'Unfortunately not. I wanted to slap her.'

'Reckon you would've been found "not guilty" in a court of law.'

They finished loading the lamb-weighing crate onto the trailer in silence and Mark tied it on.

'Do you want me to do anything about Ian?' He pulled the rope tight and turned to look at her.

Fiona looked back at him uneasily. 'I don't know, Mark.' She really wanted to ask what he thought, but she knew she wouldn't get a straight answer. Not yet, anyway. He'd take it on board, watch and listen. Work out what was going on. When he had something, he'd let her know.

'Maybe not. Maybe just leave it.'

'You sure?' He pushed his hat back on his head and wiped away the sweat.

'I can deal with him. I just wanted to make sure there wasn't anything more to it. Doesn't sound like there is, except him wanting to make a bit of money. I'll be right.' She turned and looked over her land. 'I won't ever sell here, Mark. Never.' There was a pause. 'Well, like I said. Not until I know what this little one wants to do.'

There was silence as Mark leaned into his car and turned the key. The engine roared to life and the mob of sheep took off at the noise and ran towards the fence. The first ones stopped, digging their front hooves into the ground as they realised there was a barrier in their way.

'I spoke to Geoff last night,' Fiona said. It had been good to talk to him, although they'd stayed off the subject of Charlie and the accident. She'd really wanted to check on him, see how he was coping. The fear of another suicide weighed heavily on her mind.

'I've been talking to him too,' Mark answered slowly. 'At the risk of taking a huge leap of faith, I think he's going to be okay. It will take a long time.'

'I hope you're right.'

They both stared out across the land.

Finally, Mark asked, 'Do you need a hand with anything? As time goes on and when the baby comes, you won't be able to do everything you're doing now. I've had kids, remember. Debby hardly moved for the last two weeks before Jarrod was born! And then the screaming . . .' He put his hands over his eyes. 'I'll never forget . . .'

Fiona giggled. 'Thanks so much. You're really making it sound easy!'

'But that's just it! It isn't, Fee. And you're not going to have someone with you to help.'

She shrugged. 'I'll manage. Mum and Jo will be around. I've always got Meita!' She leaned down to rub her kelpie, who was lying on her side, eyes closed, enjoying the sunshine. 'You never know—she might make the best babysitter ever seen!'

'You don't think Charlie's parents will come back?'

'I wouldn't have thought so. I don't need their help.' Fiona frowned as she contemplated the thought.

'Might be nice if they wanted to help you out. Especially

with a grandchild on the way. I watched them at the funeral and it was hard to believe they were mourning their own son.'

'Don't I know it.' Fiona rubbed her hands over her belly. 'They barely spoke to me and didn't come out here. In a way it didn't bother me—I'm not sure I would have known what to say to them anyway. We hadn't seen them in years. They completely wiped Charlie when he was given the farm and I didn't help things when I gave Ronda a mouthful about being so nasty.' Looking towards the creek, she stared at the leaves moving in the slight breeze and wondered how they could have borne to leave here. It was the most perfect place on earth, she thought. 'I wish I knew what all that was about. Charlie never said much other than his dad was never cut out to be a farmer and would have sold the land out from under him. It had been in his family for four generations and his grandfather didn't want it to leave the family. Can you imagine even wanting to sell this place?' With a small smile, she waved her hands as if she were a game show hostess introducing a prize.

Mark smiled and nodded. 'Not really, but who knows what happens inside people's heads. It would be nice to think they'd like to spend a bit of time with their grandchild. Family is going to be important for you in the next while. Now,' Mark changed the subject and Fiona knew it was so she wouldn't howl down his comments. 'Before I forget, I know of a young bloke who needs a bit of work. Let me know if you want to talk to him. He's reliable and pretty handy with machinery.' He gave her a hard stare. 'I'm going to act as your father now and say there is no way you should be spraying crops while you're pregnant. It's not good for the baby.'

'Thanks for the lecture!' Fiona smiled to show she didn't

mind. Mark was one person she knew had her best interests at heart. 'But honestly, I'll be okay. I'm not sure the bank account will stretch to wages yet. A contractor yes, but not full-time wages. Maybe after this year, if it keeps going the way it has been. Although,' she paused, and her eyes narrowed as she thought. 'I don't suppose you know if he's a handyman? I need someone to put locks on the doors. And I'd love for someone to cut me some wood.'

'Couldn't tell you that, but I can ask. But why don't you ask Rob? You know him.'

'Rob, as in Rob Cameron, the vet?'

'Yep. He's pretty handy. When he's not working, he donates his time to the old folks units—you know, fixing dripping taps and stuff I don't understand! Says it's relaxing. Me? I'd hit my thumb with a hammer before I could hit the nail.'

'I won't be asking you then! Don't want the locks installed upside down, thanks!'

'Good idea. Anyway, let me know if you want to talk to the bloke who's good with machinery. His name's Damien MacKenzie—he's your neighbour. Know him, do you?' He grinned widely at her and opened the door of his four-wheel drive and got in.

'Funnily enough, I do. I've already spoken to him about doing some spraying for me—you'll be happy to hear that! Lucky for me he's a contractor, too!'

'Good, I'd better get on. I'll let you know when the truck is coming to pick these up and come out to give you a hand to draft.'

'No, it's all good. Meita and I will be able to draft by ourselves, won't we, girl?'

The two-tan kelpie, still stretched out near Fiona's feet, sprang up at the sound of her name and put her paws on Fiona's stomach. She patted the dog's head before lowering her to the ground. 'You'll upset the baby with those sharp claws, Miss Meita!' She turned back to Mark. 'Honestly, we'll be fine. Just let me know when the truck is coming.'

'It's not a sign of weakness to ask for help,' he said, starting up his engine.

'It is if you don't need it!'

'I'll see you later then.' He shook his head in exasperation before putting the car into gear and driving off, waving.

Fiona waved back to him and walked to the gate to let the sheep out. They streamed into the paddock, a mob of bleating and searching chaos. It wouldn't be long before all the mothers found their lambs and returned to grazing.

She watched as the ewes ran around, sniffing at every lamb they came across in the hope it was their baby. Some were rewarded straightaway and their lambs, having been separated from them for a few hours, went directly for their udders, lifting the ewes' hind legs off the ground as they suckled enthusiastically.

Fiona smiled. If nothing else, the rain, good lambs and crops were a sign that Charlie was looking out for her and her baby.

Her Hamish.

That would be his name when he was born. If he was a boy. But Fiona wasn't thinking the baby would be anything other than that—a boy.

ശ

The creaking of the floorboards in the passageway woke Fiona. But instead of waking slowly and gently, as she normally would, she immediately felt frightened and anxious.

She was sure she could sense someone's presence in the house. Fear lay over her like a heavy wet blanket, making her powerless to move.

Her mind raced and her stomach clenched in terror. Who was it? Why were they here? What was going on?

There it was again. *Creeaaakkk, grrooaannn.*

Her stomach coiled and she swallowed hard. With her heart pounding, she huddled further down in the bed, trying to ignore what she'd heard.

Where was Meita? She hadn't barked. That made her breathe a little easier. Surely there couldn't be anyone there if her faithful dog hadn't alerted her.

The house was silent now and her body began to relax. She slid out of bed, trying not to make any noise.

Clutching her doona to her, Fiona tiptoed across to the door and, holding her breath, cracked it open about an inch.

There was no sign of an intruder.

She opened the door wider and put her head all the way out. Still nothing.

Sagging against the doorframe, Fiona closed her eyes and berated herself for being so foolish. After all, who did she expect? Charlie? His ghost to be looking out for her? A burglar? Ha! Now that was funny. Not funny haha. Funny, stupid. Not out here.

She pulled her doona tighter and plodded out into the passage to put the kettle on. She wouldn't be able to sleep much more now.

After making herself a hot chocolate, Fiona went across the passageway into the office, hoping Will would be on the end of the computer.

'You there?' she typed.

'I am,' he replied as soon as she'd hit the enter button. *'What's happening? Can't sleep?'*

'Just scared myself silly.'

'What a good idea. Any reason why? Bored or something?'

Fiona couldn't help but giggle at his sarcasm. 'Thought there was someone outside my bedroom door.'

'What gave you that brainwave?'

'The floor creaked . . .' Even typing it now, she felt ridiculous. Why had something so normal made her feel so frightened?

Something niggled in the back of her mind—it wasn't normal. That was the creak the floorboards always gave when someone trod on them.

'Don't you lock your doors?'

'Ha! You've got to be joking. This house is so old you couldn't lock anything if you tried. The screen door doesn't even shut properly.'

'Seriously, you don't lock your doors?'

In her mind, Fiona could hear Will's voice and his incredulous tone. She supposed it did sound strange to someone living in New York.

'Serious. The doors don't lock. They never have. It's quite normal in old farm houses. I don't know anyone who locks their house. The best we do out here in the sticks is lock the front gate while we're away, but even then, it's not something we really like to do because it brings attention to the fact you're not home.'

'You might need to get that fixed. Have you got someone to do it for you? I'd offer to help, but being so far way and all . . .'

Chuckling out loud, she tapped the laughing emoticon. Will wouldn't know one end of a screwdriver from the other. Then she started to type again:

'You know what I think it was?'

'No.'

'I reckon it was a dream. Dreamt something which I can't remember and it woke me. The house must have moved or expanded or did whatever it does, then the boards creaked and I got scared. That's all it can be.'

'You need to get someone to fix your dreams.'

'And your doors.'

Chapter 4

Dave Burrows slammed his hand on the table and glared at the internal investigations detective in front of him.

'I've told you. I did what I thought was right at the time. I saved her life. There wasn't any other choice.'

'You were instructed to wait for the Special Tactics and Rescue team.' James Glover clicked his pen and looked at Dave as if he were a piece of shit.

'There would have been more public outcry if he'd killed her,' he stated flatly.

Dave hadn't been able to believe his eyes when he'd received an email, ordering him to attend a hearing regarding his actions during his last investigation. It had been the case of Dominic Alberto, his wife, Ashleigh, or Eliza as she became known, and the poaching of native wildlife from the national park in the Flinders Ranges.

'And,' Glover drew out the word. 'You were instructed to wait in the case of Amelia Bennett the previous year, and you didn't then, either.'

He raised his eyebrows, as if daring Dave to argue with him.

But there was no argument to be had. Yes, he'd gone rushing in, but he'd saved both girls. Surely that was a good thing. Not something to be hauled in and questioned over.

'Sure didn't,' he finally answered, shrugging his shoulders as if he didn't care. But he did. In a massive way.

'So you admit you disobeyed orders?' Glover made a note on his pad before tapping the pen on the paper and staring disapprovingly at the words he'd written.

'And what the hell do you want me to do about it now?' Dave asked, anger brimming inside him. 'I can't change my actions. I had to react the way I saw fit at the time. It was me on the ground there, not you lot. The outcomes were good for both the victim and the police department. We had arrests. Brought the crime-rate stats down. That's what you blokes need. What more do you want?' Agitated, Dave ran his fingers through his greying hair and wondered if Kim was still waiting outside. Embarrassment welled up inside him. He hadn't wanted her to know about this, but he'd had no choice.

He also knew she would stand beside him, whatever the outcome. The humiliation came from being a top-shelf cop who never thought he, or his actions, would be questioned. He considered briefly why it had turned out this way. It wouldn't have happened ten years ago. Policing was changing and he wasn't sure he was up to it.

'This will all be documented on your file.'

Dave fought the urge to slam his hand down on the table again and swear.

'Of course it will be,' he said after a moment. 'So can I go?'

'You won't be able to go back to work until the investigation is complete. It will take a few days. Expect to hear from me next week.' Glover snapped his notepad shut and turned off the recording machine, before looking at Dave closely. 'You've been very careless, Detective Burrows,' he said. 'Very careless indeed.' He sighed. 'Trouble is, the police department needs people like you. If it was up to me, you'd be badgeless for the duration. In reality, we're short-staffed in the rural areas and you know how to run and investigate those areas if needed.

'I'm not happy; however, I'll be recommending that you are fit for duty.' He sighed again, this time deeply. 'But let me tell you, if I have to interview you again for reckless behaviour, I won't be so lenient. In fact, I'll throw the book at you and make sure you don't work for years.' He leaned over the desk and looked Dave in the eyes. 'And that will kill a cop like you. Pull your head in, Burrows. You're not a one-man band. Even if you do live in the sticks without backup. You've been told that before.' He stared at Dave, who stared back.

He wished he could say, 'Bugger off,' but deep inside he knew Glover, the 'Toe-cutter', was right. And that was what hurt the most.

'This way,' Toe-cutter indicated which way to leave the interview room.

Bloody internal investigations. 'Toe-cutter' wasn't the nicest name for these investigators—actually, 'Feather Feet' was what they called the unit in WA, where Dave was from originally. It came from the Aboriginal Lawmen, who used to wear feathers on their feet so they could sneak up on an unsuspecting target. Well, that was a pretty appropriate name for him. Dave hadn't seen him coming but it certainly wasn't what he would have called Glover right at that moment.

ও

As Dave walked out into the police station foyer, he saw Kim sitting there, reading a magazine. When she looked up, he could instantly tell there was something wrong.

Raising his eyebrows, he looked at her quizzically. He could see fear and panic in her eyes and his stomach constricted. What could possibly have happened while he was being interviewed?

His need to get out of the police station was overwhelming. He turned back to Glover and waited until the forms were completed before snatching them and holding out his hand for his badge.

'Remember what I said, Burrows. This is the last time.'

Dave nodded curtly and turned to Kim, ushering her out, his hand on her back.

He waited until they had passed the glass sliding doors before asking her what was wrong.

Kim put a hand on his arm. 'Let's get a coffee,' she said, walking in front of him towards a café across the road.

Dave felt a sense of foreboding he'd never had before. Something was off kilter.

He pulled out a chair for her and went to the counter to order drinks. When he came back, he reached for her hand. 'What's up, sweetie?' he asked, his voice as gentle as he could manage.

Kim swallowed and ran her thumb along his. Dave didn't like the way she was avoiding making eye contact.

'So the breast-check van has been in Port Augusta. I went and had my normal mammogram a couple of weeks ago.'

Dave's stomach dropped and fear rippled through his whole body. He knew exactly where this was heading. He wanted her to stop talking, because saying it out loud would make it true. 'No,' he said softly, pleading with her. 'Don't say it, Kim.'

She raised her face to look at him. 'Chelle has just called and asked me to go in and see her when we get home.' Chelle was their local doctor in Barker and also Kim's niece, Milly's, school friend.

They sat in silence as the waitress brought their coffee and muffins. Neither of them remembered to thank her.

Dave couldn't breathe. It had taken him all his life to find her and now, two short years in, he might lose her. He felt as if he were on a speeding train he couldn't get off.

'What does that mean?' he asked. 'Wanting you to go in. She didn't give you any indication of why?'

Kim shook her head slowly. 'She just said she wanted to discuss my results with me. We'll have to wait and see what she has to say. I'll go and see her when we get back. She said she'd make time for me whenever I got there.'

Dave gripped her hand with more force. 'That's bullshit,' he said through gritted teeth. 'How can she leave you hanging like that?'

'I guess it's not something she wants to talk about on the phone.' Kim shrugged. 'I don't know. Don't get angry with me. I haven't caused this.'

That sobered him. 'Sorry, sweetheart,' he apologised. 'Sorry.' He didn't know what else to say, but he bumbled along anyway. 'Well, you never know, it might be nothing. Or something different to what you're thinking. A cyst or something. I'm sure it's nothing serious. I promise.'

When Kim responded, her tone was tight with anxiety. 'Don't say things like that, Dave, because you can't promise me anything at the moment. I know you want to, but we've got no idea what we're facing here.'

The coffees sat untouched, cooling as they both stared down at them. As if on automatic pilot, Dave poured sugar into his cup and took a sip. As the liquid hit his stomach, he felt ill. His eyes searched every aspect of her face—the face he knew so well. He knew her moods just by watching her eyes; he knew what she was about to say by the way her mouth tilted as she spoke. Today her face told of terror. It seemed as if she'd aged ten years in the space of ten minutes.

He didn't know how to comfort her, so he moved his chair around to sit alongside her and slipped his arm around her shoulders. She let her head rest against his chest and he felt the warmth of her tears on his shirt.

ᔓ

The drive home was silent; both were lost in their thoughts. Dave didn't know what the future held for him, but he knew one thing for sure: he wanted, no, needed Kim in that future.

After hearing this news, the run-in at headquarters meant nothing to Dave. He'd already decided he had done the right thing in both situations, and stuff the police department if they didn't like it. He'd do it again. He'd saved both those girls and brought a band of criminals to face the courts. Single-handedly. To him, that spoke volumes.

Dave wasn't even sure if he wanted to keep policing if Kim had breast cancer. He knew he'd want to spend every moment he could with her. Be there for everything and anything she needed. He glanced over at her as they pulled up at the surgery.

Her usually beautiful face was tight and she wouldn't look at him. Dave thought she could have been walking to the gallows.

'Stop.' He put a hand on her arm. 'I'm coming, too.'

She twisted away from him. 'No, I need to do this by myself.'

'But, Kimmy . . .'

'Dave! For God's sake, just let me do this, will you? I'm sorry!' She grabbed her handbag and walked quickly away from the car. There was nothing to do except let her go.

Putting his hands over his mouth, he expelled air into them, then rubbed his tired face. 'Shit.'

His phone rang, making him jump, and he snatched it up and looked at the screen.

'Shit,' he repeated when he saw his supervisor's name. 'Steve.'

'Dave,' Steve answered in the same no-nonsense tone. 'Home yet?'

'Yes. Look, can I call—'

'We've got a problem.' Steve spoke over the top of Dave; if he'd heard the request to call him back, he ignored it.

'What's that?'

'I've been looking at the file on Eddie McDougall. The vic that was killed in the shooting accident up your way. There're some things that don't add up.'

Dave racked his brains. 'I was on holidays when that case came through,' he told him. 'I can't help you with that. You'll need to talk to Jack or Andy.' He was referring to the two other officers who worked with him in the Barker Police Station.

'I want you to review the case. I think some mistakes have been made.'

'I don't think I can, Steve.' Dave ran his hand over his hair, trying to decide whether to tell him what was going on with Kim. 'I've got some, ah, personal problems at the moment.'

'Don't be difficult because you're pissed off, Dave.' Steve sounded exasperated. 'I know your pride's hurt because of the roasting you've been given, but . . .'

'It's not that,' he interrupted. 'It's Kim. She might have breast cancer.'

The silence stretched out between them.

'I see,' Steve said finally. 'Nothing to do with anything else then?'

'Well, yeah. I'm angry and annoyed and probably a bit embarrassed. But we've only found out about Kim today. I need some time, Steve. Anyway, I've been told I can't work until sometime next week when the Feather Feet get back in contact with me.'

'Don't worry about them. I'll clear it. I need you on this case.'

'Can you give me until next week? Let me just find out what the hell is going on with Kim and what we need to do. Eddie McDougall has been dead for four months; it's not going to be urgent.'

'I'll send you the file. Have a look at it when you've got time.' He paused. 'And, Dave? I hope everything will be okay. You always expect the worst, but it doesn't have to be.' He cleared his throat. 'My wife was diagnosed eight years ago—they caught it early and she's okay now. It's her fifth year clear. It's a hell of a time, Dave, but you'll get through it. That I can tell you from experience.'

Dave's throat constricted and he wasn't able to say anything.

'Anyway, catch you later.' Steve hung up.

Chapter 5

Leigh Bounter walked down the main street of Booleroo. He nodded at a couple of people, then saw Mark Simmons, Ian Tonkin and Rob Cameron crossing the road, deep in conversation. He was about to call out to them—they were all interesting men to talk to—but Ray Newell crossed his line of sight before he had the opportunity.

'G'day, Ray.' Leigh extended his hand and forced a smile to his face.

'Leigh, how're you going?' Ray sounded just as strained as Leigh felt speaking to him.

'Good, mate, good. Great win yesterday. Torrica should be very worried about us here at Booleroo, leading into the finals.'

Ray nodded. 'Exceptionally worried.' He rattled off a few names of players who had kicked goals or made good tackles. 'But what about that young Myles Martin? Isn't he something special, the way he weaves and dives? Don't think

I've seen a youngster with such ability in quite some time.' The passion in his voice shone through.

Leigh nodded enthusiastically. If the two of them talked only about footy, they could talk for hours, but if they strayed from the subject or went down memory lane, they had to end the conversation before the punches started. Didn't matter who started the fight, they would both retaliate in a fiery way.

'Totally agree with you. In fact,' Leigh drew out the word, thinking, 'are we playing against Laura next week?'

'Sure are.'

'I think I'll keep him in mind for the Leigh Bunter Medal.'

Neither spoke for a moment, Leigh remembering the day his future had been snatched away from him.

'Good idea,' Ray agreed, shoving his hands in his pockets and rocking on his heels. 'Well, I'd better be off. Thanks for coming and watching the boys yesterday. Catch you round.'

'Sure.'

Leigh scratched at his beard as he watched Ray wander off. He wished he could forgive this man, but he just hadn't been able to. Seventeen years ago, while on the footy field, they'd both been going for the ball, but at the last minute, Ray, realising he couldn't make it in time, had changed direction and taken Leigh's legs out from underneath him. Leigh's head had snapped back as he'd landed awkwardly on the ground, resulting in a fractured C2 vertebrae.

A four-month recovery period, with heaps of physio past that date, had annihilated any hope of being able to play again, even at a local level.

For years, he'd been so angry with Ray he would make a detour if he saw him in the street. These days, so many years on, he managed to hold a conversation with him. Leigh couldn't talk about Ray's success in life—the trucking business he'd built up from scratch, his pretty wife and even more beautiful three-year-old daughter. It made Leigh think of all the things he could have had, but didn't.

Sure, he was successful in his own right—he had a large farming enterprise, handed down through generations, no debt and a large stack of money he'd inherited when his parents died. The combination of a few good seasons and cleverly invested money meant he was exceptionally well off. He was the mayor of Booleroo Centre. But he'd never planned on that. Never even considered it. Not wanted it.

No, what Leigh had wanted was nothing less than an AFL career. A drop-dead stunning wife on his arm as he paraded down the carpet for the Brownlow Medal. Mateship and a bond that came from playing in a team. Fame and success. To be in the spotlight. Respected.

In reality, Leigh went home to an empty house every night, and his body hurt. He didn't have a family of his own, and both his parents were dead. His two sisters were scattered across Australia, busy with their own lives and families. He rarely spoke to either. He was alone at thirty-four and, although the Booleroo Council area was his to run as he saw fit, there were no team players within the council. Everyone was out for what they could get. He saw it as his duty to oversee that.

When it was clear his AFL dream could never be realised, Leigh set about trying to make a difference. His farming operation increased, and he employed more workmen. He worked hard for the town of Booleroo Centre, becoming mayor at twenty-five—only for a year. He took a break and then ran again when he was thirty. He'd been mayor for four years now and didn't have any intention of letting his position go. Fame and success had come through different channels. He now knew everything that happened within the council boundaries, and everyone who lived there.

He'd often contemplated what a difference it would have made had Ray apologised. Ray never would, Leigh knew—to him injury was part of the risk you took when you played. But to be involved in snatching away his dream . . . Well, he thought he would have at least fronted the bloke he'd injured. But not Ray.

ᔕ

Leigh absent-mindedly rubbed the back of his neck. He could still feel the lump there. Really, he should just be grateful he was alive. An inch or two either way and he would have been looking at the inside of a coffin, not the warm winter sun of today.

He tried to shake off the melancholy by thinking about Fiona. He was on his way to Charona with a few others for Carly's birthday. From what Fiona had said, it sounded like Carly had a cackle of friends heading out there. Only reason he wanted to go along was to check on Fiona and show his face to the old girls. The re-election was coming up in a few months. Be good for him to remind them he was still around.

Although why Carly had chosen to have the lunch at Charona, when she would have been much more comfortable back at her house in Laura, interested him. Leigh had wondered if it was more about making sure Fiona attended. She'd been avoiding a lot of the social activities she used to enjoy.

Leigh worried for Fiona. He was sure the upkeep of the farm was too much. Life would be a lot easier for her with three million in the bank and no debt or stress about seasons. How she would manage when the little one was born was beyond him. Still, it was her call.

He worried for Geoff as well—he seemed unreachable. Staying busy on his farm, so he didn't have to think. Fiona had told him she'd spoken to him recently, and although he was still traumatised, he was okay. But even with that reassuring bit of information, he couldn't stop being concerned. It was his job to look after people.

He felt his stomach twist as his thoughts moved on to Charlie. How he missed him. That was one feeling he couldn't have anticipated. Missing Charlie.

Charlie had been one of the few blokes who had come and seen him while he was in hospital with a broken neck. That stuck in his throat a bit, too. He would have expected the whole town to have been behind him, help look out for him. They should have. After all, his family was important, so he should have been, too. But no, it was really only Charlie and Geoff who had made the effort.

Leigh smiled to himself as he remembered the visit when Charlie had smuggled in a few beers and a couple of kebabs. With Leigh's head in a SOMI brace and unable to bend his neck, Charlie had smuggled in straws as well! The look on the nurse's face when she'd walked in had been worth the scolding he'd got.

Charlie had looked after him when he'd been down and now it was his turn to look after Charlie . . . although it had to be through Fiona.

He pushed open the door into the pub. Once inside, he looked at his watch, then checked to see who he knew.

'How're you going, Leigh?'

'G'day, Leigh.'

There was a chorus of voices. A couple of people came to shake his hand and ask if he'd heard anything more about the new mobile phone tower that was supposed to be installed. He gave them the standard line: 'We're waiting on confirmation from the government and Telstra. It takes time.'

He made his way to the bar, still nodding and saying hello to people. He liked this. It made him feel like a celebrity. Things had certainly changed from when he was laid out flat on his back, in hospital, worrying about his future, his farm, his career. Everyone wanted to know him now, but they didn't back then.

'Can I grab two bottles of sav blanc, Kristy, please?' he said to the young blonde girl behind the bar.

Leigh handed her a fifty-dollar note and took the change and the bottles in a brown paper bag.

'Hello, what are you up to?' Jo appeared at his shoulder and gave him a smile before ordering a six-pack of beer to take away.

'Heading out to Charona to help celebrate Carly's birthday. They don't know I'm coming, thought I'd surprise them,' Leigh answered. 'You?'

'Oh, good plan! Carly will like that. I'm going out there, too, but I'm running so late. I went out to Geoff's today to do some tissue tests on his crops and it took a lot longer than I thought it would.'

'How is he?'

They gathered their purchases and walked out together.

Jo thought for a while. 'Stoic, I think, is the best word for it. Almost pretending it didn't happen.' She paused. 'No, that's not right. More not thinking about it. Making sure there's so much else going on he doesn't have to.'

Leigh nodded. 'Yeah, I'd say the same thing.' Silence filled the air between them before he said, 'Right, no point in standing about. See you out there.'

ᔕ

Fiona handed around a plate of chops and indicated for Jo to pass the salads. Eight women sat gathered at a wooden table, glasses of wine in hand, touching Fiona's belly as she walked past and cooing over the patterns of baby clothes that Nana Carly was planning to knit.

'Isn't that just too sweet?' Angela asked, pointing to a picture of a miniature pink beret Carly was holding out.

'No point in knitting that one, Mum,' Fiona said with a smile as she saw the colour. 'This little one is going to be a boy.'

'Oh no,' Sylvia said. 'You're carrying too high. If it was going to be a boy, you'd be carrying really low, down in your pelvis.'

'How can you tell?' Leigh wanted to know. 'I know she's got a bump but surely you don't know how she's carrying?'

'We're old hands at this, Leigh,' Carly said, grinning at him. Her cheeks were a soft pink, an indication she'd had more than one glass of wine. 'We've seen lots of babies born!'

'Are you always right?'

'More often than not. You'd be surprised what we girls can work out between us!'

'So, love, have you settled on a name yet?' Monique asked.

Fiona shook her head as she sat down next to Leigh and loaded up her plate with salad. 'Hamish for now.'

'Hamish? Why Hamish? Surely something like Charlotte or even Charles if it's a boy?'

'Monique!' Carly said with a frown. 'That's a little insensitive, don't you think?'

Monique had the grace to blush.

'Fiona, I *am* sorry. It came out without me thinking about it. I thought it was a away to remember Charlie.'

'It's fine,' Fiona said picking at a splinter on the table. 'I guess most of you would assume that's how I was thinking.' She gave a little half-shrug. 'It's going to be a boy, no matter how I'm carrying, and I'm sure I'll get a feeling for the right name in time. But at the moment, I'm leaning towards Hamish.' She didn't tell them that at the end of a passionate love-making session she and Charlie had discussed names—even though they weren't ready for children.

'Do you want kids soon?' she'd asked Charlie as his fingers had trailed over her stomach, tickling her.

'Not yet. I want all the practice I can get,' Charlie had answered. 'We haven't quite got it right yet.'

Giggling, she'd swotted him gently with the back of her hand. 'I think we're doing pretty well. Can you imagine what they'll look like?'

Charlie rolled onto his stomach and heaved himself up on his elbows to look at her. 'Like you,' he'd answered, 'your eyes, your nose—so cute.'

'Haha, you know I hate my nose.' She self-consciously touched her nose and tried to rub it away.

'I want our children to have your nose,' Charlie grinned at

her. He leaned forward and kissed her. 'Hamish for the boy and Emily for the girl?'

Fiona felt her lips turn upwards. 'You've thought about it?' she asked, incredulously.

'Yeah.' Charlie had turned serious. 'But I'm not ready for a baby yet.'

Fiona blinked as she felt Jo nudge her. Looking around the table, she realised everyone was looking at her. 'Sorry?'

'But what if it's a girl?' Marge repeated, looking at her curiously. 'You can't be so sure.'

'I am. It won't be.' She looked peacefully at everyone.

'Fiona, have you talked to someone about putting locks on your door?' Carly asked, changing the subject.

'Not yet, but Mark thinks Rob—you know, the vet—might do it. I just haven't rung to ask yet.' She picked up her soft drink and wiped the condensation from the side.

'Maybe that's a job for Leigh, since he's here right now?'

He straightened at the sound of his name. 'Anything for you, Carly,' he said with a wink, before turning to Fiona. 'What's this about locks?'

Fiona waved his question away. 'It's not urgent. Just thought it might be a good idea to have some locks fitted, since I am here by myself now.' She wasn't going to mention being frightened out of her wits sometimes.

'I can do it, no problems,' Leigh said, getting out his notebook and clicking his pen. 'What do you want? Deadlocks?'

'Honestly, Leigh, it's fine. I'm going to ring Rob tonight. You've got more than enough on your plate. But let me tell you what happened two nights ago . . .' She leaned forward. 'I'm sure I heard the wild dog howling. In the distance, I mean, not close by, but I got out the gun just in case and went for a squiz around the yard. I only heard it once, so I can't be sure . . .'

Carly looked as if she were about to faint. 'You were going to shoot it?' she asked in a shaky voice.

'Well, yeah, Mum, of course I was. Far out! The amount of damage that bloody thing has done.'

'I didn't know you could shoot.'

'I can shoot very well,' Fiona said with a smile. 'I'm just really pissed off I didn't see it to get a shot away. Bastard.'

Carly blinked. 'Fiona! Your language.'

Leigh intervened. 'Two nights ago? Yeah, I thought I heard it too. I knew it had been around because I found three dead lambs the next morning. I've been laying baits, but none have been taken.'

'I've heard a couple of other farmers talk about it down the pub,' Jo interjected. 'But no one wants to have a go at shooting it again because of what's already happened.' Her voice trailed off. 'An old dogger I met ages ago told me it's pretty unusual for wild dogs to take baits—like they've got a sixth sense it's poison.'

'Domestic dogs love baits. I hope you've all got notices up saying you're baiting?' asked Sylvia, before raising her glass again.

'Of course we do.' Leigh looked at her, a puzzled frown on his face. 'We have to. It's the law!' There were murmurs of agreement.

Changing the subject, Leigh asked, 'Did you get many lambs off the other day?'

A smile lit up her face. 'Yeah, Mark and I did. I was so pleased. They were bloody good. Got a really good price for them in the sale yards, too.'

'That's great. Hey listen, I was checking my pastures

yesterday and noticed a few red-legged earth mites getting around. Have you checked any of your paddocks? Buggers will clean out the clover before you've got time to say, "Let's order the chemical and spray!"'

'Yeah, I've noticed a few in the pastures I've been checking, too,' said Jo.

Fiona pursed her lips in thought. 'I haven't had a look, actually.' She pushed some meat and salad onto her fork. 'Better get out there and have a crawl around!'

'Think it would be worth it,' he advised.

'Now, Leigh, you can't be boring all of us old ladies with your farming talk,' twittered Kay. 'Baby talk is so much more fun. Oh, Carly, I can't tell you how excited I was to hold my little granddaughter, Jaime. She was born five weeks ago. Look, I've got some photos here.'

Leigh stole a glance at Fiona and Jo, and rolled his eyes. They did the same.

He leaned over to talk to Jo. 'You won't be bored with my farming talk, will you?' he asked seriously.

'Not at all. I quite like hearing a language I understand,' she joked.

Leigh switched his gaze to Fiona. 'Actually, Fee, I've got something I wanted to talk to you about. You mentioned a while ago, you weren't sure how you were going to cope with everything. I've been giving it a bit of thought. Maybe leasing is an option? Or even selling? Have you thought about either of those two options?'

Fiona's jaw dropped. 'You are kidding me, right?'

'Nope. I'm not . . .' He opened his mouth to continue, but she interrupted him.

'Why would you want me to do that? I'm not going to.'

Her low, furious tone shocked him and he reared back slightly.

He saw Jo shift uncomfortably and quickly realised the situation had escalated from nowhere. He couldn't help himself, though. Anger flooded through him. Jeez, he was only trying to *help* her. She could be so stubborn at times. 'Right, you need to listen to me and hear me out,' he fired back at her, in a stern but gentle tone. 'I don't *want* you to do that.' He emphasised the word she had used. I was trying to find an option that might help you. This isn't just about you. It's about that bub that's coming along, too.' He looked at Jo and Carly for support. 'Can you just make her hear me out?'

Jo snorted. 'You know how determined she is when she makes her mind up about something!'

Carly just shrugged.

'Hang on a minute,' Sylvia spoke up, but Leigh talked over her.

'Please, just listen to me,' he said to Fiona but knew from her posture that she wouldn't. She was glaring down at the table, her hands in her lap.

He pushed on anyway.

'Sorry, Sylvia,' he threw a quick, apologetic glance her way before continuing. 'A newborn baby, not a lot of sleep, farming doesn't stop.'

Fiona's head flew up. 'Bloody hell, Leigh, you don't think I *know* that? Look at what I've just been through! Farming hasn't stopped. Geez, anyone would think that Ian Tonkin has got you on commission!'

Leigh froze. 'Sorry?'

'Ian Tonkin,' she said. 'The real estate bloke? The one who's been hassling me to sell ever since the funeral. If I didn't know better, I would have thought you two were in bed together.'

'I'm only suggesting this for your sake and the baby's,' Leigh said, his patience wearing thin. 'It's not like I've suggested it before, it was an idea that came to me a while ago, after *you*, not me, *you* were worried about coping with everything. Three mill sitting in the bank will keep you a lot more secure than the vagaries of the weather and stock prices. The baby will have your full attention at home. But he won't be getting much of that when you're running around treating fly-blown sheep or feeding the lambs because it hasn't rained. Or seeding, or spraying . . . Do I need to go on?'

He watched as Fiona's face suddenly changed, and she smiled at him. 'I know you're only doing this because you care, Leigh. I know you feel like I'm your responsibility, or something, now. But don't. I'm okay to make my own decisions. Honest.' She reached out and put her hand on his arm. 'I'm not selling,' she told him simply but firmly. 'I can't take this little one's heritage away before he has a chance to work out if he wants to farm or not. There're enough people around to help me when I need it. I'll be fine. And I promise I'll ask for it if I need to.'

Sylvia spoke up. 'She's right, Leigh. I know. My husband died thirty years ago. My children didn't know if they wanted to farm at that stage and I wasn't going to do anything until they knew. We'd worked too long and too hard to sell something they wouldn't have a chance of getting back if they wanted to farm. You let Fiona alone. Just be there if she needs a hand.'

Chapter 6

Kim pushed the key into the lock and swung open the door. Walking into the roadhouse was an effort, but one that would be worth it. She had to find a new kind of normal. One that didn't include sleepless nights and worry.

Her appointment with Chelle hadn't been as bad as she'd thought. There wasn't a conclusive diagnosis of breast cancer—she just needed more tests. An ultrasound first, then a biopsy.

Kim shuddered a bit at the thought of a biopsy; she'd heard they could hurt, but Chelle had assured her that not all of them did. It could be more a sensation of pressure than pain. She hoped hers was the pressure, non-hurting kind.

The lights flickered to life, and as she walked past the TV attached to the wall, Kim hit the on button.

Going through her routine as she did every morning, she turned on the deep fryers, got out the bread rolls and started to set up the kitchen for the morning rush. From the fridge she removed a chocolate mud cake and started to slice it into wedges in preparation for the after-sports crowd.

Saturday mornings always seemed to be about coffee, cake and hot chips. Sometimes bacon-and-egg or steak sandwiches, but not many.

Realising she hadn't turned on the pie warmer, she stopped what she was doing and went out to the front counter and switched it on, before loading a few pies, pasties and sausage rolls into it.

The top-of-the-hour news came on the TV and reported a car accident that had killed two people on the Port Wakefield Road and how interest rates were expected to remain steady. She listened to it half-heartedly, wondering how everything was able to seem so normal when her world was about to change—or had already changed—forever.

Back out in the kitchen, she stopped, her fingers finding their way to her breast. She pushed them in, searching for the lump that everyone was telling her was there.

Again she couldn't feel it. She couldn't doubt the results—after all, Chelle had confirmed them—but shouldn't she be able to feel something? Even if it was tiny?

The bell in the shop dinged as a customer came in. Kim pulled on her 'game-day' face, determined not to let anyone know yet what was going on. She hadn't even spoken to her sister, Natalie, about it. Oh, and then there was her niece, Milly. That was a conversation she didn't want to have.

'Good morning,' she said to the truck driver who had just walked in.

'Mornin'.'

'Dining in or take away?'

'Just a coffee to go, love, thanks.'

Kim jotted down the order on the pad before asking about sugar and milk.

'Neither, thanks.' He handed over the money and Kim went back into the kitchen to make it.

She'd just put the cup under the nozzle of the machine when the bell went again. She turned and looked through the reversible mirror and narrowed her eyes. Wasn't that Fiona Forrest, the woman whose husband had committed suicide?

Kim hadn't known either of them, as their farm was seventy kilometres from Barker, close to the larger town of Port Augusta. She could see the telltale sign of Fiona's pregnancy pushing out the jacket she was wearing.

'Won't be a moment,' Kim called and reached for the coffee cup lid, trying to gather her knowledge of suicide so she could be kind and caring towards her without overstepping the mark. It would be good to think about someone other than herself.

Dave hadn't been involved with either tragic event, as they'd been away on holidays at the time, and then he'd been asked to take leave pending an internal investigation. She didn't know the ins and outs of everything, as she would have if Dave were on the case.

Thinking about the two previous cases Dave had been involved in, the familiar feeling of indignation on his behalf swelled inside her. She still couldn't believe the police department could make Dave take leave without talking to him and explaining the process. After everything he'd put into his job, the dedication. She frowned.

Clipping the lid onto the takeaway cup, Kim pushed open

the swinging doors and handed the driver his order before turning her attention to Fiona.

'How can I help you there, sweetie?' she asked. 'You look like you've got to eat for two! I've got mud cake out the back or I can put some chips on. They'll be a few minutes if you want a serve of them though.' Kim smiled as she shook back her hair and watched Fiona.

The woman looked at her with embarrassment. 'I'm so sorry, but I've got this overwhelming craving for a meat pie! I never eat them, but I was passing and it just came over me. Guess it's got something to do with being pregnant.'

'More than likely, I'd say.' Kim grinned. 'Although, I can't speak with any authority. My niece is the closest I've come to having a daughter.' She reached over and checked the temperature of the warmer, before screwing up her nose slightly. 'They're not quite warm enough yet, love. Do you want me to whack it in the microwave for you, or do you want the pastry crispy?'

'Will they be long? I can wait for a while. I don't have anywhere to be.'

'Reckon if you give them another fifteen minutes, they'll be about right. Can I get you a coffee or tea while you wait?'

'A hot chocolate would be lovely, thank you.'

'Take a seat in the dining room, it's more comfortable in there.' Kim pointed through the door. She went back into the kitchen and started frothing the milk. *That poor girl*, she thought. *She looks just awful, like the rug has been pulled out from underneath her. She should be radiating happiness and being fussed over by her husband. Puts my news into perspective.*

She dropped two marshmallows onto the saucer and took the cup out to Fiona, placing it in front of her. 'There you go.

I'll keep an eye on the pies and let you know when they're ready. When are you due?'

'January. I'm four months and two weeks now.' Fiona took a sip of her hot chocolate. 'You know I went to boarding school with a girl from up here. Can't remember her name, though. I remember she was so kind to all the new, homesick boarders. Tall, willowy girl with dark curly hair—a little like yours!'

Kim sensed Fiona wanted to talk, so she pulled out the chair opposite her and sat down. 'I'm Kim,' she said, holding out her hand.

'Fiona.'

'Well, it's nice to meet you, Fiona. Where did you go to school?'

Fiona named a boarding school in Adelaide and Kim gave a loud laugh. 'There you go. My niece, Amelia Bennett, went there. What years?'

'Seriously? That's who I was thinking of. That's right; Milly, we used to call her. She was lovely. Bit scatty and forgetful but lovely.'

Kim nodded. 'That sounds like my Milly,' she said fondly. 'She's beautiful, inside and out! Married now to a farmer. Loves it!'

'That's so strange,' Fiona mused. 'I felt like I knew you when I walked in here, but I'm sure I've never met you before. It must be because Milly looks like you.'

'Could be,' Kim agreed. 'She does look more like me than her mother. She's a throwback!'

Fiona laughed and Kim noted it was just a little too loud and a little too long. Fiona sighed as she picked up her cup again and held it to her cheek.

'I'll tell you why I remember Milly—or, rather, why I remember her face. She was a couple of years older than me and I was really homesick. I can remember her sitting next to me at the sports day. I'd been crying because my mum hadn't been able to make it down. It wasn't long after my dad had left. Mum couldn't get time off work—she was always busy with work or something.' She gave a crooked smile.

Kim put her hands on the table and twisted the salt-and-pepper shakers around, listening.

'Anyway, she must have known I was upset, but she never said anything about it. She just came and sat with me, told me she knew I was from up this way, too, and all the fun things she found about being in boarding school. After that she always kept an eye out for me. Always made a point of saying hello, or if we were going home on the same bus, that I had a seat near hers.' She paused, her eyes fixated on a point in the distance. 'I haven't thought about her in years.' Fiona smiled and refocused on Kim. 'What a small world!'

'It sure is,' Kim agreed.

Their conversational flow was interrupted by sirens and flashing lights on the TV. Kim saw Fiona's face freeze and looked up at the screen. She was pretty sure Fiona was remembering traumatic scenes from a few months ago. She wondered what Fiona might have seen; if it had been dark when her husband's body was found, if the flashing lights had penetrated every remote corner of the farmyard—something Fiona would never be able to forget.

'*In breaking news*,' the newsreader said, '*the body of a woman has been found in an alleyway off Hindley Street in the city centre.*' The urgency and excitement in his tone sickened Kim.

'To date, the information is that the woman was strangled. Police are continuing their enquiries.'

Fiona's face was awash with sadness. 'That poor family,' she said.

Kim turned around to look, just as Steve, Dave's boss, flashed onto the screen. Intrigued that he should be the spokesman instead of a media officer, she focused on what he was saying.

'We are in the process of identifying the woman.'

Microphones were pushed into his face, but Steve held up his hand with authority and said, *'That is all the information we have at this time. We are asking that if any of the public saw or heard anything to phone Crime Stoppers. Thank you.'*

'That poor family,' Fiona repeated. She fidgeted with the empty cup and tore her eyes away from the screen as the newsreader came back on.

'Not often there are murders in Adelaide,' Kim commented. 'And yes, how horrific for the ones left behind.'

'Unless you catch the murderer, they won't have closure,' Fiona said. 'And even then, they'll forever ask the question why. Why it was their child, why she was there on that day, at that time. Why, why, why?

'It's a little like suicide, you can't understand. You think that all the love and support in the world is going to help them, to pull them through it. But it doesn't. And afterwards you're left with a great big empty hole and a question that can never be answered. I think that's the hardest thing. The why.'

Leaning back in her seat, Kim looked at Fiona. 'I agree,' she said. 'A little like cancer, too. Why me? Why did it have to come now?' Without warning, her eyes filled with tears and she blinked them away rapidly.

Fiona looked startled. 'You have cancer?' she asked.

'It's looking that way,' she replied, before shaking back her hair and tilting her face upwards in a defiant way. 'But the other side of the coin is: why not me? What are the stats now? One in eight get breast cancer, or something like that. But even knowing that, there's still that great big question—why?' She looked down at her hands and took a breath. 'Still, nothing like what you've faced, sweetie.'

Her gaze dropped straightaway. 'You know?'

'Yeah, I do.' Kim made her tone soft. 'Bit hard not to hear of something like that no matter how far apart the towns are. And we're not really that far from you, what—seventy, eighty-odd k's? We're country people and we care about our own. You've had a lot to contend with. Especially with the little one on the way now. Plus, the papers didn't leave you alone for a while, did they?'

'They were *bastards*!' The word was ripped from Fiona. 'They even turned up at his funeral.'

Changing the subject, Kim asked, 'Why are you up here today? You're out of your way, aren't you? And it's pretty early.'

Fiona scowled. 'I couldn't sleep. I'd been talking to my brother, Will, on Facebook and he suggested that I just get out and go for a drive. Let the road take me to wherever I ended up. So I jumped in the ute and drove. I don't know why I turned right instead of left when I headed out the front gate, but I did and here I am.' She adjusted her jeans around her waist and wriggled to get more comfortable. 'Will was right, though. I had to get away. I had to see something different. I love being at home, but I'm surrounded with memories of Charlie there and occasionally I just have to not remember.

I have to be normal, pretend like my life hasn't changed forever, that I'm still the person I was before all of this.' Then she laughed. 'And then I felt like a pie, so I stopped.'

Leaning forward, Kim took Fiona's hand. 'You know what I think?' she said, smiling at her. 'I think we were destined to meet. I'm feeling just the same as you. I have to pretend that my life is still normal. That it hasn't changed forever. Two completely different circumstances, but entirely the same feelings. Maybe we could help each other.'

'So weird,' Fiona said. 'Like I said, I felt like I knew you the minute I walked in. It seems safe here.' She paused before taking a deep breath. 'Tell me about the cancer?' Then she flushed. 'If that's not too forward.'

'Not at all!' Kim told her what Chelle had said, finishing with, 'I have to go back to Adelaide next week, just as Dave, my partner, is starting work again, to have the ultrasound and biopsy.'

'Where's the lump?'

Kim lifted her right arm and felt towards the back of her breast with her fingers. 'It's supposed to be here, but I can't feel a damn thing. That scares me even more. Maybe there're others and they haven't been found yet. I tell you, I've gone over them with a fine-tooth finger and I haven't been able to find anything else that feels unusual or sinister. So who's to say there aren't more there?'

Fiona grinned. 'Maybe your husband should check for you, too. Just in case!'

Kim let out a belly laugh—they both needed to laugh now. 'I like the way you think, Fiona!'

Chapter 7

Walking into the police station for the first time in nearly five months, Dave felt the familiar surge of excitement, but it was quickly clouded by disillusionment.

'Good to see you, Dave,' Joan said from the front desk as he walked past.

'Nice to see you, too, Joan. Anything interesting happen while I was away?'

She shook her head, her tightly curled grey hair a stiff helmet. 'It's all quiet on the Western Front,' she quipped.

He made his way to the tea room, relieved to see the coffee machine still in place. That had been one of the first things he'd changed when he'd arrived: the instant coffee had been thrown in the bin and replaced with a sparkling stainless-steel machine that radiated beautiful, rich coffee smells. He switched it on and waited for it to warm up before pouring himself a cup.

The door to his office had been shut, and judging by the

cool temperature within the room, it had probably been kept closed the whole time he'd been gone.

He switched on the computer and idly flicked through the paperwork on his desk while he waited for it to boot up. Nothing grabbed his attention.

There was a clatter of boots on the floorboards outside and a few moments later Andy Denning stuck his head in.

'Well, look what the cat dragged in.' His smile was broad as he held out his hand. 'How goes it, big fella?'

Dave leaned over and grasped the young man's hand. 'Good to see you, Andy,' he responded, wishing he still had his colleague's youthful enthusiasm. He could see it in Andy's face—the expectation of what was going to happen next, the desire, the eagerness. *As they got older, did they all lose it?* he wondered. *Or was it just blokes like me who get hauled over the coals when they least expect it?* He took a breath. 'So, what's news?'

'Not much going on around here since the Eddie McDougall and Charlie Forrest incidents. We've been checking speeds in the school zones now that the holidays are over. Although,' he paused for effect, 'I've had word I'm getting a transfer.'

Dave's eyebrows shot up. 'Is that right? Where are you off to?'

Andy looked slightly bashful. 'I've been asked to do a detective course in Adelaide. I saw there was a job coming up and applied. Then one of the head honchos rang and said he'd heard some good things about me, thought I'd make a good detective and did I want to have a crack. Of course I said, "Is the Pope Catholic?"'

Immediately Dave schooled his features. He couldn't let Andy know what he was really thinking.

No one had contacted him and asked for a reference regarding Andy and his abilities. That's what should have happened. If they had he wouldn't have agreed that now was the right time. In the two years he'd worked under Dave, Andy had certainly improved, but not to the extent of being ready for the detective course. He was a reasonable copper. However, there was a difference between being a reasonable copper and a detective.

Still, he knew that no one was applying for detective jobs and the department was scraping the bottom of the barrel. The word had got out about how hard it actually was to work as a detective and suddenly very few wanted to take it on as a career. The job had changed so much and there was so much work around. Detectives kept long hours, and quite often their marriages—if they were married—didn't survive. They were known for being hard drinkers and never being home. All in all, it was a tough and lonely life. Dave's marriage had been an exception for the first twenty years, but it had gone the way so many went—not talking, no connection, easier to work than be among all the stilted silence of an unloving home. He would never let this job come between him and Kim.

'Well, mate, that's great news. When do you leave?'

'End of this week. Course is six weeks, so I'm hoping I'll be a fully fledged detective in seven weeks' time.'

'Good for you.' Dave turned back to the computer and saw the screen was alight. He clicked the emails and cringed as he saw there were over one thousand to read. Bugger. 'What're your plans for this morning?'

'Jack and I are going to do a patrol over towards Port Augusta. Been a few reports of a grey Holden ute doing fairly high speeds and taking corners on the wrong side. Four, actually—one couple were nudged off the road.'

'Idiot.' Dave rolled his eyes in annoyance. He was one who believed it should be mandatory that every young driver be taken to an accident scene. Let the kids see the twisted and mangled bodies, let them see the deaths and the survivors—the wheelchair bound and worse. Shock tactics. There would be fewer accidents that way, he was positive. 'I'll catch you when you get back then.'

Andy stood there a bit longer. 'Um, Dave? Any chance I could get some information from you about this course? You've already been through it and you're my mentor.'

'Sure, Andy, no problems. It's changed a lot since I did it and it's not as hard to get through. I've taught you a lot of the basics of detective work. I'm not sure I can catch up with you tonight. Kim and I have a bit going on, but I'll make sure I do before you go. We'll need to organise drinks as a catch-you-round, too.'

'I saw Kim yesterday, she looked pretty ragged.' Andy eyed him curiously.

Dave's immediate reaction was that if Andy was going to be a detective he'd need to learn to hide his feelings better and to ask questions more strategically and cryptically. In Dave's experience, people rarely responded well to direct questioning.

'Yeah, there's just a bit of crap going on at the moment, mate. Nothing that we can't handle.' He nodded. 'Better get on with answering these emails. Seems like the whole force has missed me.' He turned away, thinking about Kim and their conversation the night before.

He'd been so relieved when she'd sat down next to him on the couch. Taking the beer from his hand, she'd put it on the coffee table and held his hands in hers.

'I'm sorry.' Kim had given a half-smile that Dave now recognised as sad. He'd seen it so many times over the last week that he never wanted to see it again. Instead he wanted to see her wide grin, hear her belly laugh, and that delighted tone she usually had when she talked to people.

'I'm sorry I shut you out. I didn't know . . .' She broke off. 'I didn't know how to do anything—how to react, how to be, how to understand.'

'Hush, love,' Dave had said to her, taking her face in his hands and looking into her eyes. 'It's fine. We'll deal with this when we know what we have to cope with.' He'd wrapped his arms around her then and held her as tightly as he could, wanting to make everything go away. They'd gone to bed and made love as deeply and intimately as ever, and when Dave had kissed her goodbye this morning, he'd felt even closer to her.

The pain in his gut was the fear of losing her. But he couldn't let her know he was terrified. He had to be her rock.

Running his eyes down the list of emails, he quickly deleted the ones that were newsletters and updates—they were out of date now!

The phone on his desk rang and he snatched it up. 'Burrows,' he snapped.

'Steve Morris.' His boss's voice echoed down the line.

Dave paused for a moment, unsure how to respond. Finally, he said, 'G'day, mate, how's things?'

'Glad to have you back, Dave. Sorry about all that bullshit you had to go through.'

'I won't say it's okay,' Dave retorted, his tone flat.

'No, well . . .' Steve stopped, obviously trying to find the right words. 'As I've said before. We need you. Just not the way you react sometimes.'

Dave opened his mouth once again to defend his actions, but then shut it. He didn't care. He knew he wouldn't change anything.

'How's Kim?'

'We're still waiting on more tests. She has to have an ultrasound and biopsy this week. We'll be heading back to Adelaide on Thursday.' Dave sounded more clipped than he'd intended. He just wanted Steve to get on with his reason for calling.

On the other end of the line his boss cleared his throat. 'I hope you're both holding up okay,' he said gruffly. 'Now, Eddie McDougall. I want you to have a look at his file.'

'Sure. What seems to be the problem?'

'The whole file is a mess. There were protocols that weren't followed. The fingerprints of the three men on the back of the ute weren't taken, for crying out loud.' Steve broke off, his frustration obvious. 'It's just a fuck-up. My first impression is that the officers have gone to the scene, where everyone was distressed, decided it was an accident and left it at that.'

'Didn't Andy Denning and Jack Higgins cover this?' Dave asked.

'They did,' Steve confirmed. 'However, from what I'm seeing, it's mainly Denning who put this file together.'

Dave leaned back in his chair, stretching the telephone cord and pulling the phone towards him. 'I heard today that Denning is heading to Adelaide to do a detective course.'

There was nothing but heavy breathing on the other end of the phone.

'Steve?'

'I heard. Yes, yes, I'd also heard that he'd been approached.'

'Well, then,' Dave said sarcastically. 'Let's hope the course teaches him something.'

'The file has been sent back to you.'

'Wait. Hold on.' Dave straightened at his words. 'Why did the file even leave the police station?'

'Went with the body when it came down here for the autopsy. Should never have left. Instead it landed on my desk—came to me, because I'm the supervisor for your area. I've had a look through it and straightaway I could see there are problems with it.

'I want you to go back through things. Start from the beginning. Re-interview the men who were on the ute that night, then follow up on that suicide—what was his name? Charles Forrest? Talk to the wife. And take Denning with you. See if you can give him some decent understanding of basic detective work before he gets down here. I've been through the electronic version of the file and it isn't any different to the hard copy, which is a small blessing. At least that bit was done correctly.'

'Not much point in taking Denning with me. He leaves at the end of this week.' Dave's mind was racing. It was unusual for Steve to be involved in something as minor as this. And why would Andy have let the file leave with the body? That was not on. The people running the detective course had their work cut out for them with Denning.

'Right, well, I guess the training department will have a bit to teach him when he arrives in Adelaide.'

Dave ignored Steve's last comment, because the bubble of excitement he always got during the initial stages of an investigation began to trickle through him. 'Don't worry, Boss,' he said casually. 'I'll get right onto it.'

'Good man. Hope all goes well on Thursday for you and Kim.'

Dave hung up and walked thoughtfully out to the front desk. 'Joan, has a case file from Adelaide turned up for me?' he asked.

'Something came for you last week. I think Andy was going to put it on your desk.'

'Right.' He strode back into his office and went through the mail again. It wasn't there. 'Andy?'

'They've gone already,' Joan called from the front.

'Bugger.' He cast around, looking for something that looked out of place. On Andy's desk he saw a yellow envelope under some books. When he lifted them he saw his own name and address on the front. Interesting. He pursed his lips.

Inspecting the seal, he noted it hadn't been opened. He must've forgotten to put it on Dave's desk. He riffled through the papers, piled high, looking for anything else that might have been missed, taking in the messy nature of it. A detective needed to be organised; he couldn't keep an untidy desk or forget to do things. That was how notes, ideas and evidence got lost.

He took the envelope back to his office and shut the door behind him, needing quiet and full concentration.

First he looked at the photos, then he started to read the report. It didn't take long to see Steve was right. No one thought this death was anything but an accident; it was just a disorganised and chaotic investigation on Andy and Jack's behalf.

Disappointment and realisation coursed through him. That was what Steve wanted him to do. To clean up the sloppy work and make these two accountable. As he read on, it was clear that there was only one cop who really needed to be shown up, and that was Andy Denning.

Chapter 8

Driving through the front gate of Charona still gave Fiona chills. The few hours of freedom she'd had in Barker during last weekend had been precious, but coming home and seeing the familiar driveway and ramp made it hard to keep her foot on the accelerator.

The light was beginning to fade so she flicked on her headlights, just in case there were any kangaroos. Pulling up at the shed, she felt Meita's wet nose on her hand before she even saw her.

'Hello, beautiful girl.' Fiona stopped and bent down, her stomach squashing up against her breasts. 'Geez, that feels weird,' she complained. 'Now, Miss Meita, Jo is coming out tonight, so don't be barking your head off when the lights show up, okay? Unless you get wind of that bloody wild dog. Then bark as loud and long as you can. Where's Mum? I guess she'll be staying again tonight. It's not like I need the company,' she complained quietly. Her mother thought she was doing her daughter a good turn by staying every so often. But most of the time she seemed to pick the nights that Fiona craved to be by herself.

Meita stood quietly as Fiona grabbed a few bags of shopping from the back seat of the dual cab.

The lights of the house weren't on and the darkness made Fiona shiver.

'C'mon, Meita, you can come in with me tonight, I think.'

Flicking on the lights as she went in, she saw a note in her mother's handwriting on the table. As she read it, a small smile lightened her face. Ah, so her mother and the local doctor, Scott, had gone out to dinner. That was good news. It gave Carly something else to focus on, other than her widowed daughter. As much as she loved her mum and appreciated her support, she could be domineering. And her insistence about the locks was driving her spare. She had Will to thank for that. After one of their Facebook conversations, Will had told Carly that Fiona was getting frightened at night. Now Carly had taken it upon herself to make fitting the locks her top priority. She'd even gone so far as to bail Rob up in the street yesterday! Fiona had to keep reminding herself it was only because her mother was worried about her.

Meita followed her as she checked the answering machine in the office and listened to the messages, all the while gazing at the silver urn on the mantelpiece. It held her Charlie.

'Hi, Fiona, it's Mark. Letting you know that the price of lambs has increased by twenty cents per kilo, over the hooks. If you've got any ready, let me know—I've got this price for about a week.'

The machine beeped then the next voice was Rob's. 'Hi, Fiona, I got your message about the locks. Happy to put them on for you. Got the impression your mum was pretty keen to get it done, so I'll head out in the next day or two. Glad I can help you out. Let me know if you want any firewood, too. I've got a few spare loads cut up. I can bring one out when I come. Cheers.'

'That should finally shut Carly up,' Fiona thought as she wrote herself a note to ring Rob. A load, so she could keep having her fire at night, would be perfect. She wiggled the mouse to bring the computer to life. She saw there was a message from Will.

How goes it, sis? he wrote. *Sorry I've been quiet all week—the firm have had me working overtime on a case to do with mining. You wouldn't believe all the environmental reports we have to read—boring as batshit! ;-) Was good to see the photos you sent through of your jaunt up towards the Flinders. Different country up there to where you are, that's for sure. How are you feeling now? And Bub? How's he? I'll be online later tonight if you need to chat—you sounded a bit flat last night. <3 Will*

Putting her fingers to the keyboard, she quickly typed: *Jo's coming to stay tonight, we're going to try to put the cot together. We may or may not come out without blood. A flat-packed piece of furniture and two women who know best . . . Wish us luck!*

Just as she hit the enter button, Meita let out a bark and ran towards the front door. Looking out, she could see the telltale glow of lights coming around the side of the shed. Jo was here!

'Hello, hello,' she said as she bustled inside. 'It's cold out there.'

Fiona gave her a hug. 'I know. I was just going to light the fire.'

Jo put her hand on Fiona's stomach. 'All good in there, Master Forrest?' she asked, before fixing her friend with a stare. 'What about you?'

'It's been a long week, but we're both fine.' She knelt down in front of the fire and started to stack the hearth with kindling. 'How was yours?'

Jo poured herself a glass of wine and flopped into the chair. 'Oh, you know, crop-inspection time. Everything is looking pretty good, but there're all the old enemies around, beginning to show. It's so early, but we're starting to see heaps of snails. And there's a few aphids into the pastures.'

Fiona got up from the floor, rewarded as the small flames took hold. 'You're going to check all of my crops tomorrow, aren't you?' she asked, her stomach constricting slightly. She hadn't budgeted on spraying too early. She knew she'd have to do something about aphids and red-legged earth mites, but not anything else. Snail pellets were expensive; it wasn't just the cost of buying them, it was also the expense of hiring a spreading contractor to get them out onto the paddocks.

The bank still hadn't unfrozen the business account and her personal one was running low, even with the money she had transferred into it. It would be a while before she had any more lambs to sell. She wished she could take up Mark's offer of higher prices, but the lambs just weren't ready. A suffocating feeling of being trapped started flowing through her body. Quickly she reined it in. She couldn't make sensible decisions if she was emotional.

She swung back from the fire in time to see Jo drain the last of her glass and pour another one from the bottle sitting beside her. Fiona looked at Jo carefully. She noticed the dark smudges under her eyes. She looked very tired.

'You working too hard?' she asked as she sat on the couch next to Jo.

'Just a long week,' Jo hedged.

Fiona sighed and let her head fall back against the couch. She didn't think tonight was the night to try to tackle that cot. Maybe next weekend.

They sat there quietly, until Fiona felt Meita put her paw on her leg. The loveliest thing about this dog was that she had barely left her side since Charlie died. It was as if she knew something within her mistress had shifted and that she needed her.

She covered Meita's paw with her hand. 'I met the nicest of ladies when I went for a drive last week.'

'Hmm?'

'Her name was Kim and it turned out that I went to school with her niece. She was just who I needed to run into that day, I think. She seemed to totally understand how I was feeling.'

Jo opened her eyes and turned to look at her. 'That's really great. Did she lose someone, too?'

'Nope, just really seemed to understand the "why" questions.' She stretched out. 'You know, I never understand the way people come into our lives, or that things sometimes happen when we need them. It crossed my mind that Charlie might have had something to do with that.' Her voice trailed off and she shut her eyes before she could see the look on Jo's face. That wouldn't be something she would understand. 'Kim's been texting me every day to see how I'm going. She's gorgeous.' Fiona paused before asking, 'What do you want for tea?'

'Cheese and biscuits.'

'Going all out then? Is that what you usually eat when you get home?'

Jo let out a giggle. 'More like can't be bothered. And no, I'm a bit of a fan of frozen meals.'

'Jo! Doesn't sound like you're doing a good job of taking care of you!'

'Maybe not, but it's easy.'

'I need to eat something. He's getting hungry,' Fiona commented as she felt a weird sensation deep inside her belly. She gasped, her hand flying to her stomach. She felt the slight fluttery sensation again.

Jo shot up from the couch. 'What's wrong?' she asked, panicked.

'I think he just moved,' Fiona said, her voice filled with awe.

'Really?' Jo put out her hand and pulled it back before it reached Fiona's belly.

Fiona took her hand and placed it on her swollen stomach. 'I don't think you'll feel it yet,' she said softly.

'What does it feel like?' Jo's voice was quiet and reverent.

'Butterfly wings,' Fiona whispered. 'Brushing my stomach. Can you feel anything?'

'No.' Jo finally leaned away. 'Wow.'

'Yeah, wow.'

The magical moment passed and Fiona struggled to her feet while Jo reached for her wine.

'Right, I'll put on some eggs,' she said, going into the kitchen.

'Should be me looking after you,' Jo said and she stood up to put a small log on the fire. 'Not the other way around. Where's your mum? Thought she'd be here telling you what to do, as usual.'

Getting out a frying pan and the eggs from the fridge, Fiona laughed. 'Oh my God, didn't I tell you? She and Scott have had a couple of dates! She's out with him tonight.'

Jo clattered into the kitchen, her face alight. 'Are you *serious*? Ha! That's bloody classic. I can't imagine Carly going out on a date.'

'I'm really pleased for her. It's about time she found someone else. Dad's not coming back, obviously. Who even knows where he is or if he's still alive.' She sprayed some oil into the pan and cracked an egg on the side. 'I don't care. But I always thought Mum sort of hoped he would. Even though I'm pretty sure she never would have taken him back. But I think she would've liked to have seen him grovel!'

'Do you remember much about him leaving?' Jo hoisted herself up onto the bench, her glass of wine next to her.

Fiona stopped to think back. 'Nope, I was away at school. Mum rang one day and said he'd just gone. Left a note to say he wasn't coming back and she could have everything. He took about ten grand in cash, then we never heard from him again.' She shrugged.

'But didn't she get upset? You'd think if someone walked out like that, you'd at least be a little sad? Didn't you get upset?'

Fiona thought about that as she put the bread in the toaster. 'I think she concentrated on me and Will. I never saw her upset, but maybe she just didn't let us see her like that. You know,' she paused, 'maybe that's why she's the way she is now,' she said slowly, as if all the pieces of a puzzle were falling into place. 'She's overbearing and controlling, but I don't remember her being like that when I was really young. That's what it must be, the hurt and bitterness inside her.' Getting out the plates, she smiled. 'If anyone can get that out of her, it'll be Scott. As for me, my father wasn't a large part of my life. He wasn't often home, when Will and I were—it was

Mum who did everything. Took us to sport or church. He was always away. I never asked Mum what he was doing. It was just accepted.' She grabbed a sponge out of the sink and began to wipe down the bench. 'Perhaps I should have.' Her voice faded in memories.

Fiona jumped as Jo banged her glass on the bench with a whoop. 'Oh, I've just worked it out! Maybe that's why Janey was so pissed with her when we took you into the surgery the other day. Everyone knows she's had the hots for the doc for *years*! She's always making lovey-dovey eyes at him.' She raised her voice, mimicking the receptionist. 'Can I get you anything, Doctor? A cup of coffee maybe? You've had such a long, hard night delivering babies.'

Shaking off her thoughts, Fiona laughed. 'You sound just like her!'

'She's one woman who does annoy me,' Jo confided. 'I'm sure she only works for Scott because she's such a busy-body.'

Sliding the eggs from the pan onto the buttered toast, Fiona passed the plate to Jo, who refilled her wine glass for the fourth time and went back into the lounge room to eat. Before sitting down she took off her jumper.

'Doesn't take long to warm up the room,' she said.

'Might have something to do with the wine you're drinking. Your cheeks are red already!'

They ate in companionable silence, although Fiona could tell that Jo was shooting glances at her. She knew her friend well enough to know she was working up to something.

'What?' It might be better to head off what she was about to say than wait until she was questioned.

'What do you mean, what?'

'You keep looking at me. Like you've got something to tell me, or ask. If it's so difficult I would have thought the wine would've given you enough Dutch courage by now!'

'Do you want to clean out Charlie's clothes yet?' Jo blurted out after a moment.

Fiona stilled, trying to understand the words. 'Um . . .'

'Not that you have to,' Jo rushed on, 'but I thought I'd bring it up in case you wanted to but didn't want to bother anyone for help.'

The thought of parting with the things Charlie had worn—been inside of. No, no, she just couldn't. Fiona put down her plate and brushed tears away. 'I don't want to do that.'

'Sorry, it's been on my mind for a while.'

'Well, you have my answer now—no.' She stood up and went into the office to look at the urn holding Charlie's remains.

Jo appeared next to her, touching her arm. 'We've never really talked about that night.'

Fiona picked up the urn and held it to her cheek. 'There's nothing I want to remember about it, but I see it every day. I don't want to talk about it.'

'Okay.' Jo didn't say anything more. She left the room and returned with another glass of wine, but this time she brought back a glass of water for Fiona. She took the urn out of Fiona's hands and placed it carefully on the mantelpiece before leading her back to the couch in the lounge.

The fire crackled and sent sparks shooting up the chimney. Fiona stared into the fire, remembering everything.

'He looked like he was sleeping,' she said. 'Like he'd fallen asleep in the front of the car. Charlie did that sometimes. Especially when he'd been seeding and working really long hours. If Leigh hadn't come and got me and I'd seen him, I would have assumed that was what he was doing. Until I looked in the window. He was so blue around his lips, and when I held his hand, the skin underneath his fingernails was blue, too.' She took a breath as memories continued to pour from her. 'I thought he should have been pink, but he wasn't. Just blue and so still. So still.'

Jo reached out to hold Fiona's hand.

'I can't believe he used Carly's car,' Jo whispered.

'It was ours. We'd bought it from her, but what else would he have used? It was the only petrol car around here. Diesel won't do it.' She swallowed. 'I wish he'd left me a note—something to say he was sorry, or he just couldn't cope anymore. I mean, I know now he couldn't cope. Obviously, or he wouldn't have done this, but just something to say he was sorry; sorry about leaving me. That's all I need, for him to be sorry about leaving me. But, Jo,' she raised her tear-filled eyes and met Jo's sympathetic gaze, 'I don't think he was.'

The fire cracked, throwing sparks up the chimney again, and Meita whined, sensing her mistress's distress. She tried to get onto Fiona's lap, but she leaned down and put her arms around the dog, hugging her to her chest.

Then she spoke even more softly. 'The one thing I never understood about that night was the scotch in the car. He never drank Johnnie Walker Red. Said it was repulsive. He always drank Jameson. You'd think if it was going to be his last drink, he'd drink what he liked, wouldn't you?'

Chapter 9

Once they'd disengaged the security system—a chair jammed underneath the handle of the front door—Fiona and Jo started their crop and pasture inspection. Jo crawled through the ankle-high clover, searching for the microscopic bugs that could destroy an entire paddock of feed in a matter of days.

'I think you're in luck,' she finally said to Fiona, who was stretched out on the grass, patting Meita. 'See these?' She pointed to the telltale white spots on the clover leaf. 'That's red-legged earth mite and there are definitely a few of them crawling around on this poor little plant. I can't see any aphids, which is good news. Still means you have to spray though. Can you get a contractor in?'

Fiona moved over to look at what Jo was pointing at.

'I've spoken to Damien MacKenzie, my neighbour, and he says he can come just so long as I let him know by the end of the weekend how much there is to do. He's fitting me in as a favour.'

A flock of white corellas soared above them and came to settle in the gum trees that lined the deep creek. She could hear them tearing and stripping the leaves from the trees.

'Why do they do that?' she asked out loud.

Jo sat up and looked over at them. 'It's to exercise their beaks, and it stops them from being bored.'

'Really? You'd think with the whole of the sky to explore, they'd never get bored.'

'Come on, we need to go and check your barley crop. I could see from the road last night that it's grown heaps.' Jo stood up and dusted off her knees. 'The soil tests that Charlie had done last year were pretty good and so is your fertiliser history. It depends on how much rain comes through in the next while as to whether or not I'll recommend you put on some urea, to keep the pastures pushing along.' She looked up at the cloudless blue sky. 'The rain has dried up for the time being, but there should be more here by the weekend and the long-range forecast is still positive.' Jo took off her jumper and tucked her short-sleeved shirt into her jeans. 'It's almost hot.'

'I know! This is about the second week in a row there hasn't been a frost. I hate frosts, they just dry everything out so much.'

Fiona's eyes rested on her friend and then widened.

'What are they?' she asked, jumping up from the ground and grabbing hold of Jo's arm, before pushing up her shirt to expose yellowing bruises on her upper arm. 'I didn't notice them last night.'

Jo pulled away. 'Oh, they're nothing. You know what it's like—you bang into things when you're out and about, crawling along the ground and around machinery. Never even know how you get them half the time. I've got a dozen on my legs, too!'

'They're not normal bruises, Jo! I can see the finger marks. What the hell is going on?' Fiona stared at her, hands on her hips.

'Nothing is going on,' she answered in a light tone. 'Come on, we need to look at that barley crop.'

'No, talk to me about this,' Fiona demanded.

Jo shrugged. 'Look, it's nothing. I was with some guy and he got a bit rough. That's all. Nothing big.'

'He got a bit rough?' Fiona felt as if her eyebrows were going to lift her hat right off her head. 'What the hell is that supposed to mean? That's awful, did you report him?'

'Nothing, it's what happened, and no, I didn't.' She turned and started to walk towards the car. 'Don't worry about it.'

Fiona couldn't understand what Jo was saying. She walked after her quickly, grabbing her arm to turn her around so she could see Jo's face. As Jo flinched, Fiona let go. 'Sorry. But why not? That bloke needs to be taught a lesson. Are you alright everywhere else?'

'Again, no, he doesn't. Just relax, Fee. The pool isn't that big out here and you know it. We've all got needs and wants. Sometimes it comes off a different way to what you expect.'

Fiona gaped at her. 'When you come away with your arms looking like that? I don't think so. Who's the bloke? Do I know him?'

Jo held up her hand. 'No. That bit I'm not telling you yet. I just want to see where it goes. It's been on and off for a while. At the moment it's about sex and that's all. We both like it like that. No commitment. Not sure if it will go any further. If it does, you'll be the first to know.'

Fiona blinked. 'What the hell?' She looked at her friend as if she didn't know her.

'Look, don't worry about it. It happens from time to time.'

'Do you know this guy or are you on a weird dating site?'

'I met him through a dating site.'

'Is he a local?'

'No.' Jo grinned coyly and wagged her index finger. 'Now, you're not getting anything more out of me. Sorry if you've been shocked by uncovering my secret life, but don't worry about me—it's how I roll and I like it.'

Fiona got into the ute without a word. Rarely did Jo shock her, but she absolutely had just now. What else didn't she know about her friend? Feeling like she was thinking underwater, she tried to form a question: 'Sorry, I'm still not clear. And I'm sorry to get personal.' She stuttered out the next part of the question. 'Do you like it to get rough or was it something that happened and you weren't expecting it?'

'Wasn't expecting it. Didn't matter though.' The light, flippant tone was back again, but Fiona couldn't help thinking she was hiding much more.

They drove along the stony road that followed the edge of the creek and led to the next paddock.

'I just want to check this pump,' Fiona said, breaking the silence that had filled the car for the past few minutes.

'Have I really stunned you? Do you think any less of me?' Jo asked, staring out the window.

Fiona sensed that Jo didn't want to look at her until she'd heard the answer. Taking her time, she tried to formulate what she was thinking. It was different for her; her relationships had always been based on a mutual liking for each other, not just on sex. But she also knew how lonely Jo had been over the past few years and how badly she wanted someone to love her. Did one lustful night take away that longing, just for a little while? Or did it heighten the loneliness, as it would have for Fiona?

'I don't think anything, Jo,' she responded carefully. 'I'm sad it has to be that way for you. I wish you could find someone who loves you so you didn't have to shag some random stranger, but if it works, who am I to judge? I might be asking your advice on how to do that in a few years' time.' She didn't add that just the thought of it made her skin crawl. She stopped the ute. Turning to Jo, she forced her friend to meet her gaze. 'Just be careful. That's not just being rough.' She indicated her friend's arms. 'That's abuse. I don't suppose a vibrator would do the job?' she asked hopefully. 'It would be a lot safer.'

A laugh bubbled out of Jo, then died in her throat. She rested her elbow on the windowsill and sighed. 'You know, I've tried so many dating websites and I can't get anywhere. No one seems to want a thirty-plus woman. Especially one who works in agriculture. I'm sure it's got something to do with being too independent for a bloke's liking.'

'Weird, isn't it,' Fiona said thoughtfully. 'According to the reality TV shows there're heaps of farmers out there who are desperate for love. Wish we knew where they all were when we're looking for them.'

Putting the ute into gear, she chugged forward over the creek crossing. There was a crunching noise as the stones flicked up under the chassis. A mob of corellas painted the sky white as they rose in one big flock. The noise was deafening as they flew off down the creek and settled in another lot of gum trees.

'I'd like to know that, too!'

'Have you thought about asking for a transfer? Surely your company is big enough to shift you to a different area. Or going down to Adelaide on the weekends, getting in with some singles groups or something?'

'I've tried to transfer a couple of times. Hasn't worked yet. There's always been someone higher up more qualified than I am for the jobs I've applied for.' She shrugged. 'That's the way it is. Got to keep working at it.'

Fiona pulled up at a cocky gate and stared through the front windscreen. 'I'm sorry,' she said. 'I'm sorry I never knew you felt like this. I feel like I've been such an awful friend.'

Jo leaned over and gave her a one-armed hug. 'Not at all. You're the best friend I've got.' She smiled and got out to open the gate.

They drove around the paddock and Fiona marvelled at how much the feed had grown in the past few weeks. Sometimes it didn't grow much through winter, even though there was rain. The ground was just too cold.

The warmer days over the past two weeks had made a difference. She wound her way from the creek around the side of the hill to the top, where there was a water tank, and pulled up.

'Look there,' she said, pointing to the west. 'See that shed in the distance—you can just see the roof shining in the sun.' She got out of the car and motioned for Jo to do the same.

'That's Gunner's Run. Charlie and I tried to buy that place when we first got engaged.'

Jo leaned against the front of the ute and closed her eyes, her face tilted towards the sky. 'Why didn't you?'

'Too much money. Funny looking back, we thought our hearts had been broken. We always wanted to have our own farm—something different and separate to Charlie's family and we thought Gunner's Run would be it.' She pushed her hat back and flicked away a fly. 'But then his granddad gave Charona to Charlie and the rest is history. If we'd done that and we had this place, there is no way I'd be able to do what I'm doing now.'

'You know you're doing fabulously, don't you?'

'Well, what else am I going to do?' Fiona said in a huffy tone. 'It's not like there's a choice, is there? We're country women, we just get on and keep going because if we don't, no one else is going to do it for us. Sometimes things seem to happen for the best, even though we don't know it at the time. We've got no idea about the big picture, have we?'

'No, you're right there. But there is a choice,' Jo said softly. 'Why don't you sell, Fee? Leigh's right when he says how much easier it would be for you.'

Fiona's head whipped around. 'Not you, too?'

Jo held up her hands as if to ward off a blow. 'I'm going to support you in whatever decision you make. And I do understand where you're coming from when you talk about making sure Master Forrest here has the opportunity. I'm just thinking about you. Maybe not selling. Leasing—you've always got the land then. You could come back to it. It might be a better option.'

Fiona was quiet as she looked over the land. A gentle breeze ruffled her hair and the smell of eucalyptus brushed by. In the distance she could hear galahs, corellas and magpies.

'No,' she answered in a low, certain voice. 'No. Farm kids learn by osmosis. They know things about the land, the weather, the stock, from such an early age because they learn by watching. Even if I leased it out, he wouldn't have it ingrained in his soul. Growing up on Charona is what I want for him.'

'Fair enough. I promise never to mention it again!'

In the next paddock Fiona could see the ewes and lambs hanging right on the fence. She smiled as a few lambs took off, running along the fence, playing chasings. They'd run flat out, then sometimes stop so suddenly the ones behind would accidentally barrel into them. 'See?' she pointed. 'He needs to be able to see this, to love it—if he grows up loving it, he might never leave . . .' her voice trailed off as she realised she couldn't see the old season's lambs that were supposed to be in this paddock. She swung around and looked carefully. From the top of the hill, she could see every corner and they definitely weren't there.

'Where are they?' Her voice had risen in slight panic.

'Where are who?'

'The lambs. There are supposed to be four hundred in here and I can't see them.' She quickly walked over to the tank and checked that it was full. The pump next to it was full of fuel and oil, so it was ready to be started when it was needed next. She yanked the rope and the engine roared into life. After making sure it was pumping, she swung around to check the area again. She could see absolutely no sign of the sheep anywhere.

'Come on, let's check the fence!' Jo called to her.

They drove along one fence line and followed it to the gate. There was nothing amiss there.

'I hope they haven't got through into the neighbour's place,' Fiona groaned. She paused as she glanced along the fence. 'But look at that.' There was the telltale sign of wool on the barbed wire and some bent steel posts. She was sure the sheep had been held there until the fence had crumbled under their weight. Just what a wild dog would do, when it was trying to catch its next feed. 'Looks like they've gone over the top. Two guesses what's happened here and the first one doesn't count.'

'The baits aren't working, obviously. It's too clever to take them,' Jo commented.

'Other than when I heard it howl the other night, I hadn't realised it was still around. It's a lot quieter than it was. There's the occasional loss of a ewe or lamb. Geoff mentioned he thought it must be doing its killing away from here, because there's a problem only once in a blue moon. Not like before.' She stopped the ute next to the fence and got out. 'But like you, I wish it'd take the baits.' Grabbing a pair of pliers from her ute, she gave Meita a quick pat, before trying to stand the fence up. The stony ground made it hard for her and by the time Jo was by her side to help, she was puffing.

'Bugger, that means a heap more drafting, then getting them all back across the paddocks to here. Just makes more work for me.' she grumbled, trying to catch her breath.

Jo put her hand on her arm. 'I'm not going to harp on about this, but this is why it would be so much easier to sell.'

'You promised!' Fiona turned on her.

Giving a cheeky grin, Jo skipped out of the way. 'I know, but I couldn't resist. Hey, who's that coming in the driveway?'

Fiona turned and saw a muddy-coloured dual cab slowly making its way down her drive.

'I bet that's Rob come to put the locks in. Nana Carly will be pleased. Come on, let's go and meet him.'

ᔕ

'Around here,' Fiona waved Rob towards the back of the house, where an old rainwater tank lay tipped on its side. A row of wood was stacked up, but it was clear that the supply was running low.

Following her directions, Rob reversed up to the tank, then got out of the car. Jo nudged Fiona. 'Now there's something to look at. Hot or what? How come I haven't noticed him before?'

As she looked at Rob, dressed in tight Wrangler jeans, Rossi boots and a navy shirt, which set off his blond hair, Fiona had to agree—he looked very nice. She'd never noticed how good-looking he was. Maybe she could set him up with Jo. She knew Rob was kind and was pretty sure he wouldn't cause the types of bruises she'd seen on Jo's arms today.

Fiona rolled her eyes at Jo before saying: 'Shh,' hoping Rob hadn't noticed. 'Hi, Rob!'

'Hi, Fee, how are you? Jo, good to see you again.' He smiled at them both. 'Isn't it an awesome day? Nice to see the sunshine for a while. In here?' He indicated the tank.

'Yes, please,' she managed to get out before Jo broke in over the top of her.

'Oh, it is!' Jo gushed. 'Need it to get some of the pastures growing. Too many around with cold, wet feet.'

'Thanks so much for bringing all this out. I'm running really low and can't use the chainsaw.' Fiona interrupted before Jo made a fool of herself. She indicated her growing belly with a wry smile. 'Junior tends to hold me up a little these days.'

'I'm glad I'm able to help you, Fee.' Rob pulled on some leather work gloves and started to unload a trailer full of logs.

Jo elbowed Fiona again and nodded at the muscles rippling up his arms as he handled the heavy logs. Fiona threw her an incredulous look and tried not to giggle as she leaned over to help unload the trailer.

'You're right, Jo.' Rob said. 'The animals need a bit of sunshine too. Quite a few ewes getting around with sore feet because of the water lying in the paddocks.'

That made Fiona prick up her ears. She'd noticed some ewes standing away from the mob and when she'd tried to shift them, they'd been very lame. *That must be what's causing it.*

'Oh, I've seen a few sheep like that here,' she told him.

Jo's mobile phone rang and she answered it as she walked away.

'Are you busy at the surgery?' Fiona asked above the noise of the wood thudding into the aluminium tank.

'There's a lot of small animal work at the moment,' Rob answered. 'You wouldn't believe the amount of cats I'm desexing, and I've two cases of dogs who've eaten chocolate. Not good for their health! Lots of antibiotics for the sheep with sore feet, like I said, but other than that, the big animal work is a bit quiet. It'll fire up again when preg-testing time starts.' He flashed her a grin. 'Do you remember . . .'

Fiona laughed and took a break, leaning up against the side of the ute. 'I know exactly what you're going to say, and yeah, I do!'

'Poor Charlie. You know, I always make my clients mark their dry ewes now. I don't know why we never thought of it beforehand. But it certainly makes a difference when all you have to do is draft up the sheep when they get boxed up, not scan the whole lot again!'

'Thank God for alcohol that night. I'm sure it made us all feel better. I know my arms were sore the next day from pushing the sheep up for you!'

Jo reappeared from the side of the house and motioned to Fiona. 'I gotta go. There's a problem at a farm on the other side of town.'

Fiona squinted at her, sure she was lying. 'Really?'

'Yeah, I'll give you a ring a bit later on.'

Fiona tried to work out what to say. 'Be safe.' She reached out to give her friend a hug and watched her go.

Rob came and stood beside her. 'Right, finished that job. Should we get on with the locks?'

'You'll be in the good books with Mum if you do,' she answered, leading the way into the house.

'Why is it farm houses don't have locks?' Rob asked, inspecting the door.

'I don't know any of the old ones that do. Never used to have to lock up.'

'I'm with your mum. I think doing this is a good thing. I'll just grab my tools.'

Chapter 10

Dave stared at the pages in front of him, unable to believe his eyes. The crime-scene photos he was looking at should have been in focus and well lit. Instead, they were dark, and some were even blurry. He made a note on his pad: *Photos—who took them?*

He'd glanced at them when he'd first opened the file, but hadn't realised how bad they were, being more interested in reading the report.

He took a magnifying glass out of his drawer and tried to make sense of what he was seeing in one of them. The scene had shifted slightly from where the accident had first taken place and Dave could understand that—after all, the three men had panicked as they'd tried to save their friend. They dragged him away from the ute, grabbing what they could to press against his chest. It looked like the guns had been thrown clear because they were scattered haphazardly across the ground. A toolbox was lying near the side of the ute, as was a shovel and some other odds and ends. Obviously all had been in the tray earlier in the evening. He could see the glint of broken glass in the flash of the camera—on closer inspection it was thick and he thought it could be from the spotlight.

The ute was on its side—Dave could imagine the wheels turning helplessly, unable to find traction while in the air. Then the impact of it hitting the ground, the tools scraping, shattering glass, the echo of the shotgun, the silence before the screams.

Even though Eddie wasn't in the pictures—he'd been taken to hospital by ambulance—the rags that had been used to stem the flow of blood were lying next to where he must've have laid.

Next, Dave turned his attention to the autopsy report, although it was obvious that a shot to the chest had killed him. Nothing unusual there . . . Except his hands and head hadn't been bagged, soil analysis had not been handed in and there were no fingerprints.

Dave frowned and chewed the inside of his cheek, before checking his watch and picking up the phone. He waited for Leigh Bounter to pick up. No answer. *Damn.* He crashed the phone back into its cradle. Was there time to drive the seventy kilometres, do an interview and get back before Andy and Jack returned to the station? Probably not.

Instead, he picked up the phone again and rang Geoff. He seemed to be the silent one in all this. He was the driver, but he was also the one who had dropped out of sight since it had all happened. Trauma, Dave guessed, but maybe he would be the easiest one to talk to.

The mobile rang out and he left a short message, asking Geoff to call back. He'd just put down the phone when it rang and Dave recognised the number as the one he had just dialled.

'Detective Burrows,' he answered, reaching for his pen and new notepad.

Geoff's tone was subdued as he introduced himself.

'Thanks for calling me back, Geoff,' Dave softened his tone. 'Busy on the farm?'

'Nothing out of the ordinary,' he replied.

'Must be just about time to peel off some wool in your neck of the woods, huh?' Dave was relying on the TEDS system to get the man talking. Tell me, Explain to me, Describe to me, Show me. It was tried and tested. He'd seen inexperienced coppers go in and ask direct questions and the interviewee shut down. There had been one incident back in WA when twenty-five tonnes of superphosphate fertiliser had been stolen and the young cop had just gone in and said, 'What do you know about the fertiliser being stolen?' Dave had wanted to put his head in his hands, because the younger man had just alienated a witness. The neighbour had fired up, asking what they thought he had to do with it, when at the time, the police hadn't thought anything . . . they had just wanted to talk and gather information.

'I finished shearing last week,' Geoff responded. 'Two weeks' worth.'

Dave let out a low whistle. 'Timed it just right, the prices are pretty good at the moment.'

'They're not bad,' Geoff agreed. 'Helps keep the wolf from the door. What with lamb prices on the rise and crops looking good, it'd be nice to think I could make some money this year.'

Dave jotted down a note. *Financial pressure??*

'Good results with the shearing?'

'Pretty happy with the wool quality. They cut about six kilos per sheep and averaged between eighteen and twenty-three microns. Should go up for sale at the end of next week.' Geoff offered the information without Dave having to dig too hard. 'Do you know much about sheep, Detective?'

'I used to work in the Rural Crime Squad in WA,' Dave said as he made a note of when the money would be coming through. 'Had a lot of experience with sheep and cattle. I'm actually the third son of a farmer, but there was never room for me at home, so I chose to be involved in agriculture in a different way. Loved working with sheep though. Prime lambs were great fun, but of course, back when I was a boy, they weren't "prime", they were "fat" lambs.'

'Yes, people don't want to buy "fat" now, do they?' There was a pause and then Geoff asked, 'You're not farming now, obviously. You're a copper.'

'Yep, a copper, but I spent a lot of time in the Stock Squad. The government, in its wisdom, gave it over to the Department of Agriculture about nine years ago.'

'Got no idea, the bloody government,' Geoff said slowly, his disgust loud and clear.

Dave wasn't going to enter into that side of things, so he changed the subject. 'Your place must be pretty good stock country to be able to get that type of cut per sheep. Whereabouts is your place exactly?'

'About ten k's from Booleroo Centre. Towards Morchard.'

'Ah, you're pretty close to Fiona Forrest then?'

'On the other side of town, compared to where she is. If you go up the hill on their place, you can almost see mine on a clear day.'

Dave rubbed his eye, and pushed his coffee cup around, waiting to see if Geoff added anything. He didn't, but in the background, Dave could hear the bleat of sheep and the barking of a dog.

'Out and about now, are you?' he finally asked.

'Got a few mobs to shift down the road and back into their paddocks.' There was another pause. 'Look, Detective, is there something I can help you with? I have things I need to do.'

'Geoff, I'm sorry to have to do this to you, but we're looking into the death of Eddie McDougall.'

There was a pause a heartbeat long, then: 'Why?'

'It's nothing really, but the investigating officer didn't get all the information needed. I wanted to run a few questions past you. Perhaps get you to come out to the scene with me.'

Again, all Dave could hear was the background noise of the sheep yards.

Finally, Geoff said yes and they organised a time.

Interesting, Dave thought, as he hung up the phone. He was expecting some type of pushback—that was usually what happened when he conducted an investigative review. Witnesses and other people who'd been affected didn't want to have to relive it all. Geoff just agreed. But the way he'd volunteered the information about shearing . . . maybe he was desperate to talk. Perhaps he didn't have anyone who would listen. Dave was happy to be a listening ear—that was when he heard the best information.

He heard Andy and Jack return to the station and took a deep breath. Opening the door, he called Andy into his office.

'Take a seat.' He pointed to the chair on the other side of

his desk. 'Can you tell me how you went about investigating this suspicious death?' he started without preamble as soon as Andy had sat down.

'There was nothing suspicious about it,' Andy said. 'It was an unmistakable accident.'

'That's not what I asked.' Dave kept his voice patient and level. 'I asked how you went about investigating a scene you'd been called to, with a suspicious death involved. How did you do your best to be accountable to, and get answers for, the family of Eddie McDougall?' He fixed Andy with a hard stare and watched as a red stain appeared on his cheeks.

'I did what I was supposed to do.' There was defensiveness in his tone. 'I locked down the scene, restricted access.'

Dave nodded. 'Good,' he said lightly. 'Sounds like an excellent way to start.' He saw Andy relax and the hint of cockiness return. 'What else did you do?'

'Took photos of the scene, spoke to the people who were also there at the time. I got the ambulances in, although there wasn't much point. It was pretty clear he wasn't going to survive. But we needed them to treat the others for shock as well as do what they could to help the victim.'

Dave wanted to shake the man for his nonchalance. He was dealing with someone's loved one. Instead he nodded. 'Tell me what else you could have done.'

Andy narrowed his eyes. 'Are you saying I didn't investigate this properly? Or are you giving me hints for the detective course I'm about to do?'

Dave leaned forward and put his elbows on the table. 'Why don't you have a think about that and see what you come up with?'

That stumped Andy, who opened his mouth and closed it again, his jaw tightening.

Dave pushed the file across the table. 'If you were handed this, as a detective, would you think this file was complete?' He had purposely put the shoddy photos on top of the file.

Andy flicked through them, then quickly looked at the reports, his eyes scanning them, before he cleared his throat.

'The photos are a bit dark and hard to see,' he admitted.

Dave waited him out.

'The interviews with the other victims could have been a bit more in-depth.' He turned over a page, ready to make more comments, but his frustration got the better of him. Andy threw the report down on the table. 'Hang on. I said before. It was obviously an accident. Why would you bother with all that other stuff, when it's a fox shoot gone wrong? Look, that's exactly what Leigh Bounter says here.' He pointed to a line: '*Oh my God, what a terrible accident. How are we going to tell his mother?* And here: Geoff says, *I couldn't stop the ute from sliding. One minute everything was okay—Charlie had just shot a fox and we were going over to make sure it was dead, then the next, I hit something, with the front tyre. The noise . . . like ripping. I remember it hurt my ears, then the ute just rocked over. I couldn't do anything.*' Andy sat back and looked at Dave. 'See? Just an accident.'

'But how do you know?' Dave persisted.

'Because they told me!' Andy almost shouted. He half rose from his seat before he sat back down again.

Dave could feel Andy's anger, aimed at him, but took his time to respond. Let him wait. After all, Eddie's family would be waiting for the proper answers, since the young man had so readily accepted what he was told.

'Sure, Andy, you're right. That's exactly what you were told. But did you ask if there was any bad blood between the victim and any of the men on board? Did the victim owe money, or was there some type of motive that could have indicated he was killed and that it was made to *look* like an accident?'

There was an uncomfortable quiet in the room before Andy blustered: 'Get real! This is Booleroo Centre we're talking about. Nothing ever happens there. Of course it was a bloody accident.'

Dave stood up and put his hands on the table, leaning across to get in Andy's face. 'Like the stock stealing that was around here in the early two thousands, like the rodeo theft a couple of years ago and the poaching of wildlife from the Flinders Ranges last year? Yep, you're right, nothing happens around here.' He pulled back and paced the room. 'You've got a lot to learn before you make it as a good detective, Denning.' He stopped and turned back to the young man. 'The first rule of detective work is to never, ever make assumptions. And why, for God's sake, didn't you take fingerprints from all the men there that night? One of the men is dead! How are we supposed to get his prints now? He's been buried.'

Andy kept his seat, staring straight ahead. Dave wanted to feel sympathy for him. After all, it wasn't long ago he'd probably had the exact same look on his face while Toe-cutter grilled him. The difference was Denning had brought this on himself by second-rate work. His own reprimand was brought on by disobeying orders.

'I've been asked to go back and reinvestigate this case,' Dave finally said, sinking down in his chair. 'Is there anything you want to bring me up to speed on? Anything that isn't documented in here?'

Andy shook his head, his eyes still forward and avoiding Dave's.

'Right, then. I'd like you on board with this—to watch and learn only—but I guess that's impossible since you're leaving at the end of this week. You asked for some help with the detective course. The best piece of advice I can give you, Constable Denning, is that investigating is all about gathering information and then proving the conclusion without a doubt. It's not about jumping to conclusions and substandard, not-thought-through and chaotic work. It's about being methodical, working through things slowly. Asking the right questions. Your work here wouldn't stand up in a courtroom. But mine will.'

Chapter 11

Darkness had fallen across the streets of Adelaide. The soft glow of streetlamps cast small circles of light that didn't reach the darkest corners.

He sat in his car, waiting for the one. He would know her when he saw her. And he was patient. He would wait until the early hours of the morning if he had to.

He watched as people walked the street. There were couples laughing, walking hand in hand—they were the ones who made him sick. *It will never last*, he wanted to scream at them.

There were the groups of men, tumbling, inebriated, out of bar doors, arms around each other, singing Cold Chisel and other iconic eighties music, their voices loud. He wanted to yell at them, too, but he restrained himself, not wanting to attract any unnecessary attention.

Then there were the families, the parents hustling their youngsters along the footpath, protective hands on their arms, making them walk quickly so they didn't see too much of the seedier side of town.

Tonight there were two women haunting one corner—perhaps they were offering two for the price of one. That tickled his fancy, but he would hold off.

He had something particular in mind for tonight. A celebration.

He thought about the incident that had changed everything, and started to feel angry again. Like he had to assert himself. It wasn't an uncommon story, he realised. A young boy in a change room, left alone with a man he trusted. Told he had talent and asked to stay behind after practice.

The man had stroked his ego, before stroking his leg. The actual act, he couldn't remember. He'd blocked it out, but he remembered the pain, guilt and shame. He knew it was wrong and that he should report the man. But the threats and promises he'd made had been too confusing. And now? Well, that man was gone. He'd made sure of that. But he still needed to release his rage from time to time.

Getting out of the car, he pulled his hat down low, thinking he'd stretch his legs. At a street stall, he bought a couple of chicken kebabs. Walking on, he smelled Asian food coming from a restaurant and realised that not only was he still hungry, but a drink would go down a treat, too. Only one, for he had to drive and keep his wits about him.

Settling himself at a table, he ordered food and a beer. He looked around, just in case there was someone here who suited his need tonight.

In the dim light, there were many couples sitting at tables, but there didn't seem to be anyone by themselves. He let out a breath through his nose—partly in disgust and partly in resignation. He had known it wasn't going to be that easy because she had to be perfect. Fit exactly what he liked.

He thanked the waiter who brought his beer over, and took a sip before casting around from under the brim of his hat again.

Oh, but hang on . . . in the corner . . . There was a woman sitting by herself.

Narrowing his eyes, he looked her over carefully. Her face was angular, with high cheekbones, and she was deeply tanned. Her dark wavy hair fell over her arm to her waist. Her head rested on her hand and she was reading a book. A clear indication she wasn't waiting for anyone.

He watched her for a while, admiring her full mouth, her graceful hands as they used chopsticks, and the way she tucked her hair behind her ear. He felt the familiar ache of desire.

Beckoning to the waiter, he asked him to send her a glass of whatever she was drinking.

When it was delivered she reacted with surprise, then looked over at him. He tilted his head, gave her a slow smile and raised his own glass to her. Embarrassed, she looked down and returned to her book, pushing the glass of wine to the corner of the table, untouched. That just enflamed his desire. And his anger. He didn't like to be dismissed.

He imagined her in his bed; he would tie her up. He would spank her, pull her hair. Oh, how he'd love to hear her scream. He knew she'd enjoy it. In his experience it was the quiet ones who were always the feistiest. Blindfolding them seemed to really heighten their senses. Once they were blindfolded, he could do anything with them.

He licked his lips, desperate to taste her skin, and tried to control his breathing. This was no good. He was already too worked up. He shifted uncomfortably. He was so hard, his dick stretched against his denim jeans, the material unyielding and painful. He had to stay where he was.

So when she walked out the door, there was nothing he could do but let her go.

Half an hour later, he walked into a whorehouse and requested a prostitute. One who liked it rough, he insisted.

Chapter 12

That evening, Fiona stoked the fire, grateful for the wood Rob had brought. She turned on the TV, before looking over at Charlie's chair. She needed to feel close to him.

She missed him all the time, but tonight she'd wanted to talk to him, to share her excitement of having new lambs on the ground. To talk crops, feeding regimens and things that only a farmer would understand. To tell him about the lambs going over the fence and how there were snails around so soon in the season.

But he wasn't here. She glanced at the urn, which she'd brought into the lounge with her, just so she could be near part of him. It hurt her eyes to look at it.

Could she sit in his chair? Would she feel closer to him if she did? It was one thing she hadn't done yet. Oh, she snuggled into his side of the bed and wore his jumpers, just so she could be inside something of his, but she hadn't sat in his chair.

She ran her hands over the arms of the chair before lowering herself into it. Closed her eyes and imagined Charlie sitting there, talking to her, drinking a beer. Smiling at her, before changing the channel or reaching out to hold her hand as she sat in the chair next to him.

'You're doing great, Fee. Don't worry about anything. She'll be right.'

Her eyes flew open and she looked around. His voice sounded so real, even though she knew it was only in her mind. Tears pricked her eyes and she swallowed quickly. She couldn't get maudlin. It would be the end of her tonight, if she did. Knowing she needed a distraction, Fiona tried to make her brain focus on what else she could do.

Tea. She'd get herself some tea.

In the kitchen she grabbed the lamb chops that had been defrosting on the sink and ripped the bag open. Methodically she cut up a salad and seasoned the chops, before starting to heat the frying pan.

Outside, Meita set off a round of ferocious barking.

Fiona froze, her heart starting to thump in her chest. She waited, listening. Meita never barked unless there was a reason. It was a bark Fiona had never heard before—certainly not one warning of arriving visitors.

She sounded savage.

Fiona could almost imagine her lunging at the end of her chain, trying to get at whatever was out there.

There was only silence now. An engulfing silence that threatened to swallow her. She started towards the door, but Meita let off a new round of barking, even more vicious than before.

Fear prickled her skin into goosebumps and her stomach

was in knots. She stared at the blank window, seeing nothing but darkness.

Then she heard it. A low, guttural howl.

Instantly, she knew it wasn't Meita.

Fiona couldn't breathe.

The howl sounded again. In her head, she heard Charlie again. '*Get the gun, get the gun.*'

Abruptly, Fiona ran to the gun cabinet and pulled out the shotgun. Jamming two bullets into the barrel, she cocked it and made sure it was ready to fire, then ran towards the front door.

She stopped, listening. Where was it? Where was that *bastard* of a wild dog? She'd never felt an urge to kill like she did now.

She flicked off the lights, then opened the door. Peering outside, she realised she didn't have a spotlight or any other way of seeing where it was.

Fiona wasn't about to let Meita off the chain in case she took up its scent and followed it.

Easing onto the verandah, she tried to make out if the dog was anywhere close by. It moved stealthily so it would be hard to hear.

But there it was. Standing at the end of the verandah, looking at her. Yellow in colour and its tongue hanging out, unmoving, its eyes reflecting the moonlight.

Fiona stared at it, all her fear gone. Slowly she raised the shotgun and aimed. It stared back at her, its eyes not shifting from her.

Meita started to bark again and the spell was broken. The wild dog took a step into the darkness and was gone.

ആ

Dearest Kim, Fiona wrote in her text message. *I know you're heading to Adelaide today for more tests. I'm thinking of you and sending you every good wish I can. Let me know how you go when you feel you can.*

As she hit 'send', she heard her mother call out to her. 'Yoo-hoo, Fee! Where are you?' Then she lowered her voice, but Fiona could still hear her. 'I know you're here somewhere, because Meita is here and so is the ute.' She called out again, 'Fee?'

'In here, in the shed,' Fiona finally answered as she wiped her hands on an oily rag and walked out into the dull light of an overcast day.

She'd been checking to see what stores of wool packs and lice treatment she had for shearing, in case she needed to buy anything extra, then decided to check the oil in the tractor that hadn't been used since Charlie's death. She thought she might pull it out today, make sure it started, and give it a run.

Summer would be upon them in no time. The paddocks would become a baked golden—barley and wheat crops standing tall and straight, the heads plump and full of grain. The sky an endless blue, heat mirages shimmering in the distance. It wouldn't be too long before she would need to hook the tractor up to the chaser bin for harvest. She needed to make sure it was all in working order.

'Oh, that reminds me,' she muttered to herself and took out her notepad to jot down a couple of points. When Damien MacKenzie turned up tomorrow to start spraying, she'd need to ask him if he would contract harvest for her. Fiona was sure she'd be able to drive the chaser bin, but not the header.

'Hello, darling.'

'Hi. Soooo,' she dragged out the word and turned to Carly, who was patting Meita. 'I haven't seen you since. How was the big date?'

Carly flicked her hand coyly. 'Oh, that seems like an age ago! A lot has happened since then! I can't even remember.'

'Yeah, right, Mum! It was last week. But,' she waved her hand around airily, knowing that Carly was dying to tell her. 'You don't have to tell me if you don't want to!' She lifted her eyes to the range of hills behind her mother. 'Come on, get inside, quick! We're about to get rained on.' She turned and went back into the shearing-cum-machinery shed and turned on the lights. As they flooded the interior, the misty drops started to land on the tin roof. She stopped and looked out of the doorway. Raindrops fell into puddles and created ripples. There had already been an inch of rainfall this week and the pools that hadn't soaked into the soil were very large.

The sound of running water came from the side of the shed, where the rainwater tank was overflowing—something that rarely happened. Fiona sighed happily as she huddled into her jacket and pulled the hood over her head.

'Isn't this beautiful?' she asked above the noise of the rain, which had become heavier, as she sat down on a wool bale. 'I love the rain.'

'Oh, me, too,' Carly agreed. 'Me, too.'

They both stared out at the countryside through a curtain of rain. The sheep were tucked up under the bushes and gum trees and Fiona could just see them. The creek closest to the shed still had water from the previous downfall and she knew it would start to flow very soon.

She couldn't hear the whoosh of cars that passed by her front gate, but she could see their lights as they came around the corner, into the dip of the creek and up past her driveway.

Thankfully, she didn't feel as cold and bleak as the day itself. She turned her attention back to Carly.

'Now, quickly, before I forget, Rob came and put the locks in for me, you'll be thrilled to know. And he brought a load of firewood! Means I don't have to be stingy in lighting the fire anymore.'

Carly smiled. 'Great. That's one job I can cross off my list. What a lovely man.'

'So,' Fiona looked at her mum expectantly. 'You're not getting away with it. Spill! Tell me how it was.'

Carly toyed with a bit of wool that was escaping the confines of the bale before saying, 'It was really very nice.'

A half-grin played around Fiona's mouth. 'Is that right? Well, I'm really very pleased!' She got up to start tidying the workshop bench. 'I can't sit still, Mum, I have to do something. I'm just going to put all these tools away, while you keep talking.'

Carly followed her over to the bench and looked at the shadow board and the mismatched tools lying around. 'Don't think I can help much here, I'm afraid!'

'It's easy, all you've got to do is match up the tool to the picture.' With deft hands, Fiona hung a hammer and a spanner over their outlines and turned back to do it again. 'I should have done this ages ago, but I couldn't face being in here, touching the things he had touched last.'

Carly reached out and put her hand on Fiona's arm to still her. Startled, Fiona looked over at her.

'I am so proud of you,' Carly said in a low voice. 'So proud that you took this farming game on and gave it your best, the way you've coped with everything since . . . Well, since Charlie died. And before. You are an incredible and inspirational young woman, and I'm so pleased you're my daughter.' She left her hand there a little longer, then patted her arm and withdrew.

Fiona wasn't sure what to say—it was so unlike her mother to show any emotion. Maybe Scott was a good influence on her!

Clearing her throat, she hung up different-sized ring spanners. 'I'm glad, Mum. I had a pretty good mentor.' She turned around, brandishing a tyre lever. 'Now, tell me about your date or I might have to get violent!'

The rain eased back to a drizzle, the melodious noise on the roof creating beautiful music for a story. But when Fiona saw the look on Carly's face, she knew that, really, nothing had to be said. Her mother had been hit by Cupid's arrow.

'We went to the fish-and-chips takeaway place in Port Germein, then took a stroll down to the jetty and ate about halfway out on the benches there.'

'Cripes, must have been cold!' Fiona had just about cleared the workshop bench and was heading towards the chemical-storage room to see which sprays were left from last year.

'It was a little fresh, but I didn't really notice. Not for the first bit, anyway. We talked—do you know he's the only person I've come across who loves apple-and-vegemite sandwiches like I do?'

Fiona let out a laugh. 'You must be destined to be together, then!'

'Oh, be like that,' Carly huffed, but she couldn't keep the smile from her face. 'I thought it might be difficult—you know, him being your doctor and so on, but it's not. He never even mentions work. You wouldn't know he was a doctor.'

'So when are you seeing him next?'

'I've seen him every day since. We're going back to Port Germein on the weekend to do some fishing.'

But Fiona barely heard what her mother said. Her eyes narrowed as she looked at a dusty twenty-litre insect-spray container. Strangely, the handle of the chemical drum was clean. It shouldn't have been. All the others were dusty. She could see where a hand had wrapped around the handle. Given this would last have been used twelve months ago, she found that more than a little odd.

She checked around but couldn't see anything out of place. Maybe Charlie had come in here to check things before he died. Maybe he'd even sat in here to hide from her, hide from what she saw as love and concern but what he'd seen as intrusive and meddling behaviour. She knew he'd certainly avoided her at times. 'Oh, Charlie,' she whispered. She ran her hands over the drum, wanting to touch something he had touched.

'Fee?' Carly was at the door to the chemical-storage room.

She hoisted the drum back to the floor with a groan, banging it against her stomach as she did so.

'Fiona!'

Surprised at Carly's sharp tone, she snapped back, 'What?'

'You shouldn't be lifting something that heavy. You might hurt the baby.'

Just then Fiona's mobile phone beeped, and she was thankful for the distraction. Pulling it from her pocket, she saw the text was from Kim. *Thank you, sweetie, I'm pulling out all good thoughts too. Xxx*

'Fiona! Did you hear me?'

'Yes, Mum. Don't worry, I'm fine. The baby's fine. We're all good.'

'When's your next appointment to see Scott?'

'Next week.'

'Make sure you tell him you're lifting things.'

'If I don't, I'm pretty sure you will.'

Meita, who had been snoozing in the corner, sensed the tension in the air. She gave a short, sharp bark and Carly a look of disdain as she got up and moved to sit next to Fiona.

Carly bit back a smile. 'I'm obviously outvoted!'

'Exactly. Come on, it's lunchtime and I need something to eat.'

'Do you feel faint?' Carly immediately asked.

'No, Mum, I'm just hungry!' Exasperated, Fiona stomped out into the grey day and took a deep breath of cold air. The chill on her cheeks made her stop and gasp a little as another wave of rain started to fall. She dug her hands deep in her pockets, trying to keep them warm.

In the distance there was the growl of an engine and she swung around to look up the road. A John Deere tractor, a large orange flashing light on its roof, rounded the bend. The engine noise rumbled up the creek line. Towing a massive spray rig, it slowed down, turning into the Charona driveway.

'Who's that?' Carly asked.

'Damien MacKenzie. He's coming to do some spraying for me. I need to talk to him, show him which paddocks and that sort of thing.' She gave a wave and directed him towards the fuel bowser.

'I'll organise the lunch then, shall I?'

'Oh, Mum, that would be brilliant.' Her irritability had disappeared and in its place was tiredness. She'd experienced this before, when someone had taken charge, just for a moment. It meant she didn't have to keep going, be responsible for everything; she could just focus on one thing at a time.

Damien climbed down the first few steps of the tractor, his Driza-Bone jacket flapping around his ankles, then jumped the rest of the way. He landed in a puddle that splashed up underneath his coat. 'Bugger!' he swore.

Fiona giggled a little. 'Wet jeans now, Damien. Aren't they awful? Cold and heavy!'

'Every time I've got out of the tractor today, I've managed to jump into some bloody water. Look!' He lifted his jacket to show his mud-splattered jeans.

'Don't complain! There's money in mud, not dust, and it's usually dusty here. You'll just have a bit of washing to do tonight.' Grabbing the maps from the dashboard of her ute, she indicated for him to follow her, then scurried out of the rain and into the shearing shed, Damien following.

'I know, I know. Not often we get seasons like this here. But in this country, well, we'll end up spending all the time bogged if this keeps up. I've still got so much to do.' He sounded exasperated.

'You can't spray when it's raining,' Fiona reminded him.

'Yeah, fair call,' Damien shot her a grin. 'I need patience, apparently. That's what my gran is telling me all the time.'

'How is your gran?' Fiona asked, knowing just the two of them lived in the family home on the neighbouring farm and that he looked after the elderly lady as much as he could.

'She's getting a bit frail. So, what have you got for me?' The younger man looked at her expectantly. He was only in his twenties and he ran this business to help make some money on the side. It seemed to be how so many younger farmers had to do it these days. Many went shearing, while others ran a contract business, like Damien, and she'd heard of a few who had taken jobs at the mines, leaving their family or wives at home to manage the farm while they were gone.

'Okay.' She handed him the recommendations Jo had written out, then spread out the maps on top of a wool bale and spoke above the drumming of rain on the tin roof. 'I need you to spray the Creek Paddock, Hollies and this one here, up against the boundary fence.' She pointed to a clearly marked gateway. 'In this paddock there's a mob of lambs that I've only just got back from the neighbours. Reckon that wild dog pushed them over, so if you could be a bit careful around them coz they're still a bit flighty.'

Damien nodded and they swung around as Meita began to bark. A muddy LandCruiser pulled up next to the shed and Leigh Bounter got out. He sprinted across to where they were standing.

'Ah, here's my ride,' Damien said. 'No point in starting now with the rain around—can't spray in the wet, as you just reminded me!'

'I was a little surprised when you said you were coming today, with the forecast,' Fiona turned. 'Hi, Leigh.'

'Howdy, all.' He took off his Akubra and shook the rain off its brim.

Fiona finished giving Damien her instructions, then rolled up the map and handed it to him. 'Okay?' she asked.

'No problems.'

'I'll be somewhere around if you need a hand. The two-way channel is thirty-two, if needs be. But you know all that, being the neighbour and all! When do you think you'll be back?'

Damien wrinkled his brow, and Leigh spoke up. 'Weather looks like clearing by Monday, Damo.' He winked at Fiona. 'You'll be right to come and play footy on Saturday and still not miss any good spraying weather.'

Laughing good-naturedly, Damien shot Leigh a look. 'You just want to make sure we win on Saturday. Are you sure you've checked that forecast properly?'

'Never muck around with a weather forecast!'

Damien turned to Fiona. 'How about I check the weather and get back to you? I just saw a clear time to get the tractor here and get a ride home, so I'll give you a ring and let you know. Where's the chemical?'

Fiona showed him the storage room and said she would pick up the extra drums she needed when she was in town next.

'Good-oh. I'll ring you.'

'Now, the other thing I had to talk to you about was, are you able to take me on as a long-term client? Harvesting, seeding and spraying? I can drive the chaser bin for you, over harvest . . .' She stopped when she saw the strange look on his face. 'What? Are you already booked up?'

'Nup, but I thought you were selling. I'd heard you were just finishing off the season then shooting through.'

'That would include finishing harvest,' Leigh said, pointing out the obvious.

'What? Where'd you hear that from?' Fiona spoke over the top of Leigh.

'Don't even go there, mate,' Leigh advised. 'You'll get your head bitten off.'

'Must have been gossip. Sorry.'

'But who told you that?' Fiona was bewildered.

'Fee, you know how everyone loves to talk. Someone will have made something up or pretended they knew what you were going to do and everyone else will have jumped on board. It's a small country town. What do you expect?'

Fiona stared at the ground, stunned there could be such rumours around when she thought she'd made it as clear as she could that she wasn't going anywhere.

'Changing the subject,' Leigh said, as he and Damien loaded themselves into the ute. 'Are you coming to the footy on Saturday? It's my match.'

'I know, I'll be there.' She tapped the roof of the ute and said goodbye. Watching them drive away, she put her hand to her stomach and patted it. 'What's up in there, Hamish?' she asked quietly. 'You're feeling a little weird.'

Chapter 13

The silence in the car was deafening as Dave and Kim drove towards Adelaide. They'd tried to make small talk for a while, but it was too hard. Instead, they held hands. Dave had one hand on the steering wheel and Kim's tucked in the other.

They'd agreed the night before that they would face together whatever came. Kim wouldn't shut Dave out, and he would try to be as open as he could with his feelings.

The traffic started to pick up as they hit the Port Wakefield highway. Kim's breathing became a little faster and shallower. The fear sat in her stomach like a heavy stone.

When they finally pulled into the parking area next to the specialist's rooms, she found she couldn't get herself out of the car. It were as if she was glued to the seat.

'This is bloody ridiculous,' she said. 'Yes, I'm scared, but I'm stronger than this.'

Dave rounded the side of the car and took her face in his hands. 'You can't change the direction of the wind, but you can adjust your sails to reach your destination,' he said in a soft voice.

Kim looked at him. 'Where did you find that?' she asked.

Grinning, he pulled her from the car. 'Last night. On Google. I was looking for inspirational quotes. I wanted to be able to say something positive when there wasn't anything positive to say!'

'I'm impressed. And tell me,' she said with a small glimmer of her normal personality, 'who said it?'

'You think I don't know!'

'Do you?' She shrugged her handbag over her shoulder and kissed him as a lazy, frigid breeze rustled the leaves of the trees that had grown up in the middle of the cement footpath. Cars dashed by in both directions and Kim had an odd thought. How many people she didn't even know existed were about to go through the same experience as she was? How many of these people were driving past her right now?

'I do, actually.' He raised an eyebrow at her. 'The one and only . . . Jimmy Dean.'

Kim kept walking, looking at the ground, but a grin crossed her face. 'Is that right? You've surprised me.'

'Glad I can still do that. Come on. Here we are.' He indicated the door of an historic building.

Kim straightened and blinked, willing herself to be brave. It was then that she saw it. 'Look, Dave,' she breathed, reaching up to trace the outline of the stained glass that framed the door. 'Galahs. My favourite.'

'Must be a good sign.' He pushed the door and held it wide open for her.

The quietness of the room was what hit Kim first. Footsteps muffled by thick carpet, and the hushed tones of the receptionist sitting behind the desk. *They must see some dreadfully sad things*, she thought. *But then again, there must be some beautiful times, when the results are negative, too. That could still be me*, the fighting part of her said.

Kim had lain awake many nights wondering if the results could indeed be negative. If Dave's comment, that it might be a cyst, would be right. All these 'what if' questions haunted her.

She knew she had to hold onto hope, but in the end she'd decided it was better to be prepared for the worst. Besides, there was no point in worrying. She couldn't change what was about to happen.

After Kim had filled out the appropriate forms, they finally sat down and stared at each other. There were other women in the room; two had companions and one didn't. Kim felt an overwhelming need to reach out to the woman sitting there by herself, and talk to her, but everyone else was avoiding eye contact by staring at their phones, magazines or just the floor.

Dave squeezed her hand and she knew he'd picked up on the fact that not one person who was holding a magazine was actually reading it. Indeed, the man to her right was holding a copy of *National Geographic* upside down!

Opening her mouth, Kim went to speak to the lady on her own, but the door swung open and everyone turned towards the doctor.

'Kim.' The kindly looking woman stared straight at her and Kim felt her stomach drop. This was it. There was no turning back. She rose, sensing Dave beside her, and walked towards the surgery door.

Once they were inside, the doctor introduced herself.

'Hi! Nice to meet you both. I'm Stephanie Harper.'

Shaking hands, Stephanie indicated for them to take a seat. There was a peaceful feeling about the room and Kim half wanted to stop and take it in. The other half of her needed the doctor to talk as quickly as she could, giving her the results so they could get on with treating the problem.

'So, Kim, your mammogram shows there is a bit of shading in this area of the breast.' She gestured at a diagram on the wall. 'What I'd like to do today is an ultrasound of the whole breast and a biopsy of the troublesome part.'

Kim nodded.

'We'll start with the ultrasound—you won't feel anything odd while having that. I see from your notes that you haven't had children, but it's exactly the same type of thing that pregnant women have. Have you ever had one before?'

'No.'

'All I'm going to do is squeeze a bit of gel onto your breast . . .' She went on to explain everything, then asked Kim to go behind the curtain screening the examination area and get changed.

Kim could hear Stephanie washing her hands and getting ready. She swallowed hard, determined not to show any type of weakness. She was resilient and would deal with whatever she was told.

'Have you driven down to Adelaide today?' Stephanie asked, as she swished the curtain out of the way.

Kim answered in the affirmative as she settled herself on the examination table and looked around the room. On one wall there was a large photo of a peaceful-looking seascape, and on another there was one of a thick-trunked gum tree next to a stony creek. Kim could see the galahs in its branches. It made her feel so at home.

'The photos you have here are beautiful,' Kim commented. 'Oh!' She screwed up her eyes as the cold gel made contact with her breast. 'Cold!' she gasped.

'Yes, sorry, I should have mentioned that. My brother took those photos. He's a bit keen on photography. Loves getting out and exploring all parts of Australia and documenting it. That one there,' she indicated the creek, 'was taken up in the Flinders.'

Dave cleared his throat and mentioned that was where they were from. Stephanie wasn't paying attention. A puzzled look crossed her face and Kim felt her push the transducer handle in a bit deeper.

The doctor looked back at the screen, moving the wand around a bit more. Pursing her lips, she applied more gel and stared hard at the moving images.

'Sorry, I can't . . .' She broke off and leaned in towards the screen, slowly making circular motions. Then Stephanie did the same thing again from another angle, pushing harder and watching the black-and-white screen for longer. Then another angle, repeating the steps.

The butterflies Kim had managed to keep at bay since they'd entered the room returned with a vengeance. It took all her willpower not to ask what was wrong.

'Bear with me a moment,' Stephanie said, and picked up the notes on her desk. Kim could see she was reading intently.

To distract herself, Kim looked at the picture and tried to put herself in the creek. She would sit on rocks warmed by the sun and feel the warmth seep into her body. The gentle wind would caress her face and softly toss her hair. There would be galah cries and the rustle of leaves. If she was lucky she might see a wallaby sleeping underneath a bush.

'Kim.'

It obviously wasn't the first time Stephanie had said her name. Dragging herself back to reality, Kim took in her grave face and turned to Dave, reaching for his hand.

'Kim, can I ask you to get dressed and go out into the waiting room? I just need to cross-check a couple of things with the lady who performed your mammogram, and with your doctor.' She gave an encouraging smile. 'Don't worry. I know that's easy for me to say, and I also know you're desperate for news. This isn't an unusual occurrence, just a bit of checking.'

'For what?' Kim blurted out.

Dave took charge. 'Honey, she'll tell us when she knows. There's no point in jumping the gun and giving you information that isn't right. Let's just head out and wait.' He helped her down from the bed and waited while she slipped her shirt back on.

Within minutes they were waiting once more.

ᘓ

A short time later, Stephanie called them back in.

As they sat down, she started to speak before either of them could ask anything.

'Kim, I'm truly sorry you've had to go through this. Especially when it wasn't necessary.'

Both Dave and Kim looked at her, not understanding.

'What do you mean?' Dave asked.

'Your results have been mixed up with someone else's. We've

traced it back. I couldn't find the lump when I was doing the ultrasound. There isn't one there. You don't have breast cancer.'

'I don't?'

'No. You don't.' Reaching forward, Stephanie patted her hand. 'It's been a terrible mix-up.'

Euphoria flooded through Kim and she started to laugh. 'But that's wonderful!' she said, then stopped. 'Are you sure? How do you know? What if you're wrong?'

'I'm sure I'm right! There isn't a lump. I can't find one there at all.' The doctor looked at her file, then back at Kim before closing it. 'I hope I don't have to see you back here again. It's been nice to meet you, especially under these happier circumstances.'

'So you mean we've been through this for nothing? All the angst and—' Anger mixed with relief burst from Dave.

Kim put her hand on his arm. 'Doesn't matter,' she interrupted. 'Sweetie, it doesn't matter. What matters is I don't have cancer. What matters is we don't have to feel like this anymore.' She stood up, energised. Desperate to get out of this small room and live her life. Kim never wanted to be inside another hospital room or doctor's surgery again.

Stephanie held the door open for them and shook both their hands as they left.

They tumbled out into the street, not saying anything, looking unsure and shell-shocked. Without warning, Dave picked her up and swung her around. 'I don't believe it! It's bloody fantastic news! You're right! It doesn't matter.' Kissing her soundly in front of the passing traffic, neither of them noticed when a couple of horns tooted. What mattered was they had each other, and Kim was well.

She put her hand on his arm. 'But we should spare a thought for the other woman,' she said softly. 'Someone is about to go through exactly what we've just endured. And it'll be worse, because she's already been told she's fine.'

That was a sobering thought.

∽

The celebratory glass of wine turned into a bottle as they sat in a small bar overlooking the Torrens River. They hadn't intended to stay in Adelaide overnight unless they were asked to, but needing a release and to just enjoy each other, they had splurged on a fancy hotel.

Kim had laughed lots—and loudly. Dave felt like he'd won the jackpot—the relief for both of them was immense. They were caught up in each other and nothing else mattered.

When they returned to their room and turned down the lights, Dave slowly undressed her, drinking in every detail of her body, her curves, her skin. He wanted to memorise the way she looked tonight, without any cares in the world. She was beautiful, and she was his.

Chapter 14

The oval was already surrounded by cars when Fiona and Jo pulled in. It looked as though the Leigh Bounter Match was just about to start, with the umpire standing in the middle of the oval, the footy above his head.

'Going to miss the bounce-down,' Jo observed as she searched for a place to park.

'Look, there's one.' Fiona pointed to an empty space under a tree. Jo swung her ute in and they filed out, grabbing their chairs and eskies, before walking across to the oval. 'Can't believe it's as nice a day as this. Leigh was so wrong about the weather not clearing until Monday.'

Even though the air was brisk, the sun was shining, and if they could find somewhere out of the wind, it should be reasonably warm. She pulled the scarf around her neck a bit tighter.

'What about we set up next to the grandstand?' Jo suggested, nodding to a couple of people who walked by. 'We should be able to see from there.'

'Fiona! Jo! Lovely to see you.' Sylvia, Carly's friend, waved out the window of a car.

Fiona, needing a rest, put down the chair.

'Here, I'll get us set up, you go and talk,' Jo offered.

'How are you holding up, love?' Sylvia asked when she got a little closer.

'I'm fine, how about you?'

'No worries in my neck of the woods.' Sylvia grinned, making her face look much younger than her sixty-five years. Her zest for life was more apparent than her grey hair and wrinkles. 'I've been wanting to talk to you.'

'Oh yeah, what about?'

'I've heard you're going to sell and I wanted to encourage you not to.'

Fiona's jaw dropped as anger rushed through her. 'Where did you hear that?'

'Julie Pelly was talking about it at the hairdressers when I was in there the other day.' She reached out a gnarled hand and grabbed Fiona's tightly. 'You can do this, love, you don't need to sell.' Encouragingly, she stared straight into Fiona's eyes.

'I know that, I've got no intention of selling.' Frustrated, she extracted her hand and crossed her arms across her distended belly. 'I'm going to have words to that Ian Tonkin. It must be him who started these rumours.' She looked intently at Sylvia before asking in a quieter tone, 'Did you find it hard?'

'Oh, love, farming isn't easy whether it's you by yourself or you've got your soulmate right by your side. There were days I wanted to pack it all in, for sure. There were times when the boys were crook and I'd been up with them all night, but still had to front up at the sheep yards to load a truck at five-thirty in the morning! I won't lie to you. It won't be easy. Especially with a new bub. I was lucky that my boys were older by the time my Davy, God rest his soul, passed away. They were a big help to me. But it was still hard work.'

The crowd gave a huge cheer as a goal was kicked. The footy landed just short of where Fiona was standing.

Leigh came out of the crowd, grabbed the footy and hand-balled it back to the umpire.

'Was that us?' Sylvia asked, before leaning on the horn to cheer the boys along.

Fiona giggled. 'Nope, it was Laura's goal!'

'Whoops! Better not let Myles know that I beeped for the wrong team.' A light laugh escaped the older woman as she mentioned her grandson's name.

'Did you get lonely?' Fiona suddenly asked. Even though the circumstances were different, Sylvia had been through what she was feeling now.

'I never had time to get lonely,' she answered. 'Actually, that probably isn't quite true. There were times in the middle of the night when I felt so isolated and abandoned, my whole body would hurt. I used to go and curl up in one of the boys' beds when that happened. But mostly I was too busy.'

'Do you regret any of the decisions you made?'

Sylvia looked down at her hands. Fiona noticed she still wore her wedding rings, even though Davy must have been dead for nigh on thirty years. 'One regret,' she said. 'Just one. There was a man, a long time ago now,' her eyes softened with the memory, 'not long after Davy died. It wasn't the right time—the boys were still grieving and so was I. Told me he'd loved me for many years but could never say anything because I was married. Oh, we were great friends. Had been for a long time. Talk? Ha! Oh, we always had so much to say to each other. On the same wavelength, as it were. Both of us were as driven as the other. He would've taken the boys on, helped me run my farm and have me be part of his business. But it was too soon for me. I loved him—probably still do, but I couldn't get past what everyone in the district would have thought. Him and I together so quickly after my Davy.' Her voice faded and her face took on a faraway glaze, transporting her back to another time. She looked up and drew in a breath.

'If that happens to you, my dear, try to think clearly. More clearly than I did. Fact is, Davy wasn't coming back and neither is your Charlie.' A sad smile crossed her lips, but she was pulled back from reminiscing when a series of car horns blared around her. 'Oh that's my boy! Good goal, Myles!' she called, clenching her fist and pumping the air with excitement. 'Tell you what, if that boy had wanted to play AFL, he could have! Shame he got so caught up on the farm with his father.'

Fiona touched the older woman's arm. 'I'd better find Jo. She'll be looking for me soon.'

'Yes, off you go, love. You be strong and hang in there. Brave. That's what you are.' Sylvia nodded to her, then focused her attention back on the oval.

Fiona wandered off, watching people as she went. The calls of the footy players filled the air, as did the thud of their boots on the field and the sound of their bodies colliding with each other.

Smelling hot chips, her stomach suddenly rumbled. She

needed to find Jo. There was hot chocolate in the thermos and she'd also packed some sandwiches, but a bucket of chips and gravy would be much more satisfying.

She took out her mobile phone and saw a text message from Kim. Butterflies filled her stomach as she stopped, letting the crowds walk around her. Her fingers hovered over the phone before she finally opened the message.

All is wonderful here. Long story, but I don't have breast cancer. Will fill you in when I'm back home. Hope you and bub are well. Xxx

Breathing a sigh of relief, she was about to put her phone away when a Facebook message from William popped up.

What's this about Mum having a boyfriend???

Fiona giggled out loud. Quickly she typed: *What's the problem with that? She's happy.*

I need more information. Preferably, height, weight, whether he has any debts and a secret life!

Not likely, he's the local doctor.

But you can't be sure . . .

Shit-stirrer!

She slid her phone into her pocket and checked the scoreboard. Booleroo was in front by two goals. There were still three quarters to go.

'Fee! Over here!' Jo was waving at her from beneath a sunshade, where a group of young farmers was sitting. She groaned silently. As much as she loved Jo, she hung out with people who were so much younger than her, and Fiona didn't fit in. She hadn't before, and there was no chance she would now that she was a widow *and* pregnant. Taking a deep breath, she walked over and pasted a smile on her face.

'I was just going to get some chips,' she said, once she'd greeted everyone. 'Did you want some?'

'Oh yeah!' Jo said enthusiastically. 'Yum. Reckon they'll hit the spot.'

The canteen was on the other side of the oval. She walked around it, half watching the footy and half watching the people around her.

Out of the corner of her eye, Fiona realised there was someone walking towards her. It was Ian Tonkin and she had nowhere to hide.

'Fiona, I was hoping to see you here,' he greeted her.

She kept walking. 'I'm in a bit of a hurry, Ian.'

'Sure. Won't hold you up a minute.' He fell into step alongside her. 'I just wanted to let you know I've had a phone call from the company that has already bought two farms in the area and is looking to expand its property holdings. BJL Holdings is paying absolute top dollar and they want to make an offer on your place. They've picked you and a couple of others out.'

'I don't want to sell.'

'I understand, but if you'd just consider their offer—another two farmers have decided it's an offer they can't refuse. I don't think we'll see prices like this again.'

'Who else has sold?' Fiona stopped and looked at him.

Ian held up his hands. 'I can't tell you yet. It's not common knowledge.'

Fiona put her hands on her hips. 'Okay, let me tell you this once and for all. You could offer me a million dollars per hectare and I wouldn't take it. This is my husband's heritage and needs to be passed on to his son. I'm the custodian.' She leaned forward and looked him straight in the eye. 'I'm not selling.'

An amused look crossed his face. 'Have it your way, but let me tell you what a mistake you're making. In fact, I'm certain you'll change your mind in the end.'

Without a word Fiona turned and walked away. She couldn't help thinking he had just made a veiled threat. The rest of the day passed in a blur—she couldn't keep her mind off who was selling and why. And what was this company he was talking about? BJ something? In this area land didn't change hands very often and suddenly, in the space of a few months, four farms had been sold.

She thought about mentioning it to Mark—after all, he should know what was going on, but she hadn't seen him since they'd weighed lambs together. He obviously hadn't found out anything else or he would have phoned.

Leigh might know something. He was the mayor. She made a mental note to ask him when she saw him next.

Later she watched Leigh present Sylvia's grandson, Myles, with the Leigh Bounter Medal and thought back to the time when he had been in hospital with no one visiting. Charlie had told her about it in detail.

He'd been popular to a point, but Leigh had tended to brag, especially about his football prowess. He did like to big-note himself. Most people liked him in small doses. Charlie had such a large heart that he'd hated the thought of him being in hospital in Adelaide by himself. Leigh's parents had visited, but only a few times—they both had to work and even a family emergency didn't stop them. Very few footy-club members had made the trip to Adelaide; they didn't want to get caught up in the emotion of it all. Everyone knew Leigh wouldn't be able to play footy professionally again. How he would cope with that, no one wanted to find out.

That was, until Charlie had encouraged them to go. Geoff had helped too, but it had been Charlie who had done the hard work.

He'd put carloads of folks together, got a roster system happening when Leigh came home—it had all been down to Charlie. If he hadn't done it, Fiona doubted whether Leigh would have had as much help as he did.

Leigh changed after that. He was loyal to Charlie and realised his bragging hadn't helped people's attitudes towards him. He was a different man these days, and she knew she preferred this new Leigh to what she understood the old one to have been like.

How hard it must be to stand up and present a medal for a sport he loved and could never play again, to watch younger versions of himself, with glowing eyes and eager hands, grabbing the opportunity to play.

It must be awful, she decided, as she watched him walk from the field.

Chapter 15

Picking up the phone, Dave made the call he knew would be the toughest.

'Fiona Forrest speaking?'

'Fiona, my name is Detective Dave Burrows, from the Barker Police Station.'

There was a long silence, and he was surprised when he heard a smile in her voice.

'Dave? You're Kim's partner, aren't you? It's nice to talk to you. Oh, wait! Is everything okay?'

Dave cursed inwardly. He'd forgotten that Kim had befriended her a couple of weeks ago. He knew they'd been exchanging daily text messages.

'Uh, yep, that's me. And everything is just fine. With Kim,' he added.

'Okay.' She drew out the word, obviously intrigued as to why he was calling.

'Fiona, I'm sorry to bother you, but would it be possible

for me to see the shooting scene? I understand it's on your property.'

'What? Why?'

'There've been a few small problems with the investigation and I need to clarify some questions I have. What I'd like to do is come and have a look myself, then bring Leigh and Geoff out to walk through what happened that night.' He heard her swallow and rushed on. 'I know this is distressing for you. I'll try to stay out of your way as much as possible.'

'Of course,' she answered in a small voice. 'But it's been done before. Done straight after the . . .' Her voice trailed off.

'Yes, I know.' He heard her take a breath.

'When do you want to come?'

'Today, if possible.'

ꟹ

The road leading to where the accident had taken place was a small two-wheel track. Fiona had given him a map and pointed him in the direction of the hill.

The file was on the passenger seat, but Dave didn't look at it until he arrived. The area was still cordoned off with tape and it was obvious that Fiona didn't use this paddock for anything. He suspected she hadn't been back here since that night. Charlie, on the other hand, after the accident, could have spent hours up here, or no time at all. He would have to ask Fiona.

He looked around. The sky was clear and blue today, and he could feel the sun's winter warmth on his back. The spray-painted markers indicated where the ute had lain, but Eddie's body and where the guns had landed hadn't been identified in the same way. Groaning with frustration, he turned his attention to the shattered glass from the smashed spotlight, still lying where it had fallen all those months ago. Then he dug out the photos from the file and tried to work out where the guns and body had been.

There was a lot of heavy, slippery clay in this area and the outcrop of large granite stones that had tipped the ute over was just to his left. Leaning down and inspecting it, he wished he could see the tyre tracks. He suspected that if Geoff had swung the wheel only a few inches either way, this tragedy could have been avoided. He knew it had been raining that night—flicking through the pages of the report, he read there had been an inch of rain earlier in the day. Scattered showers had been sweeping across the country on and off throughout the night. This type of soil would be very greasy. Hard for tyres to get traction.

He shivered. There was something here telling him this story wasn't right. But what on earth was it? He could certainly understand why Andy had given everyone the benefit of the doubt that night. It would be hard to imagine anything else. Still, standing here on the lonely windswept hillside, the only noise the wind rushing around his ears, he just knew something sinister had happened.

He'd had feelings like this before; usually they were small niggles. Or an instinct about people—whether they were lying or not. A long time ago—maybe his fourth year as a detective? He'd been part of the team that had led an enquiry into an accidental death in a country town, out in the Wheatbelt region of Western Australia. As soon as he'd walked into the house, he'd known there was much more to the so-called suicide of the twenty-one-year-old man than met the eye. It took him a long time to finish that investigation. By the time he had, he had arrested all nine people involved in a drug ring who had murdered not only the lad but also another two people.

He'd learned to listen to these gut instincts, even though his colleagues had howled him down at the time.

Dave referred back to the photos. He placed them on the ground, holding them down with rocks so they didn't blow away. Stepping out the distance between where the ute had lain and, judging from the photos where he imagined the guns had fallen, he marked two spots. Then he referred back to the report.

There was no extra information there. What a surprise.

Where could the third gun have fallen? Dave was so lost in thought he hadn't heard the sprayer swoop past the fence line of the next paddock until it had gone by. The engine rumbled and a horn sounded as he looked up. Dave raised his hand in acknowledgement and went back to his job.

ꕤ

Dave swung into the council office car park and came to a stop. He glanced at the clock on the dashboard and realised he was thirty minutes early.

He stared up at the majestic and historic council chambers, marvelling at the incredible engineering feat. It was a two-storey structure, with small windows set into each quarter and a little foyer right outside the entry. Across the base of the building was a line of slate as decoration and around each window was a wide border, painted white. He often wondered how those buildings had been constructed—the man hours, muscle and sweat must have been massive.

Looking around, he tried to see if there was a little café where he could get a coffee. He'd been to Booleroo Centre before, but only to pass through. He didn't see anything that took his fancy.

As with any country town, there was a war-memorial statue with many names listed on it, and towering cement silos that would store grain during the harvest. The main street was quiet; only a few cars were parked and they were in front of either the hospital or the local supermarket.

The red doors of the council chambers swung open and a man emerged, a takeaway coffee cup in hand. *Of course! The chambers would have a coffee machine*, Dave thought, and decided to go inside to wait. It didn't matter that he was early.

He pushed the door but it wouldn't open. Pushing harder didn't make any difference. It was locked.

Strange. Maybe there isn't anyone else there today.

Further down the street, he noticed a stock and station agent building. Maybe he'd have a chat to whoever was in there.

Again, the building was stone and the heavy door indicated its age. Dave stopped and looked at the farms for sale and was surprised to see four had 'SOLD' in red across the pictures.

He pushed open the door, which buzzed as he went in. Inside was quiet and dim, the front desk empty of everything except four books of invoices and a couple of pens. *Computers must be out the back*, he thought. *Surely they couldn't run a business without them.*

A white door, in the corner behind the desk, swung open and a heavy-set man with greying hair hurried through. Dave caught a glimpse of a large shed full of chemicals and other farming supplies.

'How're you going?' he asked.

'Good, mate, good,' Dave answered. 'Not real busy today?'

'It's steady. Just not at the moment.'

Dave held out his hand. 'Dave Burrows from Barker Police Station, just passing through. Thought I'd pop in, let you know I was around.'

'Ian Tonkin, real estate agent.' He stared with open curiosity but didn't ask Dave why he was there. That meant Dave was on the front foot.

'You have been busy!' Dave commented, nodding towards the shopfront window. 'Bit of land moving, is there?'

Ian leaned against the desk and crossed his arms. 'Yeah, there's been a bit of a spate of buying recently. Be good to have some new blood coming in.'

'New blood? So not locals then?'

'Nah, a big company from over east. BJL Holdings. They tell me they're looking to spread out their risk. Must've taken a bit of a beating with the drought in New South Wales last season. Said they're buying up a heap of land in the west as well.'

'Big order then?'

'Much as I can get 'em, they'll take. Paying above the going rate, too. They've got their eye on two other blocks in particular, but they'll take what I can get 'em. Canvassing for them pretty hard at the moment.'

Shoving his hands in his pockets, Dave rocked backwards and forwards on the balls of his feet. 'Who's been selling?'

'Mostly the older blokes with no one coming up behind to take over. I've been trying to convince a few others who I think should take the money, but I'm not having too much luck. You know that Fiona Forrest? Her husband, Charlie, topped himself a while back. She's up the duff and I reckon she should sell up—in fact, they'd like her land. But let me tell you, never met a woman so stubborn!'

'Ah well, guess everyone has their own thoughts on what she should do and the only ones that really matter are hers.'

'Then there's the Goulburn family. Dad has to work away to make ends meet. Mum and the kids end up running the place. They could just take this money and set up somewhere else. Probably end up debt-free. Anyway, there's just some people you can't make see reason.'

Dave wondered what made Ian such an expert on everyone else's business before asking, 'When's the takeover? Early next year then?'

'Yeah. First of February. So why are you here? Didn't think there'd be too much that warranted a visit by a copper.'

'Just doing the rounds. We have to do that every so often. But if you've heard of any issues, stock stealing, diesel or chemical theft, that type of thing, I'm around.'

'Well, I haven't heard of anything along those lines, but I'll be sure to let you know if I do. Another bloke who would hear of those sort of things is Mark Simmons. He's the stock agent.'

'Mark Simmons, you say?' He committed the name to memory, then glanced at his watch. 'Great, thanks for your help. I better get on. Nice to meet you, Ian.'

'You, too.'

Outside, Dave couldn't work out what bothered him most: the way Ian spoke about other people's business so freely or the certainty of his own opinions.

ଓ

'Thanks for seeing me,' Dave said, holding out his hand to Leigh Bounter. He recognised him as the man who had left the council office a little while before.

'Glad to be of help. Although I've already been through this with your other officers.'

'Yeah, we realise that and we're sorry to take up more of your time. There're just a few things that weren't followed up properly at the start and now we need to go back over them. Unfortunately, it just makes more work for us and takes up your time. How long have you been the mayor? Must be a big job.'

'Four years.' Leigh leaned back in his large leather chair and crossed his legs. Dave noticed there was an Akubra hanging on the wall behind him along with a Driza-Bone jacket. It was clear Leigh wanted to make sure everyone knew he was a farmer as well as a politician.

Leigh's cheeks were tanned a deep brown above his black beard. There was a serious expression in his vivid blue eyes as he looked at Dave.

'Do you enjoy it?'

'Mostly. There are parts that aren't any fun. There's always someone complaining about a road that needs grading, or someone's barking dog.' He shrugged. 'But that's all part of it. The fun stuff is when you make changes for the benefit of everyone within the council boundaries.'

To Dave, this sounded like a practised line. 'How do you fit it in with your farming? That must be tough. I imagine there are times when you're needed in both places at once.'

'Well, I'm lucky enough to be able to employ a few blokes. If I'm not around, they cover for me. Eddie was one of them.' Leigh looked down at his desk and cleared his throat.

Dave watched as he got a grip on himself and started to tap his pen on a blank pad before giving Dave a stare. 'So how can I help? What do we need to go over?'

'What I'd really like to do is get you and Geoff back out to where it happened. Talk through the night and exactly what occurred. You can explain to me and I can see it.'

'Sure. Anything you need.'

'I've spoken with Geoff and he's agreed to this as well.'

'Right, well, let's get it over with. I don't want it hanging over my head.' He stood up and Dave instantly got the impression that he was used to getting his own way.

'Are you able to get away right now?'

''Course I can. Practically everyone's got my mobile number; they normally ring that anyway.' His tone was scornful and Dave wondered if it was anxiety making him edgy. It was so difficult to go back and face something as traumatic as this.

'Well, we can't go straightaway,' Dave said, making sure he was in charge of the situation. He was confident that given half the chance Leigh would take control. 'I've organised to pick Geoff up at two o'clock this afternoon, so I'll be back here at one forty-five.'

After a short silence, which Dave interpreted as one of annoyance, Leigh agreed.

Chapter 16

A low, buzzing sound made Fiona scan the horizon, trying to identify the noise. It sounded like a fly on steroids. What was Dave doing up there at the accident site? Some type of scanning or measuring or something up there on the side of the hill? What type of investigation made that noise?

She shuddered, not wanting to think about the possibilities, but her eyes had a mind of their own. She kept looking in the direction of the hill.

Maybe it was the tractor. She wanted to believe it was. Shifting her focus, she tried to see where Damien might be.

But still, she knew deep down it wasn't a tractor noise.

What the hell was it?

A flash in the sky made her turn. She squinted at it, the glare from the sun making it hard to focus.

There, right on the boundary fence, a . . . *thing*! Hovering in the air. What the hell was it? It was so small she could only see the sun reflecting off it.

Going over to her ute, she grabbed a pair of binoculars.

It looked like a space aircraft!

Suddenly she realised. It was a drone! How intriguing. Who would be flying that around? Maybe it was the neighbour. She'd heard of farmers up north checking their tanks and fence lines with them. And young, up-and-coming photographers using them, too.

'How cool!' she muttered out loud. Meita jumped into the back of the ute and nosed under her arm. 'What's up, girl?' Fiona asked absent-mindedly as she watched the drone hover in the sky above her. How much could it see and in what sort of detail?

Meita didn't do anything; she just rested her head on Fiona's chest and sighed contentedly.

Her phone rang. Digging into her pocket reminded her how tight her jeans were, even with the stretch belt Carly had given her. She'd heard so many first pregnancies didn't show until about six or seven months. She was obviously the exception!

'Kim!' she said, so happy to hear from her friend.

'Fee, how are you, sweetie? And how's that tummy of yours?'

Fiona laughed, her hand going automatically to her belly and stroking it softly. 'We're both fine,' she answered. That wasn't exactly the truth. The past few nights she'd been so uncomfortable. This morning she'd found a few drops of blood on her knickers, but she wasn't too concerned. Yesterday she'd hauled a fly-struck ewe onto the trailer so she could crutch the affected area and treat it. The ewe had been heavy and hard to handle. Fiona wasn't going to tell anyone that; she knew there'd be an outcry if someone found out.

Sometimes she wished everyone would understand she was pregnant, not sick. That was how she felt they all treated her at times but they were only looking out for her and Hamish; she had to keep reminding herself of that. Especially since Charlie wasn't around. But they had to understand she was capable. She didn't doubt herself, so why did they?

'Are you sure?' Kim asked. 'You sound a little weird.'

'I'm sure. Although, did you know that Dave was coming here today?'

There was a pause.

'Dave? As in my Dave? I missed a call from him and he didn't leave a message, so I hadn't caught up with that news.'

'Hmm. He's up looking at the crash site.'

'Oh, sweetie!' All of Kim's compassion came flowing down the phone line. 'How are you feeling?'

'Uncertain,' Fiona finally admitted. Once again, she looked towards the hill. Dave would be on the other side, looking at where Eddie died. Where everyone's lives had changed irreversibly. 'How does he do that?' she asked Kim.

'Do what?'

'Go to the scenes, see the blood, deal with the people left behind?'

Kim sighed. 'I don't know,' she replied honestly. 'I really don't. But there are nights when he can't sleep and he sits up late, drinking coffee. I've learned not to bother him when he's having an episode like that.'

Fiona gave Meita one last pat then started to walk towards the shearing shed, the phone still pressed to her ear. As she walked, the stony ground crunched under her hard-soled boots and her jacket pulled on her stomach.

'I don't understand why he's here though, Kim. Shouldn't it all be over? God, I wish it could all be over.' Her voice broke a little.

'Damn, I wish I was there to give you a hug. I'm sorry I can't be with you. I haven't got anyone to cover for me in the roadhouse today.'

Swiping at her nose, Fiona shook her head, even though no one could see her. 'No, I'm fine. I just don't get what's going on. I thought it was all finished. What more can he find? It's been five months! Do you know?'

From the silence, Fiona dimly realised that Kim was carefully composing her words. Fear shot through her.

'You do know, don't you? Kim?'

'I know a little, love, but not enough to tell you with certainty. Why don't you ask Dave when you see him?'

'You tell me.' Fiona wasn't sure if it was fair to be demanding this, but she didn't care. She had to know.

'I think . . .' Kim broke off. 'I think the original investigation wasn't completed properly.'

'What?'

'Yeah, not good, I know. But Dave will make it right.'

'So, what?' Alarm quickly found its way to the bottom of her stomach and sat there. Her thoughts whirled. 'You mean it wasn't an accident?'

'Oh, God no!' Kim screeched down the phone. 'No, no, no! You've got it all wrong. He's just rechecking a couple of little things. Dave just has to follow it all up and make sure it's right. It's a paper trail, that's all.'

Fiona closed her eyes and let out a breath. 'Far out!' she muttered. 'Geez!'

'Sorry, sweetie, I didn't mean to frighten you.'

'S'okay. Let's change the subject!'

'Yes, let's. What are you doing today?'

Entering the softly lit shed, Fiona reached over and flicked on the lights, inhaling the scent of lanoline and ammonia. She ran her fingers over the wooden boards and rubbed her fingers and thumb together. 'Well, I'm standing in the shearing shed. I've got to scrub the board today. We, um, I, start shearing as soon as I can.'

'Sounds like a lot of work. Who have you got to help you?'

'I've got someone teed up to do the cropping work but not to help with the stock. Think I might give Mark, my stock agent, a call and see if he knows someone.' She exhaled loudly. 'Lamb marking is coming up, too—I'd really like to do it while we're shearing, save double handling them, but I don't think I've got the energy. Shearing is more important at the moment. I need the money. I've bowed to public pressure and decided to get a lamb-marking contractor in. Usually, Charlie and I would have done it by ourselves, but I don't think I can manage that this year.'

'Well, hallelujah and praise the Lord. Your common sense has finally kicked in over your pride!'

Fiona giggled. 'Get stuffed,' she said mildly.

'It must be the day for light-bulb moments,' Kim said, her tone becoming excited.

Fiona hoisted herself up onto the wool table and sat there, her legs swinging through the air. Instantly, she was taken back to when Charlie had lifted her up there. He'd sat her on the table and swung it around, as if she were having a ride on a merry-go-round. As she'd approached him again, he'd stopped the table and dragged her to him, kissing her long and hard. Meita hadn't liked the attention she was being shown and had barked loudly, before jumping up onto the table and nosing her way between them. Fiona wanted to smile and cry at the same time. Instead, she focused on Kim.

'Tell me!'

'I think I was meant to go through this scare.'

'Well, you're the one who keeps telling me everything happens for a reason.'

The tin roof banged in a gust of wind and Meita strolled into the shed. She found a slither of sunlight, flopped down, sighing loudly, and shut her eyes, falling asleep immediately.

'Wish I could do that,' Fiona said.

'Huh?' Kim stopped mid-sentence.

'Oh, sorry.' She told Kim what Meita had just done. 'I find it so hard to go to sleep and stay asleep,' Fiona complained.

'Chamomile tea,' Kim said promptly. 'And surely you've got enough sheep on that place of yours to count?'

'Ha, ha. Anyway, keep going. You were saying something about reasons?'

'I want to cook meals for people who need them. I was thinking about you, going through all that you have been. I'm sure there've been nights when cooking has been the last thing on your mind.'

'Absolutely.' Fiona frowned, trying to work out where this was going.

'And Dave, if he'd been home by himself, he would have struggled to cook. I love him dearly, but the only place he is at all domesticated is around a campfire.'

'Okay.' Fiona sounded unsure.

'So, if I register with the hospital, or doctor's surgery, and they give the patients my details, I can cook for the families who are left at home.'

Realisation dawned. 'Oh, so if the wife is in hospital and Dad is left at home with the kids?'

'Yeah, or an older man who can't cope on his own. Providing home-cooked meals, a bit of company. Not everyone has family who can help them, you know.'

'I think that's a fabulous idea,' Fiona enthused. 'That's just like you, Kim. You turn something bad that's happened to you into something awesome. I wish I had your positive attitude.'

'But, sweetie, you do! That's what positivity is all about: getting up every morning and keeping on going. Not letting things get to you—or at least not dwelling on the bad things. You were telling me the other day how beautiful the sunrise was—the little bits of gold sneaking out from the edge of the clouds. That, my love, is positivity. If you can still see the beauty in things after what you've been through, well, need I say more?'

'Sometimes it's pretty hard to get out of bed in the morning,' Fiona admitted.

'But you do and that's what counts. Uh-oh, I've gotta go, just had a customer come in. I'll ring you later.'

They said their goodbyes and Fiona put the phone down by her side. Rubbing her eyes, she groaned. 'Come on, let's get on with it,' she told herself.

She grabbed the broom and waddled up the steps onto the board and started sweeping. The smell of ammonia under the shed rose to greet her and she breathed it in deeply. It didn't matter that she had started off her life as a town girl. She was now a farm girl through and through. A farm girl without a husband, but with a baby on the way. And as much as it hurt, she had to be content with what she had.

Chapter 17

Geoff and Leigh walked silently around the site. Both men were ashen-faced and Dave felt a pang of regret at having to put them through it all again. Still, he couldn't let that prevent him from doing his job.

'So can you tell me again?' he asked, his notebook out. 'Where were you all?'

'I was in the front, driving.' Geoff's voice was low.

'The rest of us were on the back, in the tray of the ute,' Leigh added.

'How were you lined up across?' Dave asked.

Leigh replied immediately. 'I was on the passenger's side, Charlie in the middle and Eddie was standing behind the driver's seat. He was holding the spotlight.'

Dave turned his attention to Geoff. 'Can you remember what was happening in the lead-up to when the ute tipped over?'

Kicking at the ground and in a tone that didn't change, he recited what had happened. 'I was driving with the window down and half hanging out of it so I could hear if one of the fellas yelled out to me. Charlie had just shot a fox and we were driving over to make sure it was dead. I felt the ute hit something. There was a huge noise—like tearing underneath or something, then it just went up on the two wheels. It felt like it hung there for hours before it crashed over. I was thrown across the other side, then I heard a shot.' He stopped, took a couple of breaths and blinked, before continuing. 'I heard screams and thuds. I tried to scramble up and get out through the window, but I couldn't. Well, not at first. It took a good couple of goes to get out. Coz the ute was on its side, the door was heavy and kept slamming shut on me. When I finally did, I saw Charlie working on Eddie.'

Leigh nodded in agreement and Geoff continued.

'I had my headlight already strapped to my head so all I had to do was turn it on. There was red everywhere. I didn't realise what it was at first. Thought there must've been a tin of paint in the back or something.' He began to speak quickly, his voice rising. 'Then Charlie was saying something like, "You're gonna be all right, you're gonna be all right."' His chest heaved and Leigh made a move to stand beside him. He put a hand on his shoulder just as Geoff let out a shuddering sob.

Angrily, Leigh turned to Dave. 'See? This is what happens when you drag up shit that should have been sorted properly in the first place. It just opens old wounds and makes it hard for people who are getting their lives back on track.'

'I can't tell you how much I regret having to do this.' Dave acknowledged their pain by turning and walking a few metres away from them, to give the men some privacy.

ℴ

Back inside the car, Dave started to ask some basic questions.

'Was there a particular reason you went out that night? I understand it had been raining.'

'So what?' Leigh asked. 'Would've gone if it'd been raining or not.'

Geoff stared out the window and watched the countryside whizzing by. He said, 'There was a wild dog. It'd been killing sheep left, right and centre. Sometimes it killed for food, sometimes it killed for fun.'

Dave knew that if a dog was killing for fun, the only thing it would eat would be the kidney fat. It was easy to get at through the side of the animal. It was sweet, juicy and a dog's favourite part of the sheep. If it was killing for food, it would eat most of the legs and other meaty parts of the animal, too.

'It had killed at Charlie's place last, but it seemed to be able to travel great distances in a short time. I talked to an old dogger who used to track dingoes out on the Nullarbor and he said they could travel up to fifty k's in one night. We didn't really have any idea where it would turn up next, so we just took pot luck.'

Taking up the commentary, Leigh continued, 'Eddie was really keen. The dog had been killing my stud ewe lambs and they were his pride and joy. Eddie always considered those sheep his own and looked after them as such. He'd told me he'd rung Geoff and Charlie and they were both eager to head out that night. I wasn't sure if I'd be home in time because I had a council meeting. As it turned out, it only lasted half an hour, so I texted Charlie and told him I'd be there. He texted back and said he wasn't sure if they were going to go; worried it was too wet and slippery. But if they did, they'd swing by my place and pick me up.'

Dave made a mental note to ask why, if they were shooting on Charlie's farm, they would pick up Leigh rather than expect him to drive himself over.

'Had you guys done much shooting before?'

'You've gotta shoot when you're a farmer.' Leigh shrugged. 'You've gotta control foxes, put animals down if you need to. There's a use for a gun on every property.'

Geoff nodded.

'Yeah, yeah,' Dave said. 'I'm the third son of a farmer back in WA. Dad used to cart his gun around with him in the front of the ute. He always said you'd never know when you might need it. Go for a row if you tried to do that now!'

'Those gun laws were needed,' Geoff said. 'But they've made it difficult. Especially if, like me, you farm close to town. People hear gunshots and then ring your mob. Think something bad is going down. Even out here. And we're all country people.'

'Tell me about it!' Dave kept his tone conversational so as not to lose the headway he felt he was beginning to make. 'When I was in the Stock Squad we'd be travelling all round, but it was on the outskirts of Perth that we had huge amounts of trouble. Often the farmers would keep their guns at the local cop shop—not something we'd normally do, but it was easier. Because every time they needed their guns, they'd have to come and get them, so we'd know they were going to be shooting. Then when the calls came in from the public we could tell them straightaway there wasn't anything to worry about.' He gave a little shrug. 'Where'd you guys get your cabinets from?'

It was Geoff who replied first. 'Just ordered mine from the local farm-merch store.'

'Yeah, reckon that's where I got mine from, too,' Leigh said. 'I know I looked at one from a specialised dealer, but they weren't really any different to the ones I could get locally. All about shopping local and keeping businesses afloat. When those laws came in,' he continued, 'we had cops swarming through our houses to make sure the gun safes were installed properly, in the places where they were supposed to be. Did you do that over there?'

Dave nodded as he took his foot off the accelerator and flicked his blinker on to turn into Booleroo Centre. 'Yeah, we didn't check everyone—that wouldn't have been feasible. But we certainly checked quite a few. Probably enough for the word to get around that we were doing it and to make sure you were putting them in the way you should.'

He pulled up at the council offices. 'So where do you fellas keep yours?'

'Got mine bolted into the cement floor right at the back of the shed,' said Geoff. 'Can't see it and you wouldn't know it was there unless you were looking for it.'

Leigh opened the door before answering. 'Keep mine in the walk-in robe at my house.'

'Both good spots,' Dave said, nodding his approval. 'Had any of you been drinking before you left?'

That caused both men to stop.

It was Geoff who spoke.

'Yeah. We'd all had a couple of tinnies before we went out.'

'Actually, I'd only had one because I'd been at the council meeting,' Leigh clarified.

'Okay. Now, two more things before you go. Who had the guns there that night and who knew you were going out?'

Geoff opened his door and got out, as if he was in a hurry not to have to think about it anymore. 'Dunno who knew.'

'Well, Fiona would have, but Charlie was the only one of all of us who had a wife. Guess it depends on who we told during the day. It was five months ago,' Leigh reminded Dave.

Dave let the pointed comment go over his head. 'And the guns?'

'Me and Charlie,' Leigh said. 'Eddie was holding the spotlight so he couldn't shoot as well as do that.'

'I'm really grateful for your time and walking through the scene with me,' Dave said to both men, holding out his hand to them, one at a time. 'And again, I'm sorry we have to bring it up again. There will be a few more things I have to clarify in the next few days.' He paused. 'I also need to take your fingerprints.'

'What? Why?' Geoff looked shocked. 'Hang on! What's going on here?'

'Nothing is going on.' Dave spoke in a calming tone. 'This is all routine. Happens at every accidental death scene we go to. However, the police work in this instance has been lacking. You should all have been fingerprinted at the time.'

The men looked at each other silently. Geoff nodded. 'Are you gonna do it now?'

'I've got a fingerprint kit in the back.' Dave got it out and walked around to the bonnet, ignoring the way Leigh kept looking at his watch. Carefully, he rolled each finger of both men on the ink pad before completing the rest of the procedure. Dave packed up the kit while Geoff wiped his hands on the back of his jeans. Leigh walked away to where a parking bay declared 'Mayor' and pulled back the tarp covering the tray of a ute. He fished around until he brought out a rag and wiped his hands.

Dave glanced over and quickly scribbled down the number-plate. He'd have to try to get Geoff's too. Wouldn't hurt to run a plate check on all four men, dead or otherwise. Earlier he had picked up Geoff from the council offices, so he assumed his ute was parked on the street nearby.

Leigh scratched at his beard and looked thoughtful. 'Are you going to have to talk to Fiona about all this?'

Dave nodded. 'Unavoidable.'

'Do you really have to? Hasn't she suffered enough?'

'You've all suffered enough,' Dave said kindly. 'All in different ways.'

Geoff kicked at the ground. 'I need to be going,' he said as he turned and walked away, then suddenly stopped and turned back to Dave. 'I understand why you have to do this. Be kind to Fee.'

Dave nodded and again thanked him for his time.

Leigh stood there, his hands in his pockets, his deep-blue eyes staring unblinkingly at Dave. 'Do you have to?' he pleaded again. 'She's just getting back on her feet. It'll open everything up again for her. You never know, the stress might hurt the baby.'

'I'm not going to be putting her through the wringer. Just a few questions. I'll be as quick and considerate as I can be,' Dave assured him.

Leigh shook his head, his cheeks flushed. 'This is wrong.' He raised his eyebrows in disdain as he spoke. 'And being in my position, I can do something about it.'

Dave tried hard to hide a scowl. It wasn't often that people got under his skin, but the way Leigh was keeping on about it was unnecessary, especially when he didn't know the full facts. Pushbacks by those involved were expected. But Leigh, in his position, should perhaps understand a little better.

'Look, mate. The fact is it needs to be done. This isn't about budget cuts or anything. It's a simple case of not having the information we require to close the case. Cooperating with us is the quickest way to put it behind you.'

The tension between the two men was palpable. Leigh gave a harsh laugh. 'Sorry, mate. You have to do your job. I get that.' He shrugged. 'I'm not worried about myself. I'm strong enough to be able to deal with it. Unlike Geoff—you can see for yourself how upset he is. Fee is a different story. She's pretending everything is fine. Running on autopilot. It concerns me that this might push her over the edge.'

'Everyone worries about their friends,' Dave agreed. 'I would, too. I'm sure you feel the need to look out for her.'

'I do. Charlie was my best mate. If I don't look out for her, who will?'

Chapter 18

He saw her sitting in the middle of the free-standing bar, staring into a glass of spirits. Next to it were two empty ones. She was tapping her fingers in an agitated way, but her eyes were sad.

She looked perfect.

He took a long slug of his beer and glanced around over the rim of his glass. The pub was almost empty and it was close to closing time. He got up from his table in a dark corner and walked purposefully to the bar and ordered another beer. He took it over to where she was sitting and slid onto the stool next to her.

Ignoring him, she turned slightly away and took a sip.

Not good. She wanted to be left alone.

He sighed. 'You, too, huh?'

'What do you mean?'

Her voice was low and husky and sent thrills through him.

'Looking at you, you've either been stood up or broken up with.'

Although he was staring at the bar mat, he could sense her twisting back towards him, just a little. He hid a smile. This always got to them.

'What makes you say that?' she slurred.

He shrugged. 'Been there. Know what it looks like. Know what it feels like.'

'And which are you tonight?'

'Stood up.' *But I plan to fix that with you*, he thought, the familiar urges beginning to ripple through him. 'Which are you?'

She didn't answer. Instead, she drained her glass and signalled for another one. While she was looking in her handbag for her purse, he saw his opportunity and leaned over.

He placed his hand lightly on her arm to still her. 'I'll get it,' he offered.

This time she looked at him. Her eyes were bloodshot and her cheeks were stained red from the alcohol.

'Thank you.'

He nodded, removed his hand and ordered for her. Bringing the drink back to the bar, he put his elbows up on the wood and rested his chin on his hands, not saying anything, trying to work out what to do next.

In the end he held up his beer to her. 'Cheers.'

'Yeah, cheers,' she muttered.

'What's your name?'

'Bernie.'

He glanced into the mirror behind the bar, looking for anyone who might see what he was about to do. Slowly his hand inched towards her handbag.

'You didn't tell me whether you'd been stood up or broken up with. I'm guessing broken up.' His hand made contact.

'Maybe.'

He gave the bag a little push and it spilled over onto the floor.

'Shit!' she said, leaning down instantly.

He swiftly leaned over and put a tablet into her drink before bending down to help her.

'Bugger,' was all he said as he handed her a hairbrush and a tube of lipstick.

'Just my luck tonight.' She bundled everything back in and straightened up, putting her handbag over her shoulder so it couldn't happen again.

To his delight, she took a sip of her drink. Under the bar, he rubbed his hands together. Wouldn't be long now.

'Want to tell me about it, Bernie?' he asked, infusing his voice with sympathy. Instead of listening, he watched for the signs. Further slurring of her voice, the slowing down. His drug of choice in this situation was ecstasy—although it was supposed to speed up the central nervous system, in his experience it made the girls become very affectionate and pliable.

He loved it when the drug kicked in.

'He's an arsehole,' she said.

'They all are, darlin'.'

Bernie looked up at him. 'I bet you're not. You're too cute.'

'Well, thank you. But what did he do to you?'

Her face fell. 'We've been together eighteen months and I found out today he's married. I never knew. We'd planned all . . .' She licked her lips and he could see it was time to get her out of here.

'. . . we'd planned all sorts of things.'

'You're looking a bit the worse for wear, there. Want me

to get you a taxi?' He stood up and put his arm around her, helping her to slide off the stool without falling.

Bernie started to laugh and wound her arms around his neck. 'So gentlemanly,' she cooed.

He gripped her tightly around the waist and smiled down at her. 'I always try my best.' He tugged down the hat he was wearing to make sure his face couldn't be seen by any CCTV cameras, then helped her towards the door.

Getting her out onto the street was the easy part, but by the time they made the first corner she was hanging all over him and almost unable to walk. That just made him angry.

Still, it wasn't far to go. His car was parked down the next side street.

He pushed her into the passenger seat and tugged her seat-belt over her shoulder in a futile attempt to keep her safe, but nothing was going to keep her safe tonight. Not while she was with him.

After a short drive his car disappeared into an underground car park beneath a house. He jabbed a button and the doors slid silently down, hiding his car from the world. He got out and looked at his sleeping passenger. He'd prefer her to be awake, just so she could fight back a bit. Resistance turned him on.

Looking over his shoulder, he checked that the doors were shut before he yanked open the passenger door and slapped her across the face.

'Wake up, bitch,' he growled.

Groaning, Bernie tried to open her eyes—but they flick-ered and then shut again. 'Lazy whore!' he snarled at her as he pulled her from the car, dumping her unceremoniously on the ground. He could feel himself getting hard and it took all of his self-restraint not to stroke himself. He knew if he did, that would be the end. He would have to masturbate; he didn't want that tonight. He wanted to hurt her, make sure she still felt him tomorrow.

Struggling with her dead weight, he hauled her onto a car trolley and began wheeling her into the house, to a room he kept just for nights like this.

Chapter 19

Fiona lay in her bed staring out at the night sky. The stars were bright and twinkling, with the occasional cloud floating quietly across them. It was so still. Usually she could hear the gum leaves tapping on the roof as a slight breeze tickled through them, but tonight there was nothing.

Well, she'd heard a fox bark earlier and that had set off Meita's barking. It had scared her for a moment, thinking it was the wild dog back again, but she'd got a grip on herself very quickly. A fox's and a dog's bark were completely different.

Fiona knew she couldn't let her thoughts run away with her or she'd become fretful. She was also safe in the knowledge her house was locked up tight, thanks to Rob.

He'd been lovely when he came to put the locks in. They'd laughed and joked. Reminisced about Charlie.

After Jo had left, he'd asked questions about the farm and she'd discovered he loved talking about farming as much as she did, so she'd invited him to stay for tea—putting the locks on had taken longer than they'd thought, and it was the best way for her to thank him.

Tonight, though, there weren't any strange noises or creaking. Just a deep sense of loneliness echoing through her. What she would give to roll over and feel Charlie's warm body next to hers. To hear his sleepy mumbles and quiet snores.

She sighed and got up, padding over to the window. She could see the outline of the sheds and yards, and further down the hill, the two silos glinted in the slither of moonlight that was trying to lighten the countryside.

If she stared hard enough, she could see the outline of a few sheep moving along the fence and the rest of the mob sitting down.

Fiona rested her head against the cold window and blew on it, watching the warmth of her breath fog it up. She drew a heart in it, then added Charlie's name. Blowing some more and adding her own name, seeing them linked together, made her smile. She waited until the outlines faded before leaving the window and checking the time.

With any luck, Will would be online and she could have a talk; well, a write. *Was that a something?* she wondered. A write. She couldn't talk. Maybe it was a write/talk or a wralk? Because he sounded as if he were talking when he wrote something to her. She could hear his voice in her head.

Jo would find that funny. A wralk. She'd have to remember to tell her.

Switching on the office light, she drew the bar heater up close and turned it on, waiting for the element to heat up. One of the things she missed since Charlie had died was the nightly wood fire. As much as she loved the cheeriness of the dancing flames, getting the wood had become an issue. Even though Rob had brought extra wood, it was beginning to run low again.

Now Fiona only lit a fire when she couldn't stand the coldness of the house. Mostly, at night or after work, she would turn on this two-bar heater and curl up on the couch underneath a blanket.

Charlie would have said it was 'farting against thunder' or 'would have a snowflake's chance in hell' of heating this large monstrosity of a house. He would have been right.

After she wiggled the mouse, the screen jumped to life and she was staring at a picture that Charlie had taken two years before. It was of Fiona—she hadn't known he'd taken it. She'd been drafting sucker lambs from their mums, the look on her face pure concentration, but even she, who hated looking in the mirror, had to admit there was a certain glow to her face she'd never seen before. It was happiness, Charlie had said, when he'd shown her. 'You look the most beautiful I've ever seen you here.'

'Oh fuck off,' Fiona said angrily, out loud. She went to the photo section and scrolled through, looking for something that didn't make her emotional. Something that wasn't Charlie, wasn't her, wasn't about their life together.

But she couldn't find a single photo that didn't have a memory attached to it. Finally, she opened the folder of stock photos, and changed the screen to a simple blue. There. That would fix it; she wouldn't have to look at that again.

Her computer made a soft ding; a signal that there was a Facebook comment.

Going to the page she saw that Will had left her a message. *You're quiet. What's going on? Any more ghostly visitors???*

That's not the sort of question I need right now, she typed quickly.

Ohhhh, you're scared already, aren't you?? Fraidy cat, fraidy cat.

That made her smile, even though she didn't want to.

Who me? I'm the brave one. It was always you who was scared of the dark.

That's why I live in New York. It's always light, thanks to the bright stars of Hollywood.

Pretty dark here, she wrote, with another glance out the window. *The stars are the brightest I've seen for ages. Maybe because there isn't any cloud around tonight, but I think the cold makes the sky clearer for some reason.* She hit enter and blew on her fingers, trying to warm them up so she could type faster.

Different worlds, sis.

You think?

So how are you? The vibe I'm getting across the interwebz is not good.

Fiona thought for a moment, wondering how best to respond. She wanted to tell him everything, because she could write it down. She didn't have to verbalise it, something she was having trouble with. If she talked about it she had to relive it again and again.

I had a detective come out to look at the accident site again—the shooting site, I mean.

Oh?

Apparently the policing wasn't done right. She went on to explain everything Dave had told her.

Less than average, Will responded. *Did the same policemen investigate Charlie's suicide?*

Yeah, a couple of younger policemen. Dave said they were just too inexperienced.

Does that mean they have to reopen Charlie's file?

Fiona froze. She had never even contemplated that. The lump in the back of her throat threatened to block her breathing.

Sis?

I don't know, she managed to make her fingers type.

Hate to be the one to tell you, but they probably will.

Fiona laid her hands on the desk as she looked at the words on the screen. Will didn't type anything either, so she guessed he was thinking about this, as she was, all this distance apart. That comforted her a little. No matter how big the world was, how far apart they were, they were still under the same sky, looking at the same moon and seeing the same stars.

It wasn't until the little ding sounded again that she realised the screen saver had kicked in. She hit the space bar, trying to get Will back.

Want to tell me about it? Mum says you haven't talked to anyone—well not that she knows about anyway! Probably easier to write it down than talk about it.

No.

Well don't think about it! :p

Too hard.

Good way to get it out.

No.

Okay. So what else is going on? Any rain?

Fiona scratched her neck, trying to ward off memories and, in the end, ignored his last message. Without thinking, she put her fingers to the keys and started to type.

I was inside getting tea ready. He'd asked to have chops and a special roast-veggie dish I make. It's his favourite. She stopped and corrected herself. *Sorry, rather it was.* She hit enter so Will knew what she was writing. Now he would stay quiet until she finished.

I heard a ute pull up at the shed—I wasn't that surprised. Eddie or Leigh often used to come over for a beer just on tea time, sometimes Geoff, too. Once in a blue moon, Damien, our neighbour, pops over. It seemed to be when they finished work. We kept a fridge down in the shed so I didn't always see them.

She focused on her fingers so she didn't have to look at the words on the screen; she had no idea if there were spelling mistakes or not. She didn't care. Will would get the gist of it. She just kept typing. Maybe she needed to do this. Vaguely, she thought how weird it was for her to push these keys and make words, then shoot them across the world. It was almost like she wasn't aware of what she was saying; it was just coming out in a huge, great gush.

I sort of forgot there was anyone there, but after a while I heard a yell and running. Then Leigh banged on the door, telling me I needed to call an ambulance. I knew. I just knew. Felt like my whole body had been drenched in icy water.

I can't really remember how I got to the shed. Somehow I was standing in front of the car. She paused, took a breath and kept typing. *It's weird, the things that go through your head in a situation like that. I just stood in front of the car, and thought, 'How can it be Charlie? It's Mum's old car.' Did you know that, Will? He used Mum's old car. We'd kept it as a run-around since she'd got her new one. He couldn't have used anything else on the farm—it was the only vehicle running on petrol.*

Leigh was telling me it was Charlie. I kept saying no, it's Mum. I remember looking at him before I got to the window and saying: 'Why are you lying to me?' Nothing was making any sense. I sort of stumbled up to the car, slowly, needing to see inside, but not wanting to at the same time. Then I looked in the window and there he was. Sleeping.

That's what he looked like, Will. Like he was sleeping. She stopped to brush away some tears. *Like he was drink sleeping. There was a bottle of scotch in the car with him and he had a glass in his hand that was sitting right near his hip.*

That was it. The ambulance came, then the police. There was noise and chaos and Mum arrived. Nothing, then nothing. Not for a day or so. Scott gave me something to make me sleep.

Fiona took her hands away from the keyboard and laid them on the table, still looking at the keys. She was cold.

A gust of wind made the tin on the roof creak, and a door further down the hallway blew shut. She jumped and her heart rate sped up. Fiona looked over her shoulder at the door. It was open out into the hallway. Beyond that there wasn't any light. Shivering half from fear and half from cold, she checked the computer for something from Will.

The screen stayed blank.

Grabbing the blanket from the chair, she wrapped it around her shoulders before going to the door and looking out. It was hard to stop the icy dread spreading through her, even though she knew it was only the wind making the door slam.

She crept out into the hall, made a dash to the light switches and turned them on. White light flooded the hallway. There was nothing there. Trying to keep her breathing steady, she walked towards the other end, checking each of the rooms one by one.

'Seriously being ridiculous,' she told herself. 'Meita would have barked.'

Meita!

The blast of cold air, as she opened the front door, cleared her head and dried the tears on her cheeks. It felt as if the skin around her eyes was stretched tight and taut. Eucalyptus, moist earth and pine scents wafted towards her and she heard the distant bleating of sheep.

Then Fiona jumped as Meita appeared silently from the kennel, her warm, sleepy body rubbing against her legs. Making a fuss over her, Fiona patted and rubbed her head and ears.

'Come on, you can come inside.'

In the office, Fiona settled herself before reading Will's message.

I love you.

It was brief, but it said exactly what she needed to hear.

The effort and memories had exhausted her and she wanted to go back to bed. But not before ending on a bright note.

I thought of a good name for our talks on here.

What is it?

Wralk.

Okkaaayyy. Your brain must be scrambled. Is that like walking and talking or something?

Fiona laughed, then stopped, surprised she had any laughter inside her tonight. She imagined Will leaning back in his large black leather chair, his blond hair flopping forward, or pulled back in a ponytail at the nape of his neck. His desk would be piled with documents and files, and he would be reading, taking notes and *wralking* with her, all at the same time. She'd seen him do it before and never understood how he managed to comprehend everything he was reading!

She started to play one of their childhood games with him. *'Wralking'—Verb. Writing and talking. Used mostly while on Facebook Private Messaging section.* ☺

Very clever, Fee, very clever! I've got to head to court. Will you be okay?

Fiona knew exactly what to type. *Yep, I need a long sleep, but I'll be fine.*

Wralk to you later then! Never forget though, I love you.

You were right. Was easier to write it than say it. I love you, too. Thank you for being my outlet.

Uh, I'm a drain now? Excellent. Bye!

Chapter 20

The pub was warm and welcoming when Leigh first stepped inside. He took off his jacket and shook his head, little droplets of rain falling from his hair and beard.

It had been a big day, what with the four phone calls from the same elderly woman complaining about a barking dog, and three from truck drivers asking when some of the dirt roads were going to be graded. The second, interesting call had been from a gentleman who had wanted to check that the boundary on his farm was in the right place. He'd been going through his grandfather's papers and the first deed of title was showing the boundary about ten feet from where it was now. Land had been taken from him, he'd insisted. Leigh had promised to pull out the old records and check it for him.

'G'day, Leigh,' Mark said from behind a beer. 'You look like you've got the world on your shoulders.'

Leigh focused, and saw Mark and Ian sitting together.

'Not so much the world as funding problems,' he improvised.

Mark snorted as he took another sip of beer. 'Nothing new there.' They all shook hands. 'Is that a heads-up that you're going to be raising rates again?'

'I'll have a schooner of bitter, thanks, love,' Leigh said to the barmaid, taking out his wallet. 'And whatever these two are drinking.' He turned back to Mark. 'Let's not talk about the rates issue now!'

'I'll go another round,' Ian said, raising his glass. 'Cheers, Leigh.'

'So what's going on?' Leigh asked the open-ended question, knowing he wouldn't get too much information out of Mark, but Ian would spill everything. That was the thing about Ian, he couldn't keep his mouth shut about much. Especially if he'd made a good sale or heard some good gossip.

'Oh a bit of this and that.' Mark was predictably cryptic.

Leigh nodded. 'Lambs? Sheep? Cattle?'

'All of the above. Prices for lambs are pretty good at the moment, so there're a few people trying to shift old seasons. Need to, before they cut their teeth and cross that magic line from lamb to hogget and the price plummets.'

Leigh looked around him. The pub was quiet tonight: there were five people in the dining area and four old codgers around the bar, and that was it.

'Where is everyone?' he asked. 'It's usually pumping.'

Ian spoke up. 'Forecasting a frost tonight. Reckon it's too cold for most people.'

'Hmm, you might be right.'

'I hear they're reopening the file on Eddie McDougall's accident,' Ian said casually. 'Why's that?'

Leigh could hear him trying to keep the excitement out of his voice.

Mark straightened beside him. 'Really? What's that about?'

Leigh took a deep breath. 'What's that about?' he echoed pensively as a blast of cold air came through the front door. Ray Newell walked in. It was clear by the way he wove his way over to the bar that he'd been drinking already.

'What's that all about?' Leigh wanted to rant and rage, but he had to put his mayor's hat on and speak carefully. Be politically correct. God knew if he said something wrong, it would be held against him forever.

'What's all about what?' Ray asked in a loud voice, settling himself next to Ian and leaning forward to look at Leigh. He ordered by holding out a fifty-dollar note, which the barmaid took before proceeding to pour him a drink. She obviously knew his 'usual'.

'Our police department,' Leigh bit out. He wished Ray would just leave.

'Oh yeah,' Ray said in a sing-song voice. 'I heard they were reinvestigating that shooting. Weird, huh?' His tone implied something but Leigh wasn't sure what it was.

'The trouble with our police department,' Leigh continued, putting on his mayor's hat, 'is that they come to country areas without enough training. When they are sent here, they're expected to do everything, from helping old ladies across the road to solving crimes. If they come out to us with no experience in some of these things, then we can't expect them to do well in areas they know nothing of.' When he didn't get a response, he turned to look at Ian and Mark. 'Well, can we?'

Both men nodded their agreement, although he could see that Mark wasn't sold.

'Well, think about it this way, Mark.' He put down his beer and addressed the stock agent. 'If all they've done is pull over cars and bretho people, how can you expect them to work a crime scene to the best of their ability?'

Mark nodded. 'Fair call.'

'So what's happened in this instance, is that two inexperienced coppers have come to a horrible and tragic scene. They've summed up, correctly, I might add, that it's a terrible accident. But in doing so, they haven't followed proper procedures in documenting or gathering the evidence to support it is just that, an accident.' He took a gulp of beer before resuming. 'How can we expect constables and the like to do detective work?'

'We can't,' Ian said.

'Exactly. And that's precisely what has happened in this case.'

Mark looked at him. 'Not bothering you, dragging everything up again?' he asked slowly.

'Of course it is,' Leigh snapped. 'Neither Geoff nor I should have to go through this again. But we are because of the incompetence of the police department. Now, I'm not saying these young lads are to blame, but they didn't know what they were doing. They should have had more training, more experience . . . '

'Now how do you get more experience if there's nothing to investigate?' Ray asked lazily. 'Should we just knock off a few people who are annoying us and get the police to investigate their deaths?'

Leigh threw him a withering look. 'Just like your small-mindedness to say something like that, Newell.' He turned away, just as he saw Ian elbow Ray in the ribs in a stop-it gesture.

Mark sat up straighter and put his beer to the side, watching both men.

'No, what we have to do is get more experienced coppers out into the bush. Like that Dave Burrows. He's got all the experience under the sun and he's good.'

'But look at his age,' Ray persisted, downing the last of his drink. ''Course he's going to have more experience! He'll only be a few years off retiring, so he won't stop around long. Don't expect him to be the be-all-and-end-all.'

Leigh took a deep breath and shook his head. This was why he couldn't talk to this man. 'Ray,' he said patiently. 'I wouldn't have to relive all this again if those officers had been trained properly.'

'But they've got to go somewhere to learn.' Ray signalled the barmaid once more.

'Yes, but I'm not sure they need to learn out here. Why can't they learn in the cities, where they've got more experienced police looking over their shoulders?'

'They get paid extra to come out here. Like teachers,' Ian interjected, looking pleased he had something to add.

Leigh felt like rolling his eyes. That simply wasn't true.

'You know it's not just Geoff and me I'm thinking about,' Leigh added. 'What about Fiona? She's about to be requestioned, too. Hasn't she been through enough?'

'I'm sure she's touched by your concern,' Ray said with a smirk, his insinuation clear.

Anger welled up inside Leigh, although he tried not to let it show. He pushed his hands into his pockets and curled them into fists. His jaw was clenched as he looked down at the dirty carpet and counted ten cigarette burns in it. When he looked up, he was back in control of himself.

'I think we need another round,' Ian said, then gestured to the barmaid. 'Same again, thanks.' He obviously felt the need to defuse the situation.

'I'm not sure we do,' Mark observed uncertainly.

'So what's happening in the world of real estate?' Ray asked.

'Busy, busy,' Ian said, his cheeks beginning to glow from the alcohol. Another blast of air came from the door and a few younger blokes from the footy club, Myles Martin and Damien MacKenzie included, walked in, laughing loudly.

'And did you hear about Copey? He didn't see the fence and seeded straight through it. How you couldn't hear the scraping of wire going under the tractor I'll never know,' Myles said with a grin. 'They never found it till the next morning. Made a hell of a mess.'

The group of men burst out laughing and crowded around the other end of the bar.

'G'day, Mylesy,' Ray said, getting off the bar stool and heading over to them.

Leigh breathed a sigh of relief. Maybe he'd stay away now.

'Hey, listen, have you heard from the AFL Talent Squad yet?' Ray clapped Myles on the back and the young man went red.

'No, mate. Won't be for a while. They've got a few other clubs to get around and look at. And I haven't told anyone about that yet, so I'd rather keep it under my hat.'

'Too late now!'

Leigh lifted his head to listen, ignoring Mark's tap on his arm.

'Don't pay it any attention, mate,' Mark muttered into his ear.

With every bit of self-control he had, he turned back to Ian and Mark. 'Where were we?'

Ian opened his mouth and started to speak. 'I've had more enquiries from this company, wanting to buy extra land.'

'What company?' Mark asked, curious.

Loud laughter erupted from the footy group and they all looked over at Leigh. He felt a flush rise in his cheeks but maintained his focus on Ian.

'It's a big company, BJL Holdings. They own a fair bit of land over east.' Ian went on to tell them everything he knew. 'The funny thing is,' he leaned forward as if to reveal a secret, 'I've done a bit of research on them and I can't find who the directors are.' He sat back, looking pleased with himself.

The three men sat there silently, working out what that meant.

'What about a CEO?'

'Oh yeah. She was easy to find. Some chick called Leah Kent. But the directors are hidden very well. It makes me wonder a little bit. Especially since they've bought so much land in this area already.'

'Any trouble with the settlements?' Mark asked.

'That's my point. Settlement isn't happening until first thing in the new year.'

'But if they own a heap of land over east, they must be legit,' Leigh said. 'And if they've paid the deposit they shouldn't default. They'll lose the money they've already put down if they do. Plus, there'd be a black mark against their name when it came to buying land.' He frowned, looking at Ian, troubled by what he was hearing.

'I don't reckon there'll be a problem with settlement,'

Ian agreed. 'All I'm saying is, I find it interesting that I can't discover who the directors are.'

Leigh spun his beer around on the bar, thinking.

'I wouldn't be too concerned about that,' Mark said. 'Sometimes they're a bit harder to find with only a Google search.'

'Yeah, well, that's all I've done.'

'I'm with Mark,' Leigh said. 'Wouldn't worry about it.'

'Hey, Bounter!' one of the footy blokes yelled out. 'Hear you're gonna take over as Police Commissioner now!'

Leigh drew in a breath.

Mark moved close and spoke into his ear. 'Ready to go? Now would be a bloody good time.'

'Nah, I'm not leaving because of Newell. He's a fuckwit.' Leigh looked over and noticed Damien was looking uncomfortable. Good. He wasn't like the other small-minded dimwits in the group.

'We all know that, but it wouldn't be good to see our local mayor getting into a fight with a wanker, would it? Come on, drink up. Let's go. There's another pub just down the road. We don't have to stay here.'

Leigh looked over to see Ray beaming with delight at his work and Damien edging away.

'I'm not leaving,' Leigh said. 'Another round, thanks, love.'

'He's all high and mighty. Reckons our police should be better than they are,' sneered Ray as he strutted towards them like a peacock with his feathers out.

'Fuck off, Ray,' Leigh said mildly. His tone was hiding what he really felt. The anger was so close to bubbling over, he'd have to be careful, because what he really wanted to do was punch this idiot in the face.

'I'd be leaving,' suggested Ian, getting up.

'Come on, mate, let's head home, hey?' Damien was at his shoulder.

'You never got over it, did you?' Ray asked, getting into Leigh's face.

Leigh could smell the whisky on his breath but just sat there, still and silent, looking into Ray's eyes. He couldn't be drawn into this. He had to be seen to be the better man.

'Never got over the accident. Not sure why you keep blaming me though. Just like this shooting out there. It was an accident.' He drew out the word. 'Ac-ci-dent . . . '

Leigh lifted his chin.

'Come on, mate, don't be a dickhead,' Mark said, grabbing at Ray's elbow. 'Leave the man alone.'

'Man? Is he? Is he really?' Ray asked. 'A man has a wife and a home. A man takes responsibility for his actions, doesn't blame a poor innocent bystander. A man,' he raised his voice and looked around the bar, 'a man isn't full of himself and think he's God's gift.'

'Really?' Leigh asked in a low voice. 'You can't be much of a man then. Accepting responsibility? God's gift? Fuck off, Newell, you're not worth my time.'

Ray swung the first punch and it connected with Leigh's jaw.

Leigh staggered backwards, his fall stopped by Damien, then launched himself towards Ray.

'Leigh!' It was Mark's voice that cut through the red mist of anger. With an effort, Leigh reined in his emotions, his chest heaving with exertion. He eyeballed Ray with his fists by his side.

'Hey! Cut it the fuck out!' Ian yelled, and between Mark and Damien, they grabbed Ray, wrestling him away from Leigh. Ian stood at the door, holding it open.

'I'll call the cops!' screamed the barmaid.

'They're going to do fuck all,' sneered one of the footy boys, coming closer. 'Just ask the mayor here.'

Leigh backed away and touched his face; there was blood on his fingers. He got out his handkerchief and held it up to his nose.

Turning to the footy boys, he said, 'Is this the type of example you boys want in a leader? Someone who picks fights and makes people feel small? Let me tell you what a good leader is. Someone who makes small people feel big. Who encourages and mentors. Who can bring people together and unite them. Someone you can trust. Not really sure that Ray here is any good at that.'

He walked to the door of the pub before turning back to Ray. 'And for the record, Ray, all you had to do was apologise. Accept that you had a part in what happened and we would've been good. But you're right. It's too far gone. I'm not interested in any apologies you might have now. You wouldn't mean them even if you said them. It's best you stay out of my way and I stay out of yours. Including at footy.'

And at that he walked out, leaving the pub in stunned silence.

Chapter 21

Dave read the second paragraph of Geoff's statement, but something wasn't ringing true. He checked through the notes he'd written out at the scene with the two men yesterday.

Two guns, they'd said. One for Leigh, one for Charlie. Eddie was holding the spotlight and Geoff was driving.

So how come this report said there had been three?

He flicked over to Leigh's statement. The mention of three guns was there, too. Leigh, Charlie and Eddie all had one. But that didn't make sense. Why would they be saying three guns then and two now? And how could Eddie have held the third gun and the spotlight?

Getting up, he rubbed the whiteboard clean and started a list titled *Inconsistencies*, then he divided the board in half. One side was *Report/Statement*, the other *My Findings*. Under the first heading, he wrote *three guns* and under the second, he wrote *two guns*.

From that point he decided to listen to his gut and start the investigation properly.

He printed photos of Eddie and the other men who were in the ute that night and stuck them to the whiteboard. Writing down the details he had on each man, he realised there was hardly any information on Eddie. All he had was that he was Leigh's employee, had worked for him for over six years and was originally from the south-east. His mother was still alive, he had one brother, and he'd been cremated, his ashes shipped to his mother in Mount Gambier.

Dave made a few notes, then started looking for Eddie's mother's phone number.

He wondered if he should have the local coppers in Mount Gambier knock on her door, asking for more particulars. In the end, he decided that would be better than a phone call from someone she didn't know. A face-to-face, where the officers could offer sympathy while gathering as much material as they could.

He emailed the sergeant, requesting assistance.

Within minutes he had an email, the sergeant confirming he would send a couple of constables around that afternoon.

His phone rang and absent-mindedly he picked it up.

'Burrows.'

'Dave, it's me, Andy.'

Dave looked up from his notes, surprised to be receiving a call from him. He took his time before speaking. 'G'day, Andy, how are things?'

'Good, mate, good. This detective course is really interesting. Having a great time.'

'That's good.'

'Hey, I just wanted to check in. Have you seen those cases about the date-rape drugs reported on the news?'

Dave thought for a moment. 'Can't say I have. What's going on there?'

Dave had barely turned on the TV since he and Kim had come back from Adelaide with the all-clear. Suddenly, TV and incidental things hadn't seemed important. But spending time with her, talking, laughing and loving, was. He'd made sure he left work on time. They cooked together—Dave helped Kim plate up all the meals for her new venture, of feeding people who needed help. They'd started walking together after work. Not that Dave would admit this to anyone, but it'd been good for him—he'd even lost two kilos in two weeks! If he kept that up, he'd be trim, taut and terrific by Christmas!

The fact remained, the cancer scare had brought them closer together.

He tried to concentrate on what Andy was telling him as he flicked through his emails, checking for any alerts from headquarters regarding date-rape drugs.

Oh yeah, there was one.

Scanning quickly, he confirmed what Andy had just told him.

'So the perp is using ecstasy,' Andy said. 'Putting it in their drinks. Of course, because that can make the girls all gooey and loving, no one really notices that there's anything wrong. It's not like one of the more common types, Rohypnol and GHB, where the girls get drowsy and end up being carted out, looking drunk.'

Dave had to hold his tongue again at Andy's assumptions. Oh, he knew that it was mostly girls who were the targets of date rape, but not always. He could tell Andy, if he cared to listen, of at least thirty cases, just off the top of his head, of blokes who had become victims this way.

'Trouble is we can't work out where he's taking them. We're sure he has a foxhole somewhere—a house, or unit.'

'What makes you say that?'

'Well, he's not gonna do them in a car, is he?' Andy said scornfully.

'What's the MO? Are you sure they're all the same?' Dave paused, tapping his pen against his lips. 'Actually, I'm curious. Why are you looking at this case? I thought you were at the course, not working cases.' God help the police department if they'd let Andy loose already.

'They've given these as case studies to all of us in the course. They're happening now, and the detectives haven't made any breakthroughs so they want fresh eyes over it. And that's where we come in.'

Andy sounded so young and excited, it made Dave wish he could still guide him in some way. He was pretty sure that Andy wouldn't come back to the Barker region, so there wasn't any point in thinking like that.

'I'm surprised,' Dave mused. 'But it's undoubtedly good training. So, going back, why are you looking for a house or unit?'

'Once they leave the pubs, there's no sign of them until the vic turns up dumped somewhere, beaten and bruised.' He was silent for a moment. When he spoke again, his voice was low. 'Dave, you should see the photos of some of these vics. I haven't seen anything like it before.'

Pursing his lips, Dave suddenly wondered if Andy was cut out for the job. Was he too soft? Maybe that's why his investigative skills weren't up to scratch. He didn't want to dig too deep, afraid of what he might find.

'Injuries?'

'Too many to mention. Not just around the head and face. *Everywhere.*' The emphasis he put on the word made Dave understand straightaway.

'Bastard!'

'Too nice a word for the fucker.'

'Is the perp using the same pub, or striking all over?'

'The city centre and a few outlying suburbs. But you know what I find interesting? The vics are being dropped mostly on the northern side of town. I reckon that's where his den is.'

'That's a good call. Told anyone that? Probably not wanting to drive too far with a body in the back of his vehicle, in case he's pulled over.' Dave nodded as he thought it through. 'Makes sense. I'm assuming no one has died?'

'Not that we're aware of at this stage. But I reckon he's escalating.'

'He?'

'Piss off, Dave. You know that in ninety-nine per cent of these cases it's gonna be a male. White, between the ages of twenty and sixty. You know this shit. You know the profile. Why're you making an example of me?' He exhaled, clearly annoyed, and Dave had to hold the phone away from his ear.

'You're right. Sorry,' Dave said. Andy was spot-on. It wasn't his job anymore. He should be supporting and encouraging him. 'Tell me why you think he's escalating,' he prompted, even though what he really wanted to be doing was writing more notes and compiling more facts on Eddie's case.

An email dinged and he saw it was from his boss, Steve.

Double-clicking to open it, he realised it wasn't anything important. Just Steve wanting to know how the investigation was progressing.

He didn't really have much to tell him yet, other than there were a few inconsistencies between the report and what Dave was hearing now. Still, that wasn't going to be a surprise to Steve. He focused on Andy again.

'. . . and now we're seeing a lot more injuries.'

'Sorry, back up. What did you say at the start?'

'At the start it was mostly rape. The injuries began as beatings, but now there's grave physical damage.'

'Holy crap,' Dave whispered. How had he not heard about these attacks? 'How many are there?'

'We've got reports of four, but the media officer is going to put a call-out next week for other victims who haven't reported it to us.'

'I'll keep my ear to the ground.'

'Cheers, Dave. And, mate?'

'Yeah?' Dave could hear him swallow before speaking.

'I know I fucked up that case. I'm sorry, man. I'm trying to do better now.'

Dave gave a half-smile. 'Mate, that's all I wanted to hear. And that'll go a long way to making you a better detective. Here's another tip.'

'What's that?'

'Check the days, dates, weather from when the women were dumped. There might be a pattern there. That's what you need to look for—patterns that keep occurring.'

Andy was quiet. 'Thanks, mate. Catch you later.'

Dave put down the phone, feeling pleased. Andy recognising

the balls-up he'd caused was a huge step in the right direction for him. Maybe he'd make a detective yet.

There was a knock on the door and Dave stifled a sigh. Was he ever going to get back to these guns!

Jack stuck his head in.

'What's going on, Jack?'

'Just heading out to do a few DUI checks. Any places you want me to go in particular?'

'You're in charge of that! I'm just the detective.'

'Thought I'd check. See if you had anything that correlated with what you were working on.'

That stopped Dave in his tracks. 'That's a bloody good point. Why don't you take a drive down to Booleroo? Maybe do a bit of a run along the main street and the likes. See what you can spot. Pull up a few random people.'

'Cool bananas. See you later.'

'Cool bananas? Good cop talk, Jack.' With a smile he turned back to his computer, deciding to run a background check on Eddie.

Well, well. It seemed Eddie had a rap sheet. 'Ah,' Dave breathed as he started to read. Three counts of soliciting a prostitute . . . and one for DV. Domestic violence. 'Nice character,' Dave muttered, reading on. He'd lost his licence for driving under the influence and had got it back just before the accident. But he'd been clean for the six years he'd worked for Leigh.

Getting his life back on track, obviously. Then the poor bastard gets killed.

He wrote the particulars up on the board and turned his attention to Charlie. He didn't have a rap sheet; neither did Geoff. Leigh, however, had one charge against him.

Dave gave a whistle as he read that report.

'Leigh Bounter was charged with discharging a firearm in public after he pointed a .22 towards Mr Ray Newell's ute and fired it into the door. It is alleged that Mr Newell was involved in an incident on the football field which saw Mr Bounter's neck broken. He had to forfeit his career as an AFL football player and was very angry with Mr Newell. The incident took place at Mr Newell's depot on the outskirts of Booleroo. Mr Bounter claimed it was an accident, and we were unable to prove otherwise. He was fined $2000.'

'Sixteen years ago and not a thing since,' Dave muttered. 'Exemplary record. Everyone is entitled to a brain freeze.' Still, he was surprised Leigh had been allowed to keep any firearms. The department usually looked at firearm offences very seriously. Dave wondered if the police of the day had gone a little easy on him, since Leigh had only just got out of rehab.

An email dinged again and this time it was from the sergeant in charge of the Mount Gambier Police Station.

Opening the statement, he scanned it quickly, realising there wasn't much in it. It covered Eddie's birthdate, schooling and work history.

He was such a good boy, Eddie's mother was quoted as saying. *But he got into a bit of trouble after he left school. He joined a shearing team and got stuck into the drugs. Married a woman much older than he was. That didn't last. She reported him for hitting her, but he swears he didn't. Of course I believe him. That woman was a nasty piece of work. Had a string of affairs and drained his bank account.*

'Of course she was nasty,' Dave muttered sarcastically. 'There're two sides to every story, Mum.'

Jotting down the main points on the board, he couldn't help but feel there was more to Eddie. Still, he would find it.

He picked up the phone and dialled Leigh's mobile. After introducing himself, he started to ask Leigh about Eddie.

'How did he come to work for you?'

'I put an ad in the paper, he was the only one who replied. I was desperate at that point. Needed someone to help out with the sheep work while seeding was going on. He proved himself to be quite handy in the yards. Turns out we became mates as well as work colleagues. He stayed on and became an integral part of my operation.'

'Did you know much about his personal life?'

'I knew he'd been married and divorced. But as for women, in the time he worked for me, there never seemed to be any. He was content with heading to the pub, doing a bit of shooting—he shot kangaroos to supplement his income, you know. And he loved camping. He'd head off for days, up north, by himself. He was happy in his own company.'

'Kangaroo shooter, too, huh?' Dave jotted that down. 'Did he go by himself or have someone with him?'

'No, always by himself unless I went along for a shoot.'

'Did you go often?'

'Not as much as I would've liked. There always seem to be meetings in the evenings.'

'Okay. Now, Leigh, you would've known I'd find the firearm charge against you? Do you want to tell me about it?'

'It was a long time ago. It shouldn't come into this!'

'But I'd like to hear your version, not just rely on what I'm reading.'

'I was angry,' Leigh said in a flat tone. 'I always felt it was

Ray's fault that my neck broke. I'd gone to pick up some barley seed I'd bought off him and he'd pushed my buttons. I never meant for the gun to go off, but it did and went into the door of his ute. Of course he reported me.'

'Right. Well, thanks for your help. I'll be in touch.'

Dave hung up the phone and sat back in his chair, thinking about what he'd found out.

Chapter 22

The sheep streamed through the gate into the compound and raced around the side of the shed, hoping the gate on the other side was open. They realised it was shut and slowed from running to a walk and started to mill around, their heads down, pulling at the grass. A few walked into the machinery shed looking for titbits, and others ran straight to the silos, pushing their heads into the boot, looking for grain.

Fiona was pleased she'd remembered to block off the boots with a few empty chemical drums. She didn't need them getting a tummy full of any type of food before she put them into the shed for shearing.

She sent Meita around them and the dog herded them towards the open gate of the yards. This was the part Fiona found hard now that she was a bit bigger. They were wily old ewes and knew what was about to happen. With Meita running from one side to the other, barking loudly, and Fiona trying to do the same, the ewes baulked at the gate, not wanting to run through.

Puffing hard and holding the underside of her stomach, she yelled at them. 'Ha! Ha! Get in, get in! Pack 'em up, Meita! Get in there, you old bitches!'

She wished she'd thought to grab something that rattled—even a plastic bag that made a different noise to Meita barking and her yelling. These girls were used to that. Something new would have helped.

She knew she couldn't let them go, because when she tried to get them in the yards next time, they would remember they'd beaten her once and give her an extra hard time. She yelled a bit louder and jumped up and down, flapping her arms. Meita rushed into the middle of the mob, barking loudly, sending them scattering in every direction, but she was rewarded with the leaders turning their heads and running into the yards.

'Go back, Meita, quick! Go back!'

Meita rounded behind the mob and pointed them back in the right direction and within a few minutes, Fiona, panting for breath, was able to chain the gate behind them.

'Right, they can stay there until this evening and drain out, Miss Meita,' Fiona said. Meita sat down, looking up at her, her tail thumping on the ground. Fiona grinned. 'You're going to enjoy the next few days, with all the drafting we're going to do. Come on, get up on the back of the ute. I need a rest, and I want to check the spraying that Damien did.'

Sloshing through the muddy yards, she went back to her ute, stopping to glance around at the sheep, making sure the other gates were all chained shut. She knew she'd done it, but a second check wouldn't hurt.

There was a glint in the sky and she looked up expecting to see a jet. Instead it was something small and silver.

'It's that bloody drone again,' she muttered, her brow crinkling. 'Why's it coming over all the time? That's the fifth time I've seen it.' She watched it dip and glide, never coming too close. In fact, she was sure it wasn't even crossing her boundary. Just flying up and down the fence line.

Well, just so long as it didn't buzz across her yards and scare the sheep, it would be okay. Still, she'd begun to wonder why it was up so often.

'Come on,' she said to Meita with a final look at the drone. 'Let's go.'

Fiona drove out to the barley paddock, avoiding the puddles on the road. She stopped every so often to look down at the feed that was pushing through. She was sure Charlie was looking after them this season. How else could the perfect timing and amount of rain be explained? Even the old-timers were saying there had never been a season like this one.

Out in the paddock, she felt a sense of satisfaction as she looked over the healthy crop. It was a vivid green and swayed gently in the breeze. As she got down onto her hands and knees, she felt the moisture in the soil soak through her jeans. Inhaling the smell of it, she closed her eyes. It was beautiful.

Five and a bit months on, she still missed Charlie so intensely that it hurt, and these sorts of moments were so bitter-sweet she couldn't work out if she was happy or insanely sad. Charlie would have been so proud of this crop.

Parting the leaves, she looked down into the base of a plant, expecting to see it clean and insect-free. She did a double take. There were little black dots with red legs all over it.

It was crawling with the insects she'd had the crop sprayed for.

That couldn't be right. The chemical Jo had told her to use should have killed on impact, leaving behind a residue. She shifted spots and looked again. It was the same.

She moved as quickly as she could, getting into the ute and driving further into the paddock. Here she could see the damage they were doing. Little white patches on beautiful, healthy green leaves.

Shit! What had happened?

Pulling out her mobile phone, she rang Jo.

'The spraying hasn't worked,' she said without preamble. 'What could have stuffed it up?'

'What do you mean?' Jo sounded distracted.

'Just what I said,' Fiona tried to keep the panic out of her voice. She didn't have the extra money to do another spray. The bank still hadn't unfrozen her account, and the granting of probate seemed a lifetime away. Not knowing how long it was going to take, she had to operate on a shoestring budget. She'd even had to take out a shearing advance—an advance on the sales of her wool— this year to be able to pay the shearers. In all the time she and Charlie had farmed, they'd never had to do that.

She saw that her hands were shaking and took a deep breath to try to calm herself. Reacting and feeling like this wouldn't do the baby any good.

'I'll come out and have a look this afternoon. I'm just a bit tied up at the moment,' Jo sounded strained.

'But why wouldn't the chemical have worked? Was it a shonky batch? Am I able to be reimbursed so I can buy more?' Fiona was standing in the middle of the paddock, surrounded by a barley crop that was halfway to her knees. This was a life-changing crop—if she could get it harvested and into the bin. Fear began to creep over her.

'Stop it,' she told herself silently.

'I don't know, Fee. I haven't heard of this happening to anyone else, so it's unlikely it's a chemical problem. Look, like I said, I'm a bit tied up. I'll be out there in a couple of hours, okay?'

Fiona swallowed. 'Sure. See you then.' She pressed the button to disconnect the call and stood there, frozen to the spot. She couldn't think either.

Finally, she decided she couldn't do anything until Jo arrived. She went back to the house and turned on the computer. Bringing up the weather website, she checked the forecast for the next week. Her heart sank when she saw that a cold front was due in three days' time. It looked like the strongest one, so far, for the season. Of course she was shearing.

'Bloody hell!' Her cursing made Meita, curled up in front of the bar heater, look up at her enquiringly.

'You know what that means, don't you?' Fiona said, turning to talk to her. 'That means we'll have to get them in a paddock with a shelter and make sure they get a good feed beforehand. Don't want them wandering out into the cold weather without their winter coats on. Geez, could anything else go wrong? I'm beginning to take this personally, Charlie!' She looked up at the roof as she spoke.

Sorting through the bills, Fiona worked out which ones she had to pay now and which could wait for a while. Then she picked up the phone to ring her bank manager.

'Hi, Wayne, Fiona Forrest here,' she said when he answered.

'Fiona, how are you? I've just been talking about you! How fortuitous that you rang!'

'I hope it was all good!'

'Well, I'd heard that you were selling and I'd planned on giving you a call about paying out the loan and what the best way forward was, so you didn't get hit with too many charges and fees. What made you change your mind?'

Fiona pursed her lips and frowned. 'I'm sorry, you heard what?'

There was a silence down the end of the line before Wayne cleared his throat. 'Oh, have I made a mistake?'

'Yeah! A big one,' Fiona snapped. 'Where did you hear that?'

'Um, a very reliable source. But I don't think I'll mention who, since it appears it isn't true. I'm sorry, Fiona. I have to admit I was very surprised.'

'I'm not selling,' she stated flatly. 'And you can tell anyone who brings it up again. I'm just not.'

'Sure. Now, how can I help you?' Wayne stumbled over his words.

'I was ringing about extending my overdraft,' she said, twisting the cord around her finger. She wondered what he'd say, considering how vehemently she'd just said she wasn't selling.

'Ah.'

The silence between them made her stomach constrict and she felt the need to fill it. 'Just a temporary one. Bridging finance.'

'Look, Fee, why don't you come in so we can talk about this,' Wayne replied. 'We do have a bit of an issue with security since the farm is still in both of your names.'

'But . . .' Fiona tried to think of what to say. She hadn't thought there would be a problem! 'But the will. It all comes to me. I don't understand.'

'Come in and talk to me. I'll see what I can do to help.' Wayne's voice was kind. 'How does three o'clock tomorrow sound?'

'I'm shearing tomorrow.' Fiona couldn't think; her heart was pounding so hard, she was getting spots in front of her eyes.

'Okay, maybe after you've finished shearing. How many days have you got?'

'Four, depending on how many they shear a day. It might run into five.'

'Fine, then ring me when you've finished and we'll arrange an appointment then. I assume you've got a shearing advance organised?'

'Yes, I have.'

'Good. Okay, see you in a week or so.'

Fiona hung up the phone, staring at the desk. Today was turning out to be a really, really shitty day.

Chapter 23

Storming into the real estate office, Fiona slammed her hand down on the desk, causing Ian Tonkin to jump.

'What are you saying about me around town?' she demanded.

'What?' Ian rose from his desk and walked over to her.

'Stay away from me,' she said, holding her hand out to ward him off. 'I want to know what you're saying about me selling.'

'I haven't said—'

'Well, who's saying it then? I keep hearing it over and over. My bank manager told me again this morning.' Fiona glared at him.

'Okay, sure, I said early on, not long after Charlie died, that you were selling. I thought I could convince you to. But I couldn't. All's fair in love and war.' He shrugged. 'I haven't said anything to anyone for months.'

'I'm not sure I believe you.'

'Can't do much about that.' He lifted his chin and looked down his nose at her.

Fiona squinted. Could anyone be more arrogant or more insensitive? Without another word, she turned and walked out of the office.

ഗ

'Your blood pressure is up,' Scott said as he unwrapped the arm cuff.

'Is it any wonder?' Fiona said cynically. 'I'm feeling a bit of pressure at the moment. Almost like I'm being backed into a corner.'

'You're doing too much.' He started typing, making notes. 'If you keep this up, I'll have to put you in hospital.'

'No can do! I'm starting shearing tomorrow.'

Scott pushed his glasses down to the end of his nose and looked at her. 'Which bit didn't you hear? You're doing too much. Hospital is an option.' He got up and walked over to a cupboard and pulled out a sample pot. 'Can you do a urine sample for me? I'll check the protein in it.'

Fiona bit her lip as her emotions welled up.

'Listen,' Scott softened his voice. 'It's the first time your blood pressure has been up. It might be just a symptom of today. Sounds like it's been a tough one.'

Fiona nodded, willing herself not to cry.

'But blood pressure in pregnancy isn't something to take lightly. It can be the start of pre-eclampsia and, trust me, that's not something you want. Go fill the cup and come back.' Scott opened the door for her and Fiona got up.

She needed to pee anyway.

In the toilet, her phone beeped with a text message from Jo.

I'm at your place, where are you?

'Shit,' she cursed and quickly typed back, *At doctors, forgot I had an appt. Give me an hour and I'll be back.*

I'll be here. Pick up more chemical before you come home. I've rung and organised it for you.

Fiona stared at the message. That meant she'd been right. The spraying hadn't worked. Still, there were other more pressing things to think about right now.

With the sample shoved in her pocket, she walked back into the surgery and self-consciously made her way to Scott's office.

'Fee?'

She turned and saw Carly sitting in the waiting room, reading a magazine. Her mother was up and out of her chair before Fiona could respond.

'What's wrong? Why are you here?' Carly looked her over and Fiona knew she was trying to work out if anything was different.

'Nothing's wrong, Mum. It's just one of the normal check-ups I have to have. What are you doing here?' She put a teasing tone in her voice and shot a glance over at Janey, who was glaring at them. 'Still haven't tamed the dragon,' she whispered.

Carly smiled like the cat who'd got the cream. 'Call me a bitch, but I love sitting here waiting for him.'

Scott opened his door. 'Ah, there you are. Oh, Carly, you're here, too. Good. Quick, both of you, come in.'

Fiona saw Scott's face light up when he saw Carly. Secretly she smiled to herself. This was great!

'I'm pleased you're here, Carly,' Scott said as he motioned to them both to sit down. 'Sample?' he held out his hand and took it over to the bench to test it while the two women waited.

'What's wrong here, Scott?' asked Carly as she eyed him closely.

'Everything's fine, Mum,' Fiona answered before Scott could get a word in. 'It's just a normal check-up. I told you.'

They both watched as Scott frowned, looking at the test stick. He walked back towards them and sat down at his desk, looking Fiona in the eye. 'Just let me take your blood pressure again.'

They were all silent, watching the cuff blow up and release. He nodded as if he'd expected the results.

'I want to see you next week. At this stage, your blood pressure is too high, but it could have been brought on by the stresses of today. You don't have any protein in your urine right now, but we certainly need to keep an eye on things.'

'High blood pressure? What does that mean?' Carly asked.

'It can be a sign of pre-eclampsia.' He turned his attention to Fiona. 'Have you had any dizziness or blurred vision? Headaches?'

Fiona shook her head.

'Bleeding?'

She hesitated.

'Fiona?' Carly's voice rose a notch.

'I had a bit a few weeks ago. But I'd lifted a couple of ewes onto a trailer so I could crutch them and I thought I'd just done too much. It was only a bit of spotting. Nothing much.'

Carly stood up and put her hands on her hips. 'Look here, my girl, that's my grandchild's life you're playing with. If you don't want to look after yourself, that's one thing, but don't risk this baby's . . .'

Scott put a hand on her arm to calm her. 'Carly, sweetheart, it's okay. Fiona knows. Sit down.' His gentle tone seemed to calm Carly, and she sat down abruptly.

'Your mother is right in a way, Fiona,' Scott said, when he was sure no one was going to interrupt him. 'You can do everything as you've done it before—after all, you're only pregnant, not sick, but you do have to be kind to yourself. I need you to slow down just a bit, okay? I know you've got shearing on, and being there is fine. But you need to take regular breaks. Is there anything else you haven't told me?'

'I get a bit breathless.'

Scott nodded. 'That's actually normal. The baby pushes up onto your diaphragm. Makes things a bit uncomfortable. Anything else?'

'I've had a couple of bloody noses, too. I don't usually get them.'

'Again, that can be normal. Blood vessels tend to be a bit closer to the surface when you're pregnant. Are you eating properly?'

Fiona nodded. Kim had sent her a basketful of frozen dinners she'd made as a trial for her new business. She'd happily and gratefully accepted them. Cooking at the end of the day, when she was exhausted, was too hard. 'That's one thing I am doing,' she said.

'Good. But be aware, Fiona, pre-eclampsia can be life-threatening to you and the baby. Make another appointment for next week and we'll check you out again then, okay?'

Fiona nodded, groaning inside. Great! Now her mother knew—she couldn't blame Scott for asking her to come in to the appointment. Especially since she'd been sitting there waiting for him to take his lunch break. That was how things worked in the country. But now she'd be fussing over her for the next three and a half months. Just what she didn't need.

'Carly, can you wait outside for a moment or two? There's a couple more things I just need to chat to Fiona about. And don't get huffy!' He winked at her and Carly's face split into a huge smile.

Fiona looked down, feeling uncomfortable about seeing such emotion from her mother. In one way it was so beautiful seeing Carly happy, but in another it was so foreign.

When the door shut behind her, Scott asked Fiona if she'd made an appointment to see the counsellor he'd suggested a few months ago.

'Not yet.' Fiona avoided his eye. It had actually slipped her mind, but she wasn't sure that Scott would believe her!

'Why not?'

'I don't feel like I need to. I'm getting on with what has to be done. There's no one else to do it, so I am. Keeps me busy and then I don't have to think.'

Scott made a note on his computer before turning back to her. 'Okay, I'm going to be frank here, Fiona. I love your mother, and I want to stay with her for a long time. Which in turn means I take you on, too. This baby as well. What I'm going to tell you, I'm telling you as a doctor but also as a friend. When bub is born, your emotions and hormones will get mucked around. Everything will be out of kilter. It might be a time, and I'm not saying it will be, but it *might* be, that you get hit hard with depression. It's going to be a poignant time going through the birth without Charlie here, let alone everything else you'll be facing. You won't be facing it by yourself, of course, but it will be an emotional roller-coaster. Make an appointment to see the counsellor and start talking about all this before the baby comes. Promise me.' He looked at her steadily.

'I've been talking to my brother,' she answered. 'I really think that's all I need. Everyone else is being incredibly supportive and helpful. Honestly, I'm doing okay.'

As she said that she had a vision of herself swimming underwater, trying to get away. If she kept moving and didn't stop, she wouldn't have to think.

If she didn't have to think, then she couldn't drown.

ꕤ

'I can't tell you what's happened here,' Jo said, running her fingers over her face. She had her phone out and was taking photos of the insects running over the leaves of the crop. 'My first thought was that Damien hadn't used the correct rate of chemical in the tank mix. But I've spoken with him, and he's one hundred per cent sure he mixed it correctly. I've got no reason to doubt him—after all, he's a contract sprayer.'

Fiona let the cool wind tease her hair, whipping it around her face as she stood in the paddock and watched Jo, who seemed tired and not herself.

'And he keeps notes of what he sprays, the mix he's used and everything else. I don't think it's his mistake.'

'What about the chemical? Could it have been faulty?'

Jo shook her head. 'I've already been onto our rep. He's asked the company to test the product—the chemical companies keep samples of every batch they make, so it's easy enough to go back and check. We've got the batch number of what you used from your invoice, but I doubt that's the issue.'

'Jo, I don't have the money to spray again.'

Her friend straightened up and dusted her hands off on the back of her jeans. 'What do you mean?'

Fiona explained the phone call from the bank, how she'd taken out extra money but that it wasn't going to be enough. Then she told her about the conversation with the bank manager this morning.

'That's just plain stupid,' Jo huffed. 'Get onto Leigh. He'll sort it for you.'

'No. I'll sort this myself.' She shrugged. 'I'm not going to rely on anyone.'

'Don't you feel with everything that's going on, that this is getting too hard?'

Fiona stared out across the crop. 'Not too hard, but very draining. I'm tired.'

'Well, you need to respray this crop. There's no other way around it.'

Fiona tapped her foot, thinking. 'Okay, I'll ring the manager of the merch store and see if he'll give me a sixty-day account.'

'I can organise that for you, if you want. In fact there's every chance the deferred payment option for chemical is still running.'

'Nah, leave it with me.' She ran her hands over the tops of the plants and felt the moisture on her hands. 'I still don't understand what's happened here.'

'Come on, let's go back to the shed and have a look at the containers there.'

They climbed into Fiona's ute and headed back home. Fiona looked at Jo out of the corner of her eye, trying to see if there were any bruises that hadn't been there last time.

'Hey, did you hear about Leigh and Ray Newell?' Jo asked,

pulling the ends of her sleeves into her hand and holding them with her fingers.

'Are you cold?' Fiona upped the heating, hoping that was all it was. The weather bureau hadn't been wrong about the temperature dropping in the lead-up to the cold front. 'And no, what have they been up to now?'

'Ray took a swing at Leigh in the pub the other night. Got him, too.'

They bumped across a small creek with a tiny trickle of water flowing through it. Tree trunks were surrounded by bark and leaves that had washed up the last time water had flowed through. Meita had enjoyed the previous little flood, too—she'd bounced through the shallow water, barking at the splashing she was making. The coldness never seemed to bother her.

'Shit, really?'

'Hmm, sounded like it got pretty heated and nasty. Ian was talking about it in the office.'

'Did Leigh belt him back?' Fiona wanted to know. 'You'd think the two of them would be over this by now, wouldn't you? I can't work out why Ray Newell is such a dick.'

'No point in trying to work it out. The fact is, he just is. No, Leigh was the righteous mayor he should be! But he gave the footy-club boys a bit of a mouthful about choosing their leaders wisely.' She rubbed her thighs as if she was trying to warm up her hands and looked out the window. 'Hey! What's that?' Jo pointed to the sky.

Fiona squinted and rolled her eyes. 'Oh, that again. It's a drone. I'm not sure what the neighbours are doing with it, but I've seen it quite a few times in the last couple of weeks.' She pulled up at the shed and turned off the engine.

'But there're laws about them—you can't just fly them over people's properties. You should call them up and ask what they're up to.'

'I don't think it ever crosses the boundary,' Fiona said, opening her door and getting out. Now that her stomach was brushing the steering wheel, she found it was easier to swing her legs out and wiggle herself to the ground, rather than hoist herself out as she'd done in the past.

They walked into the shed and Jo went straight to the chemical-storage room to look at the drums. Fiona slowly followed.

'So what's going on with you? You're looking really tired and distracted,' Fiona remarked, settling herself down on a chair. 'And you sounded really out of it when I rang you earlier.'

'Busy as,' Jo answered, unscrewing one of the lids and sniffing the container. 'Everyone wants a piece of me at the moment. It's just the way it is this time of the year.'

Fiona didn't say anything. She didn't believe her. Jo was behaving like she was nervous. Ill at ease. There was definitely something more than just being tired going on. She picked at the edge of her jacket sleeve, which was beginning to fray.

'Shit,' she heard Jo say.

'What?'

Jo ignored her and unscrewed another lid and smelled it. 'Have you washed any of these out?' she asked, grabbing the next one.

'No. I've been staying away from the chemicals. Damien might have.' She went to take the drum out of Jo's hand, but she'd already put it on the ground and picked up the next one.

'No, I asked when I rang him, so I knew what I was looking for. I wanted to make sure I was checking the same drums he used.'

'What's wrong?'

'I think the chemical has been emptied out and they've left you with wetter in the drum. So Damien has sprayed nothing but wetter.'

'But . . . the smell? The colour.'

'No, this chemical is clear and there would have been enough smell left in there for him not to notice. He was probably wearing a face mask when he emptied it in, anyway.'

Fiona stood up and made her way over to her, lifting up one of the containers and peering in.

'So what are you saying? That someone has deliberately emptied the drum?'

'Yeah. They've stolen the chemical by emptying it and refilling. You wouldn't have a clue until you realised it hadn't worked. By then, they're long gone—probably sprayed their paddocks already.'

'Stolen?'

'Stolen,' Jo confirmed.

Chapter 24

'Police are advising women to take extra care if they plan on drinking alone in the city. Details are scarce at present; however, police have informed us that during the past year, four women have been approached in bars. Monica Ferguson reports:

'Adelaide police are asking for any information relating to four women who have been drugged while drinking alone at bars and pubs in the Adelaide city area. These victims were bashed and raped before being dumped in parks or alleyways in the northern suburbs. Police suspect there may be more victims who haven't reported the attack to them and are appealing to these women to come forward. If you have any information, please call Crime Stoppers.'

The camera panned away from the reporter and focused on an empty park before the image on the screen flashed back to the anchor.

Dave switched off the TV and leaned back in his chair. He heard a knock on the door and called out for Jack to come in.

'Andy rang me,' Jack said without preamble.

'Hmm, I've had a conversation with him recently, too. The case has just been on the news. They're looking for more vics.'

'Reckon there'll be any?' Jack sat down and wiggled in the hard seat until he was comfortable.

'Sure to be. There'll be plenty of women who are embarrassed and ashamed of what's happened to them. They won't have wanted anyone to know, so they would have snuck home, cleaned themselves up and tried to get on with life.' Dave tapped a pen on his leg.

'Andy's got the next weekend off, away from the course, so he thinks he's gonna head home here.'

Dave raised his eyebrows. 'Things were pretty different when I did the course. We were shut away for the six weeks.' He shuffled some papers around his desk and looked at Jack. 'So, anything crop up while you were out yesterday?'

'Nope, nothing, nada, zilch. Didn't even catch anyone speeding.'

'Quiet then?'

'Very.'

'Hellooooo?'

Dave smiled and swung around in his chair, ready to greet Kim.

'Hello, my love,' he said as she came into his office.

'Hello, handsome,' she responded, leaning down to kiss him.

Jack cleared his throat uncomfortably and Kim broke away with a giggle.

'What have you got there?' Dave indicated the foil-covered tray she was holding. 'It certainly smells good!'

'Sausage rolls; thought you might need something to eat. Hi, Jack, how are you?

'Better now,' he said, helping himself to a roll and eating hungrily. 'They're bloody beautiful, Kim. Thanks.' He licked his fingers and tried to pick up the flaky pastry that had landed on the desk.

'You're welcome. Going okay here, sweetie?'

'Well,' Dave answered, 'I'm about to put in a request to have some fingerprints done on the guns for Eddie McDougall's murder.'

'Oh, haven't got them in the file?'

'No. The investigation has been a balls-up from go to whoa,' Dave said, his mouth full.

'Cheers, mate,' Jack flicked a pen at him and Dave ducked.

'Sorry! Not all of it, just a lot.'

'Not good.' Kim crossed her arms and looked at the desk, which was covered in photos and notes. 'I'd better let you get back to it.'

'Thanks for the sausage rolls, love.'

'You're very welcome. I'll leave you to it.'

'I might be a bit late tonight. I'm going to head down to see Fiona Forrest.'

'Call me,' Kim winked and walked out of the room.

Dave watched her go. 'Ouch!' He felt the sharp tip of another pen hit his head.

'Pervert,' Jack said with a grin.

'You're just jealous.' Dave dragged his thoughts back to the investigation. 'Right, now we have to see if there is something that would only have Charlie's fingerprints on it so we can disregard his on the guns. That will mean taking a trip. Want to come with me?'

'Sure, I'll get the car.'

'I'll be ten minutes or so. Got to send this email and ring Fiona, make sure it's okay.'

'I'll see you out the front.'

Dave quickly typed an email requesting the two guns be fingerprinted. He packaged up the fingerprints he'd taken when he'd interviewed Leigh and Geoff and sent them to Adelaide to be scanned into the computer.

Taking a deep breath, he picked up the phone and dialled Fiona's number.

Introducing himself, he asked if he could make an appointment to see her that day.

'I've just started shearing today, but I can catch up with you at the yards.'

'Great, I'll see you in about an hour and a half.'

*

They arrived at Charona and carefully drove in through the gate, not wanting to frighten the sheep around the shed and in the yards. Dave could see the shorn ewes with their heads down, chewing at the short pick of feed that covered the ground. In the yards, Fiona had a backpack strapped to her and she was back-lining the ones in the race.

The outline of her protruding stomach stopped Dave in his tracks. It was confronting to see a pregnant woman working like a man. His respect for her was enormous; her tenacity and resilience were huge.

There was another lady there Dave didn't know, obviously trying to help but not really sure of what she was doing.

'Can I help?' he offered as he swung his legs over the wooden rails and jumped into the yards. Jack followed him.

The older lady turned to him. 'Stopping my daughter from doing way too much would be a start,' she snapped.

The tension between the two women was obvious.

'Might take a raincheck on that,' he answered with a grin. 'This is Constable Jack Higgins, who works with me at the Barker Police Station, and I'm Dave Burrows.'

'Carly, Fiona's mother.'

The bitter wind swept through the yards, sending a shiver down his spine, yet he could see that Fiona was sweating as she walked over to shake their hands.

'Hi, Dave, Jack. No, thanks, I'm fine. I'll just finish this race and I can talk to you.'

He watched as she methodically ran the gun from the top of the neck down to the hips of the freshly shorn sheep. The thin blue lines were clear against the vivid white.

'Hear there's a graziers' alert out,' Dave commented, walking to the front of the race to open the gate. 'Finished?'

'Yep, let them go, thanks.' Fiona shrugged off the backpack as the ewes raced through the small opening and into a bigger yard. 'I heard about that. Need to get these girls out as quickly as I can, make sure they've got some feed in their stomachs and a sheltered paddock. Not ideal timing, unfortunately.' In the other yard the lambs were waiting for the ewes, and the noise of the mums trying to find their own lambs was deafening.

Fiona went to the fence and stood there, watching the sheep milling around, sniffing each lamb as it came up to them. When a couple of cheeky, hungry lambs went straight for an udder, the ewes gave them a quick kick and hopped away on three legs.

'Look out! Not giving anything away unless it's to their own,' Dave said with a smile. 'I loved watching this when

I was younger.' He breathed in the smell of lanoline and mud that was bringing back memories of his childhood and other cases he'd worked. Especially the first one he'd done over here, which had involved Gemma Sinclair and stock stealing.

'Did you used to farm?' Fiona sounded surprised.

'My dad and brothers did. None of them do now though. Land prices skyrocketed and it was too good an opportunity to miss.'

'They sold because of the land price?'

'Oh yeah. I was the third son, so there was never room for me to stay at home and farm, even if I wanted to.'

'Did you?'

'Sure would've. I love the country and being around farmers, but I'm not sure I'm completely cracked up for the finance side of things. The physical work I could do, no problems, but I like a pay cheque at the end of the week. Rural crime seemed to be the perfect fit for me.'

All four turned at a call from the shearing shed.

'Right to let 'em out?' the classer called to Fiona.

She gave the thumbs-up sign and watched as the next run of ewes ran out from under the shearing shed. Feeling invigorated without their wool, some of the ewes began to hurtle themselves towards the fence, bleating out for their lambs as they went. Some of them jumped and bucked, their eyes blinded by the light after the darkness of the shearing shed. They didn't see the large puddle just outside the let-out pens and landed smack bang in the middle of it. The more cautious ones ran around the edge. They kept running until they realised there was a fence and skidded to a halt.

They let out another round of baaing and the yards were overcome with noise.

Fiona laughed and yelled, 'Anyone who thinks that a farm is quiet should turn up at shearing and lamb-marking time!'

'Absolutely!'

'What did you want me to do now, Fiona?' Carly asked.

'Nothing, Mum. We've finished until it's time to back-line the ones that are coming out of the shed. I'll wait until the run is finished before I start on them. Reckon a sit-down is in order. Maybe you could run down and get the mail?'

Carly nodded and left.

Walking over to the gate, Fiona let herself through, then opened another one that led straight out into a paddock. She gave an arm signal to Meita, who trotted around the mob and pointed them towards the gate. The ewes made a dash for it, but Fiona slowed them down with another wave of her arm and stood to the side of the gate, counting as they ran through.

When the last one had gone through, she pulled a notepad out of her pocket and jotted down the number. Then she looked up at the sky, checking the weather. She pointed and Dave followed her line of sight.

'A drone? What's that doing?'

'I have no idea, but it's certainly up a lot. It's in a different area to usual—mostly I've seen it in the north. I thought the neighbours must be learning how to check their tanks and troughs with it.'

'Interesting.' He watched it for a while, then brought his attention back to the sheep.

Walking out into the paddock, Dave squatted down and

looked at the feed. He saw the ewes run towards the trough and jump over each other, trying to get a drink.

'Always amazes me how they're thirsty, even when it's winter,' he said, indicating the pile-up.

Fiona shut the gate and leaned against the fence. 'Just so long as they get a feed,' she said again. 'That's the most important part. If they've got full tummies they won't go out into the weather because they're hungry. And the change in weather and their being shorn could cause issues with exposure. I've thought about putting them back into the shed with this weather coming, but with the lambs on them it's too hard. They need to be in the paddock, where both the lambs and their mums can get a feed.' She looked up at the sky where the dark clouds were beginning to cover the top of Mount Remarkable. They were soft and fluffy, and not at all ominous-looking, but Dave knew better.

'The wind won't help,' Dave commented. 'The chill factor and all.'

'Yeah, I know.' Fiona pursed her lips and Dave could see she was worried. 'Come into the house and have a cuppa,' she said. 'I know you want to talk to me, but I want to talk to you, too. Sorry, Jack.' She turned to the policeman, who was standing well back, listening to everything. 'I forgot you were there. Come on, both of you.'

ೲ

Fiona read a note on the front door and Dave watched a smile spread over her face. She held it out to him.

'I'm so lucky,' she said as she pushed the door open and went in. 'I've got a lot of people looking out for me.'

Dave read the note: *'Hi Fiona, you weren't here when I dropped in. There's another load of wood in the tank at the back. Hope shearing is going well, cheers, Rob.'*

'Sounds like a fire is in store tonight then. Who's Rob?' Dave asked.

'He's our local vet. Doesn't just look after the Booleroo area, but all the way over to Orroroo and Jamestown and down to Laura.'

Inside the house, Dave looked at the photos hanging on the wall, his hands behind his back. Charlie had been a handsome man and Dave could see from the look of adoration on his face as he looked at Fiona that he had loved her deeply.

But not enough to face his demons. Stifling a sigh, Dave glanced towards the open office door and saw a silver urn on the mantelpiece. He knew what it contained.

Dave turned back to Fiona.

Jack stood near the doorway until she told him to sit down. 'Can I help?' he asked, as she struggled with a large, heavy kettle that had come to the boil on the gas stove. He moved to take the kettle from her. The Aga stove next to it looked like it hadn't been used for a while. 'That looks like a piece of history there,' Jack nodded at both the kettle and the Aga.

'Thanks,' she said and grabbed a couple of cups from the cupboard. 'I found the kettle over at the shearers' quarters—I love it. When I had the Aga going I could keep it warm all the time and it never took long to boil. Since Charlie isn't here I don't have the need, so I just use the gas stove.'

'I remember when I used to visit my cousin over here, her mum had one and they used it to heat the kitchen as well as cook on. It was the best thing for making soups and stews.

Aunty Peg used to put the pot on the top and stir occasionally until the meal was cooked,' Dave reminisced from the other side of the room.

'That's about the size of it.' She offered him sugar and milk, before pouring it into her own and stirring. 'Sit down,' she said after she noticed Jack still hovering in the corner.

The men each pulled out a chair and sat down at the large wooden table. 'What did you want to talk to me about?' Dave asked, stirring his coffee.

She was quiet for a moment and took a sip of her tea before she answered. 'Something strange has been happening around here recently.'

The two policemen let her talk without interrupting.

'I got in a contractor to spray my crops and I found out yesterday that it didn't work. Jo, who's a friend of mine and the local agronomist, came over to have a look and she agrees with me. It's going to have to be sprayed again. She's spoken to the contractor.' She went on to explain how they'd worked out what had happened, then told him about the chemical drums.

'So you think the chemical has been poured out of one lot of drums, replaced with something similar and then sprayed out?' asked Dave. 'Stolen?'

'Well, that's what Jo thinks. But why would someone do that? In fact, I don't know how you could be sure that it was stolen.' Wrinkling her brow, she spoke slowly. 'It could have been tipped out, but if you were going to tip it out, why not use it? Oh!' She threw her hands in the air. 'I don't know, but like I said, that's what Jo thinks.'

'Rural crime can be anything,' Dave explained. 'It's not just stock stealing. I've certainly heard of chemical being stolen before. The incidence of this type of crime is getting higher because things are costing more. The bottom line isn't quite as large as it used to be.' He put his elbows on the table and thought for a moment. 'I'll take a look at this before I go. Now, I've got some questions for you.'

Fiona nodded and breathed deeply.

'I need something of Charlie's that would have his fingerprints on it. A hairbrush or pen. Something of that ilk. Would you have something like that?'

Fiona spun her cup around slowly, thinking. 'There's a letter opener that he often used in the office. I haven't touched it. Would that help?'

'That would be great. I'll grab it while I'm here, but I may have to hold onto it for a while.'

'Okay.'

'Tell me about Charlie, Leigh, Eddie and Geoff's relationship. Were they close?'

'Charlie and Leigh were. Eddie and Leigh were too, and Charlie and Geoff were farming mates, if that makes sense.'

Dave nodded; he understood. They were brought together by farming and talked farming, but not much more.

'So there wasn't any bad blood between any of them? No business dealings that had gone wrong, or fights over women? Nothing of that nature?'

'Not that I'm aware of. Geoff, in particular, is a sworn bachelor. Eddie, I don't really know much about, and Leigh, he's had the occasional girlfriend, but they never seem to last.

'As for business dealings, I couldn't really say. Charlie would have known more. I never heard anything that indicated there was any bad blood between them.'

Jack wrote a few notes and looked at Dave—it was clear he had a question. Dave nodded and let him take the lead.

'Who knew they were all going shooting that night?'

Fiona shrugged. 'Have no idea who the others told. But I was supposed to go, then Leigh texted and said his council meeting was finishing early so I got left behind and he went in my place.'

'You were supposed to go? Do you shoot?' Jack sounded surprised.

'I love shooting!' She gave a smile. 'Charlie and I used to go all the time. I don't like killing kangaroos though. Foxes? Let me at them. Horrible, cruel bloody creatures they are. And rabbits, they're just destructive, so I don't mind getting rid of them either.'

'Who taught you?'

'Charlie. He wanted me to get my licence so I could have a gun to shoot snakes. It went from there.'

'But it was Charlie's gun that was on the ute that night?'

'I know he took two, but I can't tell you which ones. He put them in the ute while I was in the shower. It wasn't until you guys told me which ones that I knew.'

'How did you know he took two then?' Jack asked.

'He always took two. Different guns have different ranges. The gun he used depended on what he was shooting.' Her hands flew to her stomach and she shifted uncomfortably in the chair as she sucked in her breath.

Dave half rose. 'You okay?'

'Ugh.' She arched her back. 'Oh, stop that! Little bugger is kicking me under the ribs. Yep, I'm fine.'

'Active little sod!'

'Farmer in the making. Did you want another cuppa?'

Both men shook their heads.

'I've heard that they had to pick Leigh up from his farm. Why would that have been? Especially since they came back to shoot here?' Dave asked.

Fiona frowned. 'I guess it was just another way of having a look around. They were keen to get this dog, and if they took some of the gazetted roads across the back to Leigh's place, they might have come across it. That's all I can think of.'

'And what about Charlie? Tell me about him after the accident.'

Chapter 25

Fiona reached for a box of tissues and blew her nose.

'After the accident,' she repeated softly. 'He was a different man. He couldn't sleep. He said he kept dreaming about seeing Eddie on the ground, and the blood. There was blood bubbling towards him. He could hear the scream and the silence all at once. Charlie said he couldn't explain it, and I suggested he might've been slightly deaf from the shot.' She shrugged, still clutching the tissue. 'I don't know, it was an assumption on my part.'

Shifting in her chair, she watched as both men took notes. 'He couldn't talk about what he saw at the scene. He just said there was lots of blood. It was wet and dark and everything was confused. Charlie did say that he felt like he could never get Eddie's blood off him and how heavy Eddie was when he fell on him. That was early on after the accident. Probably when he was still in shock.

'Later he turned into a shell. He didn't speak much to

me. Well, to anyone, really. I begged him to talk to someone else—a counsellor or even one of the other guys, if he couldn't talk to me. He did go and see a counsellor for a little while, but it didn't seem to help. He drank more than usual.' She broke off. 'I don't know what else to tell you.'

'Did he spend much time where it happened?'

Fiona rubbed her arms as if trying to keep warm. 'No. He never went there. He said he couldn't face it. And I never saw him up there. Because it's up on a hill, I would have noticed the ute.' She paused. 'If I was here, of course.'

'So you think it's safe to say he blamed himself?'

'Without a doubt.' She got up and started to pace the kitchen. 'Charlie was kind-hearted. He loved everyone. This tore at the very core of him.' She brushed away angry tears, then raised her voice a little. 'Which is just stupid. I kept trying to tell him that. Just because it was his gun that the bullet came from, didn't mean it was his fault. The bloody ute tipped over. No one could have known that was going to happen. It wasn't Geoff's fault because he was driving, it was just the way it happened.

'He said to me once he thought the gun hadn't been secured. That he forgot to put the safety on. Of course it's his responsibility to do that.' She looked at both men. 'Which, knowing how conscientious he was about gun safety, I always found weird, but . . .' She shrugged helplessly, her voice trailing off. 'Maybe something hit it during the accident and it came off. I suggested that to him heaps of times, but he wouldn't listen. He had it in his head it was his fault and nothing was going to sway him.'

'He was very careful?'

'Always. Never, ever left a bullet in the chamber unless the gun was secured. Maybe he just didn't have time to make sure it was safe before the ute tipped over, but again—I've been through this a million times in my head—if the ute was moving, he should have, he *would have*, had it secured so it couldn't fire.' An expression of disbelief crossed her face. 'Dave, I've had nightmares about this. There must have been a reason it wasn't.'

Dave drained the last of his coffee and got up to rinse his cup, before placing it upside down on the sink.

'So, in leading up to when he died, were there any changes in him?'

Resting her elbows on the table, she let her head fall into her hands. 'Nothing more than had become normal,' she replied sadly. 'Withdrawn, non-communicative, angry.' She stopped. 'Yeah, angry. Charlie never yelled. But in the two weeks before, he would snap at me constantly. Nothing I did was right, or good enough. Oh, of course I ignored it—what else was I going to do. I knew he was hurting so badly. He certainly wasn't at all loving.'

She swallowed, not sure if she should go on. Even in her nightly 'wralks' with Will, she hadn't told him about the way her lovely Charlie had turned into a monster. How he would snarl at her. He would go from not talking at all to picking on her, and there had been one night when he had grabbed both her arms and shaken her. *You've got no fucking idea what I've been through!*, he'd screamed at her. *None! You didn't have to see a bloke die by your hand. By your own gun. There was so much blood. Blood smells, did you know that?* He'd looked at her accusingly. *Nah, of course you wouldn't. You. Haven't. Been. Through. What. I have.* She could remember cowering in the corner, hoping the moment would pass. It had, but he'd never said sorry.

She quickly summarised the memory, all the time looking at the table. She didn't want to remember Charlie this way; it wasn't the real him. It felt like she was telling tales on her husband.

'I think he lost a bit of memory, too,' she finished.

Looking at her sympathetically, Dave asked why.

'Because there were certain things he couldn't remember about the accident. Whether or not he wanted to remember is a different story, but he definitely said he *couldn't* remember when the other policeman was interviewing him.'

'Can you recall what it was about?'

'A couple of questions. One was about guns. How many they were carrying. He couldn't remember that, or who was holding what gun at the time.' She folded her hands in her lap and looked up at Dave. 'I researched this. There're actually websites for coping with causing an accidental death. They said that memory loss can be a symptom of trauma. Along with a whole bunch of other things.

'When Leigh found him in the car, he'd been drinking Johnnie Walker scotch. Something I never understood, because he hated it. His favourite brand was Jameson. Maybe he'd just forgotten he hated it?

'Do you want me to grab that letter opener?'

'That would be great, thanks. We'll come with you though, as I have to put the letter opener in an evidence bag.'

While Dave put on a pair of gloves and took a plastic bag out of his pocket, Fiona flicked the button on the answering machine.

'Fiona, this is Ray Newell from Booleroo Transport. Just calling in regards to an overdue account. This is the third request we've made. Can you call us when you come in? It's from when we carted three hundred and twelve lambs to Dublin.'

'Ah, g'day there, Fiona. Ian Tonkin calling. I know you're not interested in selling—you've made that clear. But I did want to reiterate it's not me who is spreading the rumours about the sale of your farm. I also wanted to let you know that BJL Holdings have upped their offer by twenty-five dollars a hectare. Just in case that might sway you. Cheers.'

ശ

Tapping the steering wheel in time to some country music he didn't recognise, Dave drove back to Barker with Jack. The Mount Remarkable ranges were just that—remarkable, tall and majestic, covered in trees. The road was narrow and winding and Dave had to concentrate. Even so, he kept going back over what Fiona had told him.

He understood Charlie's memory loss regarding the time of the accident, but he should never have forgotten what he liked and didn't like to drink. Fiona also mentioned that they never kept Johnnie Walker scotch in the house. So where did it come from? Just another anomaly with this case.

The letter opener Fiona had given them was bagged and in the back of the car, waiting to be sent off for analysis.

And regarding the chemical that was replaced with wetter—he'd shown Jack how to fingerprint the chemical drums and checked around to see if there was anything else out of the ordinary, but nothing had stood out.

He'd asked if Fiona had a security camera. She didn't, so before they'd left, Dave had offered the use of one of theirs for the time being.

He had a motion camera in his detective's toolkit, so he set it up at the front gate, hanging it high in a tree. At least it would let them see which vehicles came in and out of Charona while it was there.

When people drove into the property, the camera would start recording and they'd be able to get the numberplate as well as the make and model of each vehicle.

'Mightn't be much use,' he'd told her, 'but it's worth giving it a crack in case someone decides you're an easy target.'

'What are you thinking?' Jack asked Dave as the road changed from bitumen to dirt. It was slippery and Dave immediately took his foot off the accelerator and slowed down until he reached a safe speed.

'We need to check the registrations on all the guns, to start with. When I get back, I'm going to read Charlie's file and we'll make a call from there. Did you pick up on anything you wanted to follow up?'

Jack flicked back through his notes. 'Isn't it odd that she's got overdue accounts and she's claiming Ian Tonkin is hassling her to sell? And that phone call, it really sounds like that company wants her land. Why would that be? Not only to help Fiona out, I'm sure. There must be something more to it.'

Dave nodded. 'I agree. It's normal for banks to freeze accounts when someone dies—until probate is issued. And I'm not that surprised people want her to sell. Although I can tell they haven't got a chance. But what have we got?' He stabbed at the air every time he made a point. 'One, we have a dead man who was accidentally shot with Charlie's gun. Two, we have an alleged suicide. Three, since the suicide there've been numerous rumours of Fiona selling and the real estate agent strongly suggesting she sell. Four, there've been how many sales in the area—four, three? I have to check my notes. To the same company, in a very short period of time. Five, chemical replace—sabotage?' Dave leaned his head back on the seat and watched the road, all the while thinking. 'Hmm, maybe, maybe not. But certainly a crime—stealing. Six, inconsistencies with gun numbers. Oh and seven, the drone.'

'You know,' Jack said, 'by itself, you wouldn't think there was anything too sinister there, but put them all together and something isn't adding up.'

'Why you didn't decide you wanted to be a detective, Jack, I'll never know. You're dead on the money.'

The country slipped by; the crops were looking healthy and the stock grazing close to the roads were in good nick. Some ewes were heavy with wool, others had been shorn. The grey clouds had closed in while they'd been talking to Fiona and a light drizzle had started—just enough to need the windscreen wipers on.

'Hope those sheep she's shorn are going to be okay,' Dave mused as he saw the trees bend in a particularly strong gust of wind. 'Tell me about the scene of Charlie's death.' He returned to the subject. 'What he was wearing, that sort of stuff.'

It was Jack's turn to think. 'By the time we got there, Fiona had been taken to sit in the back of the ambulance. She was moaning and crying until the sedatives kicked in. The vic was in the front seat of the car—the driver's side.' Jack closed his eyes and Dave knew he was picturing the scene. Some things coppers had seen were burned into their brains. He didn't think this would be one of them. It hadn't been a particularly traumatic scene for a police officer—he was sure Jack would've seen worse.

'I remember the hose because it was large enough to go over the outside of the exhaust pipe. I think it was some type of suction hose he used to fill the boom spray—pretty sure that's what Bounter told me. He'd fastened it on with a large hose clamp. I hadn't seen anything like that before.'

'No,' Dave agreed. 'Mostly garden hoses with rags stuffed around them.'

'But the crack in the window was larger because of the circumference of the hose. It was really tidy—he'd folded up towels, not shoved them in haphazardly. But it was clear he wasn't making a mistake. The tank was only a quarter empty, so he'd filled it right up.'

'You know that for certain?'

'No, can't be sure, but it hadn't run out of fuel—it was still running when Bounter found him. Even with three-quarters of a tank, he was going to do the deed.'

Dave agreed.

Jack sat there for a while and Dave let him be. Quietness was a good thing at times.

They rounded the bend into Barker and were passing the familiar sixty-kilometre speed-limit sign when Jack said slowly, 'I don't think he was wearing shoes. He was rugged up—jacket and jeans. No hat that I can remember, but I don't think he had shoes on.'

Chapter 26

'Hey, Jo, it's me,' Fiona stammered into her friend's answering machine. 'I was . . . Would you mind . . . Uh, could you come and stay with me tonight? I've had Dave Burrows, the detective, here today and I'm a bit edgy. Could do with some company. Give me a call when you can.'

Tapping in her passcode for her phone, she texted Kim.

Hey, haven't heard from you for ages. How are you?

Good Sweetie and you? I heard you were going to have a visit from my better half today. Hope it went okay?

Yep, fine. Bit unsettled tonight, but I'll be okay.

From Dave's visit?

Yeah. But I'm still trying to shear—bloody hard with all this rain around—so I'm keeping busy.

Gotta go, love, Dave's just walked in. Best feed the man!

Have a good night.

Fiona put down the phone with a sigh and stared at the weather website she had brought up earlier.

The shearers had finished the sheep she had in the shed by afternoon smoko. The ones that had been left outside were wet. The rain had started in earnest at lunchtime, so Fiona had had no choice but to open the gate and let them back into the paddock.

It was just before dark when she'd driven around them and pushed the shorn ewes into the bush. They had been out grazing and she could see they were tucked up, a sure sign they were cold.

Thankfully, when she'd been shutting the gate and turned back to check on them, there hadn't been any sheep visible, so she was sure they were still in the bush.

Carly had left to go home just before the shearers had packed up. She'd stayed with Fiona for a night and they'd spent the evening together in the sitting room with the bar heater on. Carly had brought up the baby again and the need for Fiona to take it easy. Fiona had shut her down as quickly as she could, saying she knew she had to, but this was shearing time and that meant work, which in turn meant money.

She had promised, though, to take things as gently as she could.

Tonight she'd decided she needed some cheer, so she'd lit the fire, all the while thanking Rob for his thoughtfulness, and was now sitting on the floor in front of it, watching mind-numbing reality TV.

The wind was roaring outside and occasionally the heavens would throw down heavy rain. Fiona drew her knees up to her chin and focused on the cooking show, trying not to listen to the weather. Her thoughts kept going out to the ewes, hoping they'd be okay. Should she check them? But there was nothing she could really do now.

Another strong gust of wind rattled the windows. She got up and went to look outside. 'Silly,' she said to herself. 'It's not like you can see anything.' The raindrops on the window were like little translucent pebbles beading on the glass. Her reflection stared back at her and Fiona got a shock.

It had been some time since she had looked at herself in a mirror. Her face was drawn and thin—she must have lost weight, but she wouldn't have noticed because her pregnancy would have hidden it. Her hair was in desperate need of a cut and her eyes were puffy. Looking down at her hands, she saw the dirt and mud underneath her fingernails and self-consciously picked at them. She never would have let herself go like this were Charlie still alive. She'd enjoyed dressing to please him, dressing to turn him on.

Running her hands over her stomach, she decided to have a shower. Maybe she would shave her legs. God knows when she'd done that last. She wasn't sure if she'd be able to reach all the way to her ankles, but she'd give it a go!

Checking the time before she went to shower, she decided it was too late for her to hear back from Jo. She hoped she was just hanging out at the pub or something else very tame, not meeting anyone from a dating website.

Fiona had long come to the conclusion she couldn't stop her friend from doing what she wanted; she just hoped she'd be safe.

Finally, with Meita at her feet and the passageway light left on, she crept into bed and snuggled down in the warmth of the electric blanket.

Outside the rain continued to fall. Briefly, Fiona wondered if the creeks would be running tomorrow and if there would be any fallen branches that might block the roads.

Then she fell into a deep, dreamless sleep.

ᔕ

Dressed in rubber boots, tracky pants, heavy jacket and scarf, Fiona left the house while it was still dark. Meita was at her feet and jumped into the cab of the ute just as she opened the door. She curled up on the floor of the passenger side before Fiona could tell her off.

'Don't want to get on the back today?' Fiona said in a croaky morning voice. She set her travel mug, full of steaming coffee, on the dash and gripped the hand bar, pulling herself up into the seat. 'Don't blame you. I tipped twenty-nine mills out of the rain gauge first thing. And that wind, it's from Antarctica.'

Preheating the engine, she finally turned on the ute, switching on the heater and lights. She'd been itching to check the ewes.

If it hadn't been raining, she was sure there would have been ice on the iron gates this morning. They were as cold as an ice cube.

It was still so dark that Fiona had to swing the ute around from side to side to try to pick up where the sheep were. The thin pinpricks of lights didn't make it that easy to see them. Not for the first time, she wished she'd convinced Charlie to put spotlights on, not just go with the standard lights that had come with the ute.

'Ah, there's a few,' Fiona finally muttered, taking a sip from her cup. She put it back in the cup holder and rubbed one hand along her leg, trying to warm her fingers.

The green eyes of the ewes and lambs stared back at her and the lambs jumped to their feet, ready to run from the strange noisy creature heading their way. Fiona dipped her lights and stopped a little way from the mob. These were the woolly ewes.

Where were the shornies?

Picking out the two-wheel track that would take her to the other side of the bush, she drove slowly along, still sweeping the paddock with her lights.

Finally they picked up the glow of eyes in front of her.

Fiona's heart stopped. Changing gears, she headed over to the white body and got out. The ewe was dead.

A lamb was snuggled up alongside it, trying to keep out of the wind. It looked up in fright as Fiona loomed over it. It let out a loud bleat, jumped up and sprang out of reach. Disoriented, the lamb ran in circles, bleating loudly, before running off, swallowed by the dark.

'Shit.'

Fiona stumbled back to the ute and shoved it into first, taking off before she'd shut the door properly.

There was another, and another. Dozens of dead ewes were scattered around the paddock.

ഗ

At last count, Fiona had buried forty ewes. She'd rung Leigh and asked him to come and help her. She knew she couldn't drag the ewes into the pit she'd dug with the front-end loader.

He'd come as quickly as he could, bringing one of his workmen with him.

They'd worked silently, side by side, until the task was done. Fiona had thanked him and gone into the house and shut the door without another word.

Sinking down into the office chair, she tried to work out what had gone wrong. There were no dead lambs, just ewes. Normally, ewes that had died of exposure were found up against a fence, dying as they tried to find shelter. These ewes were scattered. Some were together, others had died, only their babies with them.

Fiona realised she was covered in mud. It was caked on her hands and pants, and she couldn't bend her fingers.

A tear slipped down her cheek. A rush of emotion overtook her. She rested her head on her arms on the desk and wept. Then there were arms embracing her, but Fiona didn't move.

Her tears were for her ewes, her Charlie, her life, her new baby. She began to release all the emotion of the last five and a half months.

'Shh, shh.' Hands ran over her hair.

Finally, when she slowed down, she looked up at Jo.

'Leigh told me what happened,' she whispered, pushing Fiona's hair back from her face. 'It'll be okay. It will.'

'My fault,' Fiona hiccupped. 'I should have cancelled the shearing. I knew the weather was coming.'

Jo didn't answer, she just pulled her closer and kept hugging her.

ග

Fiona woke from a deep sleep. Both the events of the morning and the crying had exhausted her. She lay in bed, listening to the sounds of Jo down the hall. The radio was on and music filtered through. She could hear the washing machine going and smell bread baking.

The wind was still blowing from the sound of creaking rafters and rattling windows, but she couldn't hear any rain.

Lying in the warmth of her bed, she didn't want to get up. Maybe she could lie here for the next three and a half months until the baby was born. Then she wouldn't have to deal with people wanting money, or a company wanting to buy her farm, or a dead husband . . . Or dead ewes. Hot tears slipped from the corners of her eyes and onto the pillow.

Down the hall, Jo's mobile phone rang.

'Hi,' she answered in a clipped tone.

Fiona raised her head, listening. That wasn't Jo's normal tone. She sounded annoyed.

'Yeah, she's asleep. Been there for a couple of hours.'

Silence.

'I'm doing some washing and a bit of cleaning. Don't think she's had the energy to do too much for a while.'

The floorboards creaked as Jo's voice moved closer to Fiona's bedroom. Instinct told her to roll over and pretend to be still asleep.

'Hmm. Yeah. Okay.'

The door squeaked open and Fiona assumed Jo was checking on her.

'Really?' she sounded surprised. 'Mining? Well, that makes a lot of sense.'

More silence.

'I'm not sure. She needs me here.' Her steps were quiet as she backed away and closed the door.

'No, I'm not going to convince her of that. You know that as well as I do. She won't. I'm going now. Bye.'

Fiona wondered who she was talking to. It hadn't sounded like a happy conversation and it had involved her.

Lying there a bit longer, her eyes closed of their own accord and she slept again.

ᔕ

'You *are* a sleepy head!' Jo said, coming into the bedroom with a cup of tea.

Fiona rolled over, bleary-eyed at the noise. 'Hmm,' she said, before licking her lips and rubbing her hands over her face to try to wake herself up. 'Didn't know I was so tired.'

'Really? You must have been the only person who didn't.' Jo smiled at her. 'Here, have a sip.' She pointed to the cup she'd put down on the bedside table.

Pulling herself up onto a pile of pillows, Fiona reached for the cup and took a mouthful. 'That's yummy,' she said. 'Thank you.'

'Dave Burrows called while you were asleep.'

Fiona was suddenly awake. 'What did he want?'

'To ask you a couple more questions. Something about the drone that you've been seeing.'

'Not much I can tell him there. I just see it.'

'Yeah, well, give him a call when you're feeling up to it. I told him what happened today, so he's not expecting to hear from you until tomorrow.'

'Thanks.'

'Carly rang, too.'

Fiona groaned.

'Man, are you in for it!' Jo grinned broadly. 'I had to hold the phone away from my ear, she was talking so loudly. Something about overdoing it?'

'Brilliant. Just what I need.'

'Oh, Fee.' Jo sobered. 'You know she means well. She loves you, just like we all do.'

'I know, I know.' Fiona sighed and took another sip of her tea. 'I'm lucky to have her. And you.' She reached over and grasped Jo's hand, holding it firmly. 'Thank you for coming today.'

'I wouldn't have been anywhere else.' Jo got up from the bed and walked over to the window, crossing her arms as she looked out. 'The chemical company has called and said there was nothing wrong with the batch of chemical. But I don't suppose we thought there was really, did we?'

'I was still hoping,' Fiona replied.

'Yeah.'

Fiona threw off the covers and swung her legs over the edge of the bed. 'I feel like pancakes for tea,' she said.

'That's a great idea! I haven't eaten pancakes for years!'

'My birthday falls on Mother's Day some years,' Fiona said, pulling on her dressing gown. 'When I was home from boarding school on weekends, I'd sometimes bring friends home. Anyway, this one weekend I had four girls with me, I think, and it was Mother's Day and my birthday. We got up and cooked Mum a Canadian breakfast, then we went back to bed, and she got up and cooked us brekkie in bed. It was a really fun day.'

'What's a Canadian breakfast?' Jo asked, picking up the empty cup and walking towards the kitchen.

'Pancakes, bacon, banana, walnuts and maple syrup. Exactly what I feel like now. What do you say?'

'I say you've got pregnancy cravings. That sounds so revolting it could almost be yummy.'

'Oh, don't you worry about that! It is.'

Chapter 27

He picked up the phone and barked hello.

'I'm not seeing any results yet,' said a voice at the other end.

'Look, mate, I'm trying,' he replied sharply. 'I know you want as much as you can get. I do, too.' He glanced through his office door and realised the secretary was looking at him in a strange way. Wanting to get up and shut the door but unable to make the phone cord extend that far, he lowered his voice. 'I heard from a source the other day that there's a journo sniffing around.'

'How did that happen?'

'I've got no idea.'

'You need to make it happen. We're running out of time.'

'Leave it with me.' He slammed down the receiver and blew out a breath. He had plans, but he was going to need to put them in place earlier than he'd originally thought.

Getting up from his chair, he stomped over to the window. The weather was clearing.

'I'm going for a walk,' he told his secretary, needing to get out of the office. 'Probably won't be back today.'

'I'll take messages for you then.'

He nodded and yanked open the door, heading out into the street. Pacing quickly, he made a beeline for the park, hoping the space would calm him down. There was too much pressure from all different sections of his life at the moment. He was scared he wouldn't be able to hold it together for much longer.

Taking off his shoes, he felt the cold grass under his feet. That calmed him slightly, but not enough. He needed a release. That meant another girl.

His breathing quickened.

His need for a woman was so strong. Curling his hands into fists, he banged them into his thighs as he walked. He wanted to hold onto someone. To feel soft, yielding skin under the pressure of his strong fingers. To hear her yelps and, occasionally, her whimpering pleas to be released. The appeals usually came when he put the blindfold over their eyes and tightened the straps around their wrists. If they were awake, which was rare.

The TV news the previous evening had shocked him. The fact that the police had connected four of his victims through their investigation had also upped his anxiety. He'd never been cocky enough to think they wouldn't link the women together, but he hadn't expected it to be so soon. The good thing was that only some of the women had gone to the police. And if they hadn't done it in the first place, he hoped they wouldn't come forward now.

He knew how far advanced his method of snatching the women was. There had been some perfecting needed, and finding the right drug had taken time, too. He'd experimented with other drugs, but ecstasy was ideal because of the way it made the women act—like they wanted him. No one would believe a woman who cried rape if security footage showed her hanging off a man. That was what ecstasy made them do.

Here he was, sixteen women under his belt, so to speak. He was almost a professional at it.

Still, he couldn't help the niggling fear and doubt gnawing away at his insides. The only thing that would make them go away was another woman. They were his weakness.

'Fuck,' the word came out as a long, drawn-out growl.

Choosing a sheltered section of the park, where he hoped no one would see him, he sat under a tree, with his legs crossed and his shoes neatly by his side. Breathing deeply, he allowed his mind to slow, his breathing becoming deep and steady again, then he shut his eyes.

Listening to the noise around him, he tried to think of every problem he was facing. Then he lined them up in order of importance.

There was a technique his counsellor had taught him many years ago, and that seemed to help when he became as agitated as he was now. He imagined all of the angst inside him being packaged into a box. One by one, he placed each concern into it. He filled it corner by corner, stacking the difficulties inside. In his mind, he watched himself closing the lid. He conjured up a roll of masking tape and slowly sealed the flaps in place. He did this twice, even hearing the noise as he pulled the tape from the roll. Nothing could escape if it was sealed tightly.

In the darkness of his mind, he placed the box in a fire and struck a match.

Breathing slowly and rhythmically, he watched as the first thin orange flames started to lick around each side. As they caught hold, the flames became hotter, turned blue and went higher. Smoke began to billow out and was released into the sky.

As the wind came and dispersed the smoke, it would take away all the pressure with it. Banish it.

Or at least that was the idea.

Chapter 28

Dead sheep littered the paddock. The orphaned lambs were standing next to their mothers, baaing frantically. Some tried to nuzzle their mothers into getting up, without success.

Fiona stared desolately around.

Again, they were shorn sheep, but this time, there hadn't been a cold front to kill them.

They'd left the yards after being back-lined and drenched, raced out into the paddock, healthy, eaten grass and drunk water. What had killed them?

'Poison,' Rob, answered her unasked question.

'Poison? It's never happened before. There's nothing poisonous in the paddock!'

'Look at that one there,' he pointed to a lone ewe staring blindly into space. As he spoke, the ewe lost control of her bowels and a pile of dark, watery diarrhoea shot out from her.

Fiona took a breath, distraught at what she was seeing. The ewe took a few wobbly steps before stopping again and letting out a small distressed noise. Her chest was heaving with her laboured breathing and her stomach looked bloated.

'She's blind,' Rob observed. 'And the only one left alive—the rest seem fine. You'll need to watch them for more symptoms, of course, but I think the ones that were going to die already have.' He got a knife out of his van and sharpened it with a steel. 'I want to do an autopsy on this one. Take some bloods, all that sort of thing.'

He took a few steps, and grabbed the ewe around the neck and inserted a thermometer into her anus.

Her twin lambs stood a few feet away, watching nervously.

'Temp's raised, too.' He lifted her up and swung her into a crate on the back of his van. 'I'll take her back to the surgery and do the autopsy there. What are you going to do with the lambs?'

'I don't know,' Fiona whispered, ashen-faced. 'I'll work something out though.'

'If you put a call out over Facebook, on the Buy, Trade and Sell site, you might be able to get a few people who'd like to raise orphans to take them. There's too many here to raise by yourself. They're just a little bit young for them to be without milk. Give them three weeks and they'll probably be okay to go out onto pasture.'

She nodded.

'I'll be back in touch, Fee.' Rob put his hand on her shoulder and left.

ᔕ

Fiona began mustering the mob, taking them steadily across the paddock. She carefully ensured she had the whole mob together, with the ewes who were still alive leading the way, otherwise she wouldn't be able to muster the orphaned lambs. Lambs were tricky things to get in the yards at the best of times, but without their mothers to guide them, they'd be near impossible to move. It took her over an hour, and every ounce of concentration and energy she possessed, but she finally managed to get them into the compound.

She opened a gate into the yards and hoped that the orphans would go into it, looking for their mothers—she couldn't draft them. She had no way of knowing which lambs were orphaned as they came down the race. Fiona could only tell when they were out in the paddocks, running around in search of their mothers.

Feeling as if her heart might break for the second time, she took her phone out to ring Dave. But as she dialled the number among the bleating and distressed lambs, she guessed Rob might have beaten her to it.

ও

'I think we're looking at a murder enquiry,' Dave said to Jack.

'What makes you say that?' Jack pulled up a chair and sat down, reading the notes on the whiteboard Dave had made earlier.

'Okay, look at these photos.' Dave pushed a bundle across to him and pointed to the one on top. 'Thank God someone thought to photograph the body in situ and get close-ups of him. Who did that?'

Jack looked embarrassed. 'Me.'

'You've done a bloody good job. Okay, see here?' He pointed to Charlie's hands. 'There are a few of what I would call defence wounds here. Tiny bit of bruising across the top of the knuckles, and there are some cuts on the top knuckle on the right hand. The coroner should have picked this up when he did the autopsy.'

'Why didn't he?'

'I really don't know.'

'Is there anything else?'

'The bare feet bother me. I can't see any dirt on them. Why wouldn't he have dirty feet if he'd been in the shed?'

'Good point. It's not cemented. I noticed it was a dirt floor and quite powdery when I was in there looking at the chemical drums,' Jack answered. He looked over at the board again. 'That drone is bothering me.'

'Me, too. I think . . .' Dave stopped as the phone rang. He picked it up. 'Burrows.' His jaw set as he listened. 'Okay, hang on. Can you slow down for me? When did you find them?'

Reaching over his desk to where he kept a pile of notepads, he took the top one and started writing.

Fiona Forrest—he underlined her name. *Sheep dead. Shearing, this morning.* He dated it. *Second time. First one due to cold front???*

'Okay, we'll be there as soon as we can. You said the vet has been in? Yep, yep. Sure. Hang in there.'

He hung up the phone and finished writing before he looked at Jack.

'I also think we have someone trying to scare this woman off her land. She's got another heap of dead sheep and the vet is sure they've been poisoned.' He got up and wrote a few more notes regarding the sheep on the whiteboard and stood back, examining it.

'Suppose,' he said slowly, 'that someone really wants her land. Suppose that someone knocked off her husband, thinking that she'd sell, and suppose they've underestimated Fiona, because she won't. Which, in turn, has put them in a bad spot, so they feel they have to frighten her off.'

'That's a lot of supposes that we have to prove,' Jack said, getting up. 'I'll get the car.'

ᔕ

Fiona was grateful to Carly for holding her hand in the cold kitchen. They'd only just finished burying the second lot of dead ewes. Again, Leigh had brought a workman with him and the job had been finished quickly, but Fiona kept seeing the bodies of the freshly shorn ewes dumped in their grave. Their staring eyes, unseeing.

She had to breathe deeply so she wouldn't cry.

'We'll let Rob do his job before we make a start on the ewe side of things, I think, Fee,' Dave said. 'I've taken the SD card out of the camera we put in place on our first visit and Jack will review that when we get back to the station.'

Fiona thought he sounded as grave as he looked.

'I'd like to talk about Charlie for a bit. Can you do that?'

She nodded.

'First off, how are the finances? We couldn't help but overhear the other day that you had a phone call from a creditor.' Dave sat with his pen poised, looking at her with sympathy and concern.

'It's tight at the moment. The bank had to freeze the business account and I'm fairly short on money. I'm juggling things as best I can, but I'm having trouble paying some of the bills, for sure.'

'Why didn't you tell me?' The words burst from Carly. 'I can help you.'

'No, it's not your problem, Mum.' Fiona lifted her head proudly. 'It will get sorted.'

Carly put a trembling hand to her mouth, looking tearfully at her daughter.

'Was it like this when Charlie was alive?' Dave brought her attention back to him.

'Not as bad as this. There are always challenges with farming, and cash flow can be one, but no, it wasn't as hard as it is now.' She swallowed, remembering how Charlie had told her never to worry about the money side of things. 'I've got it all under control,' he'd told her with a kiss.

'Did you two have a long-standing debt to anyone in particular? Or did Charlie by himself owe anyone?'

Fiona thought about it but quickly shook her head. 'I knew everything about the bank accounts, even if I didn't have to handle it. We talked about every purchase and bill. There weren't any secrets between us, so I would've known if he owed money to someone.'

'Okay.' Dave tapped his pen, thinking. 'Can you remember *before* the accident when Eddie was killed? Was Charlie stressed or upset in any way? Did he act differently?'

Fiona got up and started to pace the kitchen. 'No,' she responded slowly. 'I can't think of anything that was out of the ordinary with his behaviour. He was just Charlie.'

'I'm getting the impression he was a really affable type of bloke, that everyone liked him.' It was a statement.

Fiona stopped, remembering him. 'Everyone liked Charlie,' she said in a soft voice. 'I don't think I've ever heard anyone say a bad word about him. He didn't have any enemies.'

She watched Dave write *No enemies*.

'Okay, we're going to do a bit of looking around and then head off. We'll be back in touch as soon as we can.'

'I'm not an idiot, Dave, I know there's something more going on here. You keep asking about Charlie, not what's happened here since he died.' Fiona looked straight at him, wanting to know what was going on.

'I'm gathering information to get a full picture,' Dave answered in what was obviously a practised tone. That was all she was going to get out of him, so she had no choice but to let him go.

ᔓ

Dave and Jack drove out of Charona and onto the public road. About three hundred metres later, they turned into the neighbouring drive.

They knocked on the door of the homestead and introduced themselves.

'I'm Dave Burrows and this is Jack Higgins. We're from the South Australian police force.' He held up his badge for identification.

'How can I help? I'm Damien MacKenzie.'

'We just want to ask a few questions about a drone that's been sighted from your neighbour's property, Charona. Can we come in?' Jack asked.

Dave cringed. That wasn't the way to get the young farmer to open up to them. 'Nice place you've got here, up on the hill. Great views! You're in the perfect area to spot it!' Dave added quickly, hoping to get him on side.

'Drone? Is that what it is? Little silver thing flying around? Yeah, I've seen it. I've read about them. Always wanted to experiment and have a go at using one—you can take good photos with them.'

'Ah, don't own one then?'

'Nah, wish I did. I reckon it'd be too expensive for me.' He came outside and looked up at the sky. 'Not around today?'

'Haven't seen it yet. Can you tell us when you've seen it?'

'Do you want to come in?' Damien indicated for them to enter.

'Thanks very much,' Dave said. 'I've got a couple of phone calls to make, but Jack will get the information and then we can get out of your hair.'

'Sure.' Damien held the door open and Jack went inside.

Heading back to the car, Dave looked around him. He estimated the boundary fence to be three hundred metres from the house and he could just see the roof of Fiona's home, which was nestled in a gully.

Turning slowly in a circle, he tried to work out what was so important about Charona compared to this place next door.

He jotted down some more notes and looked over his shoulder to see if the door was still shut. It was. Quickly heading over to the shed, he had a swift look inside. He ran his eye over the chemical drums that were in there—nothing looked out of place. He opened a cupboard—it was full of electric fencing gear, staples and sundry items. No sign of a drone.

Hearing voices, he turned and casually walked back towards the car.

'Thanks very much for your help,' Jack was saying.

'Oh, before you go, Damien, I have a quick question,' Dave said. 'Has anyone approached you about selling your farm?'

'Nope,' he said. 'Sometimes I wish they would!'

'Finding it a bit hard?'

'Always hard to make ends meet when you've got a big debt and you've gotta share the income with your gran—she takes a bit of looking after. You would have seen all the rails and independent living stuff in there,' he said, turning to Jack. 'But I love farming and everything to do with it. Wouldn't want to do anything else.'

'Gets under your skin, doesn't it? Is there any difference in the soil type between here and Charona—are they both as good as one another in a farming sense?'

'I'm biased, but if you ask me, my land is a bit better. See, Charona backs onto a national park—see all them trees over there?' He pointed to where a block of trees ran from the boundary fence into the distance. 'If you get a fire come through, it'll go straight through Charona. Won't be able to stop it. Then you've got all the pests that come through—foxes, rabbits and the like. But as for soil type—mine is better.

'There're a lot more stones down on Charona. I've seen Charlie and Fee out picking stones in the middle of summer so they can clean up a paddock for cropping. Don't want any of those dirty big buggers going up into the header!'

'No way,' Dave agreed. 'So given half the chance, would you buy Charona if it was up for sale, even though it's not as good as your land?'

'I couldn't afford it, but I'd love to expand. But if I had my choice of land, I'd buy something back towards that way.' He pointed in the opposite direction. 'They get slightly more rainfall down there and the soil is a little softer.' He shoved his hands in his pockets and grinned. 'But there's always something to be said for buying the neighbour's farm and having all your land together.'

'You must've had an awful shock when you heard about the shooting accident.'

'Sure did. Eddie was an okay sort of fella. Never thought anything like that would've happened. They were all experienced shooters, especially Eddie. And then for Charlie to do what he did, well, bugger me. It's just really stuffed.

'Fee's a top chick. I did some spraying for her the other day, but we had a bit of a problem with the chemical. I'll have to go back over it for her. Charlie? He was a helluva nice bloke. Really kind to me. Offered lots of advice when I first took this place on. Always had time for me. I never really understood why he did what he did. It was such a waste.'

'Would you have seen Charlie and the gang out shooting the night Eddie was killed?' Dave suddenly asked. 'I'm beginning to get my bearings and I'm sure that's the paddock over there.' He pointed to a hill in the distance. If he had binoculars, he was sure he'd be able to see the crime-scene tape fluttering in the wind.

'I could've; yeah, you're right. But I wasn't here that night. I was in Adelaide. I never heard anything about what had happened until I was driving home the next day and the news was on the radio.'

'Thanks for your time,' Jack said when it was clear Dave didn't have any more questions. 'And for the cuppa.'

Back in the car, Jack passed on what he'd learned from Damien. 'As he said, he's never operated a drone, but he's a keen photographer. This one has been flying around for the past couple of months, but he's got no idea who owns or operates it.

'But what he *has* seen, is a car that's been parked all around the boundary of Charona while the drone's been operating.'

Chapter 29

'You're not staying here by yourself.' Carly stood with her hands on her hips, staring Fiona down.

'Where would I go, Mum? Laura is a ninety-minute round trip from here! I'd be too tired by the end of the day to drive that road. It's so windy, too. Anyway I don't want to stay over there with you.'

'Scott's got a granny flat at the back of his house in Booleroo. I'm sure he'll let you stay there. Are you really even considering staying here with what's been going on?'

'Yeah, I am,' Fiona said mildly. 'I'm scared, there's no two ways about that, but I think I need to be here to protect the animals.'

'You can't do that. It's a man's job, not a pregnant woman's. What if they've got guns, or, or . . .' Carly shuddered visibly.

'Let me stay here tonight,' Fiona said firmly. 'I need to do a couple of things in the office. I'll have Meita with me and I'll keep all the lights on.'

Carly huffed an angry breath. 'I don't like it.'

'Neither do I,' she admitted. 'But this is my home. Let me get things organised.'

'What if I stay with you?'

'Actually I have a problem with you both staying.'

The women rounded at the voice. Carly's face split into a smile when she saw Scott.

'How did you get away from the surgery so early?' she asked, going over to kiss him.

'There was nothing life-threatening and I thought this was more important. How are you, Fiona?'

'Fairly rattled. Emotional.'

'To be expected.' He glanced around and Fiona was aware that her home had begun to look very shabby. The kitchen floor hadn't been swept since Jo had done it a few nights ago and there were dirty dishes on the sink. The walls needed a paint—or at least some new wallpaper. The current design was more suited to the seventies than the two thousands.

'Sorry about the mess,' she muttered.

'Look, why don't you both come back to my place? The granny flat is free . . .' he began, but Fiona interrupted him.

'Not tonight. If something weird happens I'll come in, but I have a few things I need to do.'

'You won't change her mind, Scott.' Carly sighed, leaning her head against his shoulder. 'God only knows I've tried.'

Scott's lips became a thin line.

'I'll keep my mobile phone with me all the time and you can ring whenever you want to. If I don't answer, then I give you permission to storm the house,' Fiona tried to joke, even though she didn't feel like it. In fact, she was scared witless.

Finally, as the sun slipped below the hills and the chill in the air required a jumper and beanie, Carly and Scott followed each other out of the driveway and headed back to Booleroo.

Fiona stood on the verandah and watched them go, feeling numb. The sadness and fear had left her for the moment, and she knew she had to make the most of that time, while she could still think clearly.

Whistling to Meita, she made sure she had her phone and did a quick walk down to the shed, then on to the front gate. She closed it and used a padlock she'd taken out of the top drawer in the office to chain and lock it shut.

Wandering back along the creek with Meita running ahead, she stopped and listened to the water running. All too quickly, she moved on. There was something about being pregnant and needing a toilet fairly often. But the walk had done what she'd needed it to do. Clear her head, put a bit of colour in her cheeks and sharpen her mind.

That night Fiona kept all the lights on but the TV and radio off so she could hear if anyone pulled up. Not that she was expecting anyone now.

One by one, she took the notebooks that Charlie used to write in from the shelves and started to read.

There had been a whisper of a memory when Dave had been questioning her earlier, but she couldn't quite grasp it. She was hoping there was a notation that would make her remember. One of the notebooks fell open at the middle page.

Wild dog has attacked four of our sheep. Fiona's breath caught as she ran her fingers over the familiar writing. The yearning for Charlie intensified.

'Okay, Charlie,' she whispered. 'You've got to help me here. What am I looking for? You know what I think? Someone is trying to get me off our property. I'm not sure why. Do you know?'

Turning to the first notebook he'd started, the year they'd got married, she made her way through countless entries of lamb-marking results, crop yields, animal husbandry and rainfall records.

She smiled when she read some of the notes. *You should have seen Fee today. Drafting lambs like a pro. Never done it before. So proud of her.*

I seeded one hundred hectares of wheat today in paddock five, and she sat beside me the whole day, asking questions. She even drove it for a couple of runs.

Some others stood out.

Wish it would rain. Worried about the way the season has turned.

Looking at the date, Fiona realised it was just before their first wedding anniversary. Thinking back, she knew she hadn't picked up on the fact that he was worried. He'd smiled and laughed and kidded along with her, when in fact he wasn't as carefree as he'd wanted her to believe.

Prices for wool have fallen. Got no idea how I'm going to make the payment on the boom spray.

Her stomach dropped. This wasn't what she'd expected. They'd talked about everything . . . Hadn't they? That was what Charlie had always said: *No secrets.*

The next page was worse.

I had a letter from Dad's lawyer today. Seems they're happy to drop the court case just so long as I pay them $200k.

Not sure where I'll get that money from. Looks like another visit to the bank.

Sucking in a breath, she stared at the notation. What court case? It must have something to do with his grandfather giving him the farm. Did Charlie's dad sue him? Quickly she scrambled through the other pages, scanning every one. Halfway in she stopped.

Part of me is so glad Grandad gave me this farm. When I see the changes Fiona and I have made and the successes we've had, I know it was the right thing for him to do. Dad couldn't have grown the business the way I have. But when I see how angry and bitter Dad is, I wonder . . . he wasn't a farmer's boot, I know, and for Grandad honesty was paramount. He told me once that the only thing a man ever had was his word.

I know why Grandad handed it over to me without any discussion. I overheard an argument between them both, one night. Grandad was accusing Dad of stealing. Said he couldn't trust him anymore and he wanted him to leave. I never knew what he stole, but it sounded like it—whatever 'it' was—had been going on for a long time. It can't have been money because Grandad would've seen that through the bank account. I'm sure it must've been stock or wool, but I remember Grandad saying 'with the amount you stole, it was sheer luck you didn't send the farm under'. I can't imagine anyone stealing from family.

Crap, so that was it. Charlie's dad had stolen from his own dad. How horrific.

But how could Charlie not tell her?

Remember? No secrets.

Meita barked suddenly and butterflies shot through her stomach. She sat still for a moment, wondering what to do.

Then she went to look through the window to see if there were any lights coming up the driveway. It was dark, save for the soft white glow thrown by the moon.

'What's up, girl?' she asked as the dog sat next to her.

Her phone rang and Fiona jumped.

'Bloody hell, my heart isn't going to be able to take this for much longer,' she muttered. Looking at the screen, she quickly answered.

'Kim! How are you?'

'Fine, sweetie, fine. And you?'

'Had my ups and downs.'

'I plan on putting a stop to that,' Kim said, her happiness radiating down the line.

'How do you plan to do that?'

'I've got to drop off a food order for a dad and his kids tomorrow morning and it's on my way to you, so I thought I'd call in. What do you say?'

Fiona breathed in deeply through her nose and shut her eyes. 'I say I think that's the best idea I've heard all day.'

'Great! See you ten-ish.'

'See you then.' Fiona put the phone on the desk but picked it straight back up again.

She sent a text to Carly: *All quiet on Charona.* It dinged a couple of moments later.

Expecting it to be her mother, she didn't pick it up straightaway, but went back to reading the diaries. She was still reeling from Charlie's revelations, but she didn't have time to think about them at the moment. She was looking for something—she wasn't sure what it was, but she would know it when she saw it. She hoped.

Lent Damien the trailer for two weeks.

Myles Martin borrowed the generator.

There was that memory again. It kept flickering but she couldn't reach out and grab it. She was sure she'd heard him talking about lending a scope or bullets, or something similar, to someone. But only in passing. Maybe she'd heard a phone call or he'd mentioned it over tea. She was sure she didn't know who it was.

She riffled through the filing cabinet, looking for Charlie's gun licence. It would have all the guns listed on it. Apprehension seeped through her as she took the piece of paper to the spare room, tapped the code into the keypad and opened the door of the gun cabinet.

Inspecting each gun, she found the serial number and checked it off against the items on the permit. The police had taken into evidence the guns that had been used that night.

Fiona sucked in a breath. According to this, there was a .22 missing. She counted the guns on the licence, then what was inside the cabinet.

She wasn't mistaken. One of the .22s wasn't there.

Who had he lent it to? And why?

Narrowing her eyes, she thought hard before going back to the diaries.

Later that evening, after failing to find anything significant in the first book, her eyes began to droop and Hamish was restless. Calling Meita, she decided to go for a drive.

The air was so cold that her breath created white puffs of small clouds. The ute took a couple of goes to get started, but she put the heaters on full blast, shifted it into gear and drove towards the back of the farm.

Stopping on the edge of the creek, she got out to open a gate, taking in deep lungfuls of air. She let her head tip back and looked at the stars. Above her the leaves shifted and a mopoke called.

The empty feeling was still there—she supposed that wasn't going to leave her soon, but it was also being replaced by anger.

Her sheep had been poisoned. Rob had said that. His exact words were, 'poison of some sort'. She knew there were no poisonous bushes or shrubs of any kind on Charona, so did that mean someone had put something on her farm that had killed her sheep?

That was precisely what it meant.

What sort of person would do that?

And why were they targeting her? Had Charlie done something she didn't know about, like taking out a personal loan to pay his parents $200k compensation?

Looking back, she suddenly wondered if the sheep going over the fence into the neighbour's property was an accident.

Her phone beeped. She dug it out of her pocket, blinking at the bright light of the screen against inky black. Two messages. Carly and Leigh.

Glad to hear all is quiet. Let me know how you are in a few hours. That was Carly answering her previous message.

She tapped on Leigh's message to open it. *How are you going?*

Fiona tapped the phone against her hand, pondering how to reply. She wasn't sure she could put every emotion she was feeling into words.

Okay, she tapped out.

Are you home?

No.

Let me know if you need anything. I'm sorry this has happened to you.

There was nothing to say to that, so she put the phone away. She was sorry it had happened, too.

Getting back into the car, she blew on her hands and rubbed her nose—it felt icy!

She decided to drive along the boundary, just to see if there was anything sinister going on. Half an hour later all she'd seen were three rabbits, a fox and her woolly ewes.

There hadn't even been any cars on the main road. The countryside was silent and still, and there was no sign of the predators who seemed to be stalking her.

Chapter 30

'I'm sorry, Fiona,' Rob said on the phone the following morning, his gravelly voice reverberating around her head.

That was all she needed to hear. She knew.

Reaching out to hold on to a chair, Fiona took in a wobbly breath. She knew her hands were shaking and she cursed silently. She had known what the outcome would be, so why was she acting like this?

'Because it makes it real,' her brain screamed at her. 'If he says it, it's real.' Out loud, she asked, 'What did you find?'

'They've got selenium poisoning. Somehow they've been overdosed on the trace element.'

The silence screamed down the phone.

'I'll be reporting this to the police, and I want to come and have a look around. I'm guessing it's been mixed in with their water.'

'Right.' Fiona was at a loss for words.

'I'll be out in the next hour or so—will you be at home?'

'There's nowhere else to be at the moment.'

ᘓ

When Kim arrived at Charona, all she heard from inside the house was sobbing.

Running inside, she found Fiona in the office, curled up in a ball, and Meita standing over her, whining.

'God, Fee, what's wrong?' She fell to her knees and put her arms around the younger woman. 'What's happened? Fee?' Kim knew she sounded panicked, but she couldn't help it. The poor young woman was a mess.

Fiona tried to say something, but Kim couldn't understand her. She followed her arm signals and looked over at the mantelpiece.

'They've taken him,' she stuttered.

'Taken who?' Even as Kim said the words, understanding began to dawn on her. Oh God, she hoped she was wrong. 'Have they taken Charlie? His ashes?'

Fiona nodded as she dragged herself up from the floor and clung to Kim's arm.

'Dear God.' Dread and alarm coursed through her. She tried to find her phone. 'Come on, my love, you need to get up. We need to get you into town, to your doctor.' She didn't mention calling Dave to come and fingerprint the whole house.

Just as she was struggling to lift the sobbing woman, a voice called out.

'Hello? Hello, you there, Fee?'

'In the office. Can you give me a hand?' Kim called back,

relieved to hear heavy footsteps. She gently pushed Meita out of the way. 'Get out, dog!'

'Shit, what's happened?' A man dressed in blue overalls walked in and sank down beside them.

'We need to call an ambulance and the police,' Kim commanded. 'Now.'

The man ripped a mobile phone out of his top pocket. 'Ambulance required to Charona.' He recited the numbers that were displayed at the farm gate, which would help the ambos recognise where to go. 'Tell them it's Fiona Forrest's farm. Yes, I'll stay on the line.' He pulled the phone away from his ear. 'What's happened?'

'Some bastard has stolen Charlie's ashes.'

'What the . . .' He turned his attention back to the phone. 'We have a traumatised woman. We also need the police. Yes, yeah, there're two other people here, she's not on her own.' He blew out a breath in annoyance. 'Lady, I know you're in a call centre somewhere, but you tell the locals it's Fiona Forrest's farm and they'll know exactly where it is. Thank you.'

'Who would do this, Kim?' Fiona looked up at her imploringly.

'Sweetheart, whoever has done this deserves to be hung, drawn and quartered. Don't you worry, I'll make sure Dave gets on the case. Now, come on, up onto the couch.' She threw a quick glance at the man who was standing beside them, looking like he wasn't sure what to do. 'I'm Kim.'

'Rob. The vet.'

'Can you help me get her onto the couch?'

A few minutes later, Kim was on the couch next to Fiona, holding her hand with one of her own and stroking her hair with the other. Meita nestled into Fiona's side.

'Could you get me my mobile phone please, Rob?' she asked in a low voice. 'It's in my handbag, on the front seat of the car. And we need to find a blanket.' Turning back to Fiona she said, 'Sweetie, I'm going into the kitchen for a minute. To get you a glass of water, okay?'

Fiona clutched at her hand and stared at her as if she were a stranger. Kim gently extracted her hand and rushed to the kitchen, searching for a glass. When she returned to the office, she helped Fiona sit up then held the glass to her lips.

Rob appeared at her side, and handed her the phone.

'Sit with her,' Kim instructed, then went into the kitchen.

'Honey,' Dave greeted her phone call.

'Dave, you have to get here to Charona. Some arsehole has taken Charlie's ashes.' She explained what she'd found.

'And the vet is still there?' Dave asked in an urgent tone.

'Yes.'

'Put him on.'

Kim walked back to the living room and handed Rob the phone. 'My partner's Detective Dave Burrows,' she explained. 'He wants to speak to you.'

ꟹ

Rob walked out to the kitchen to take the call. 'Rob Cameron.'

'What happened to the sheep?' Dave asked. 'Poison?'

'Yes. Selenium poisoning.'

'How was it administered?'

'I can't tell you for sure. I only got here just after Kim and we've found Fiona in a bad way.'

'How could have they ingested it?'

'My guess is through water, but . . .'

'But what? What, man?' The urgency in Dave's voice conveyed the importance of the question.

'If it's through the water, I'm going to have trouble with the samples. The trough refills every time the water drops below a certain level.'

'Damn! Right, I'll be there as soon as I can. Check the troughs, if you can get away.'

'Sure.'

ᔕ

When Rob returned to the lounge room, he handed the phone back to Kim before heading down the passage in search of a blanket.

Kim talked constantly and soothingly to Fiona, stroking her hair. It was the only way she knew to make her feel safe.

'It's too hard, Kim. Too hard.'

'What is, sweetie?'

'To stay here. The farm. What's the point? Dead husband, dead sheep. Too many bad memories. Ian Tonkin can have the bloody thing. It's cursed, I'm sure. Or I am.'

'Now you listen to me. You are not cursed. Stop talking like that, right now. This isn't the time for it. Let's just get you to hospital and make sure that beautiful little bub of yours is okay and that you are, too. You've gotta think about that cherub. Charlie wouldn't want you to be thinking like that either.'

'Everyone else thinks I should sell. It would be much easier than facing disasters every day.' She hiccupped and tried to sit up, only to let out a moan and clutch at her stomach. 'It hurts,' she wailed. Meita jumped to her feet and whined loudly, trying to lick Fiona's face.

'Rob!' called Kim, pushing Meita from the couch. 'Rob! There's something wrong with the baby!'

Rob clattered noisily down the hall, but as soon as he came into the room, he acted calm and in control. 'Okay, where is it hurting?' He put his hand on Fiona's stomach. 'Hell,' he muttered. To Kim he said, 'Get on the phone and find out where the ambulance is.' He turned his face away from Fiona and whispered, 'I think she's going into premature labour.'

Kim's eyes widened and she scrambled to dial the emergency number. As soon as there was a response, she barked down the line at the operator.

'How far along are you, Fiona?' Rob asked in a soothing voice.

'Five and a bit months.'

'Okay, you need to listen to me and do exactly what I say. Shut your eyes and concentrate on the pressure of my hand. Breathe in and out. Slowly. That's right. This is going to help relax you, which is going to help the baby.'

'What's wrong with the baby?' Her eyes were wide with fear. 'I can't lose him! He's my piece of Charlie.'

'Shh, shh, that's not going to happen. Shut your eyes and listen to my voice.' He talked slowly to her until Kim suddenly looked up and ran to the window. She pointed outside.

They could finally hear the siren. Kim pointed at Meita and looked enquiringly at Rob.

'I'll take her with me,' he whispered.

ℴɔ

Dave hung up the phone and turned to Jack. 'There's an emergency at Charona. I need to go now. I want you to get on the phone and do some legwork.

'Find out about that company that's buying all the land. Do searches on everyone you can think of who could want to hurt Fiona. This is personal. They've taken Charlie's ashes.'

Jack looked taken aback for a moment. Then, seeming to give himself a mental shake, he said, 'On it.'

Dave hustled out to the car and put the mobile light on the roof. Hooking it up to the battery, he made sure it was spinning and flashing before he took off in a spray of gravel.

ᔓ

As he stared into the dirty water of the trough, Dave's brain raced through all the possibilities, but he kept coming back to the same conclusion: someone wanted Fiona's land so badly he was trying to scare her off it.

He needed to speak to Ian Tonkin.

Before that, he had to fingerprint the house, take photos, see if anything was out of place. That was going to be difficult to work out, because Fiona wasn't going to be in any fit state to answer questions for a little while.

Then he stopped.

Of course! There was the camera. He called Jack.

'Jack, have you had time to check the SD card we took out from Charona when we were here last?'

'Not yet, I've been following up the company.'

'Anything?'

'No. The reason I can't find the directors through a Google search is that there isn't any name attached to the company. The trading name is BJL Holdings, but there are no individual names.

'The search has revealed that they own fifty thousand acres in Victoria's grain-growing country and another twenty in New South Wales. The properties have managers on them.'

'Where's HQ?'

'Melbourne.'

'Website?'

'No. They fly under the radar. No top prices in farming magazines, no write-ups about good farming practices. You google them and there's basically no information on them at all.'

'That's strange for a business that size,' Dave observed. 'What about employees? Any names?'

'I've got Leah Kent listed as a CEO. I did an IMS search on her and didn't come across any connections between her and any of the people we have on our list.'

'Who do we have on our list?' Dave mused. Now that Fiona was in the safe hands of the ambo drivers, he could think a little more clearly. 'Ian Tonkin seems obvious, since he's the real estate agent. Charlie Forrest—have you done a search on him?'

'Yeah, but I haven't turned up more than you did.'

Dave scratched his jaw.

'You know, it's got to have something to do with this company. But who is the link? And how? Search everyone! Bounter, Tonkin, this Leah, whoever. Geoff. Hell, search Fiona! She might hold the link and doesn't realise it. Someone here holds the key.'

'Sure, I'll do it straightaway.'

'Oh and throw in Rob Cameron, Damien MacKenzie and Mark Simmons for good measure. Find out which shearers came onto Charona. But check that camera footage first.'

'Sure thing. Oh and, boss?'

'Yeah?'

'Andy rang and said to tell you thanks for the heads-up on the dates. He found a pattern.'

'Did he? That's great news! What was it?'

'All the attacks took place on a date that had the number four in it.'

'Well, good to know that one case is on the way to being solved.' He was pleased. If Andy had a breakthrough, it might show him how slow and methodical work got results. Even if the case was urgent like this one, slow and steady nearly always got the bad guys.

'Righto, Jack, I'll leave you to it. Make sure you stay in touch. Not sure when I'll be back.'

'I'll let you know as soon as I find something.'

'Good man.'

Chapter 31

The hospital was quiet except for the monitors that beeped around Fiona as she lay sleeping.

Carly sat in a chair with a blanket wrapped around her shoulders, her head drooping every time she fell asleep, before she'd wake with a jerk.

She wriggled in the chair to get comfortable, then decided it was a waste of time. Getting up, she went to the window and looked out over the main street. The sun was sinking and she could tell by the shimmer in the air that the dew had started to settle. It would be cold out there and Carly longed to go outside to clear her head. She hadn't left Fiona's side since she was brought into the hospital at eleven that morning.

A flock of galahs swooped and glided low between the buildings. Carly could imagine the sound of their screeches and the swish of their wings.

Two cars backed out of the local engineering business as it shut down for the night. In half an hour it would be dark, the glow of dusk sitting on the edge of the horizon. As she watched, the streetlights flickered on.

Outside the hospital, everything appeared normal. Life seemed to go on. The rest of the world didn't know she'd almost lost her daughter and grandchild today.

Thank goodness for Scott, she thought.

Sighing, she looked back at her sleeping daughter. Under the white sheets she looked so small and fragile. The IV lines were taped to the back of her hand and made resting seem uncomfortable.

A nurse popped her head in and surveyed the scene. Carly knew that everything looked much more peaceful than it had five hours ago. The nurse smiled briefly at Carly, then disappeared silently down the hall.

A few moments later there was another visitor.

'How are you?' Kim was standing in the doorway holding out a cup of coffee.

Carly went over to her and took it gratefully. 'Okay,' she answered with a warm smile.

'Can I get you anything else?'

She shook her head. 'I can't think of anything, thank you.'

Kim came into the room and looked down at Fiona. 'Well, she's given us all a big enough scare for the time being, don't you think?'

'I felt so helpless. It's not a nice feeling watching your own flesh and blood rushed into Emergency and knowing there isn't a skerrick you can do to help her,' Carly agreed, taking a sip of the coffee.

'She's very special, your daughter,' Kim said. 'She has so much courage and determination. That's hard to come by these days.'

Carly sat down again. 'I never saw her as a farmer, but she's proved me wrong in every way. She's stuck at it, even when things got so tough. I can't even tell you what I think about the person who has done this to her.'

Kim's beautiful face hardened. 'I've learned over time that there's no point in trying to explain human nature. Some people love to love and others love to hate. That's all there is to it.'

A gentle knock at the door sounded and both women looked around to see Jo holding a bunch of flowers.

'Jo, come in.' Carly motioned to her. 'How are you, love? Aren't they beautiful?'

Handing the flowers to Carly, Jo said, 'I've only just heard. How is she?'

'She's okay. For the moment.' Carly stopped, taking a breath as her throat suddenly tightened. 'Scott managed to stop the labour, but she won't be allowed out for a while. Her blood pressure was through the roof, but I don't suppose that was surprising.'

'What started it?'

'Extreme stress. Scott explained that it can bring on early labour. And she's been through that the whole time she's been pregnant. The ashes being stolen was just too much.'

'Why would anyone do this to her?' Jo cried, unable to hide her distress.

The noise caused Fiona to move and mumble softly. All three women rushed to her side, Carly and Kim reaching for her hands.

They watched, ready to talk to her, to comfort and reassure her, but Fiona rolled over and went back to sleep.

A cough sounded at the door. 'Hello?'

'Rob! How nice of you to come by,' Kim said quietly, going over to give him a hug. 'Do you know everyone?'

'Ah, you're the young man who put the locks on her doors. I really appreciate you doing that,' Carly said. 'I'm Carly, Fiona's mum.' She held out her hand. 'Thank you for everything you did for Fiona this morning. Kim said you were great.'

'It was nothing. How is she?'

Carly softly repeated the details she had given the others. 'She's a lucky girl because she'll be fine in the long run. Just needs quite a bit of rest and to remain in a calm, stress-free environment.'

'It will be a miracle if someone manages to make her relax,' Jo said with a wry smile. She focused on Rob. 'Did you find out anything about the sheep?'

'Yeah, I did. The post-mortem showed a trace-element poisoning. After Fee left in the ambulance today, I took samples of the water from the trough, but I'll be surprised if they uncover anything. The water refills every time the sheep drink from it. If there is anything found, it will be too diluted to prove there was ever a toxic amount in there.'

Hesitantly, Rob handed Carly a bunch of wildflowers. 'I found these growing in the paddock I was taking the samples from. I thought Fee might like a bit of Charona with her.'

Carly reached out and took them silently, so touched by his thoughtfulness that she was unable to verbalise it.

'That's a beautiful sentiment, Rob. Fee will love them when she wakes up,' Kim filled the gap. 'I'll find a vase in a little while.'

'Well, it's a regular party in here,' Dave said as he walked in. 'How's everyone holding up?'

The women hushed him.

'Sorry,' whispered Dave.

'We're fine, thanks,' Carly answered.

'Hello, you,' Kim said, going over to kiss him.

'Rob, got a sec?' Dave asked, motioning him outside.

ɞ

Out on the street, the two men leaned against the wall of the hospital.

'What did you find out?' Dave asked.

'Whoever has done this is extremely clever,' Rob answered, kicking at the pavement with his boot.

'Okay, explain to me what's happened.'

'Right, as I've already told you, they died from too much selenium. It's a trace element the body needs, but in high doses it's toxic. There's only one way to administer it and that's orally. But it comes in two different forms. One is in a slow-release capsule that can be placed down the sheep's throat so it sits in the stomach. It's very effective. Lasts for about two years. The other is a liquid that you can drench the animal with—again it goes down the throat, but it's a burst of it that only lasts a certain amount of time, then you have to redo it if the levels are low.

'The autopsy I performed on the last ewe to die, which was still alive when I arrived at the farm, didn't show a capsule in the stomach, therefore it had to have been given as a drench.

'Now, unless whoever did this mustered the paddock in the middle of the night and drenched forty ewes with an overdose, they would've had to have given it to the sheep in a natural form.'

'That's where the trough comes into it?'

'Yeah. Ewes that are milking get thirsty, the same way breastfeeding women do. They're drinking even when it's cold. It's the perfect way to knock off a few sheep, not the whole mob, because the trough . . .'

'Refills as soon as they start drinking, so it will dilute what's been put in there. And it will only be the first few who get a gutful,' Dave finished.

'Exactly.'

'Thanks, mate. When will you get your samples back?'

'Might take a week or so.'

'Let me know, okay? If you can hurry them up, that would be great.'

'I'll see what I can do.' Rob started across the car park to where his van was parked. 'Got any ideas?' he called over his shoulder.

'Not yet, but I will have,' Dave made it sound like a promise, and it was.

ꟹ

Rob sat in his car and looked over at the hospital. He felt a surge of affection for Fee. He'd known her, at a distance, for the five years he'd been stationed at Booleroo. What she'd been through in the last five months was beyond what anyone should have to bear.

But he knew better. Life always seems to throw what it wants at you—you don't get a say. If Rob had had one, he wouldn't have chosen to have cancer at ten, or lose his dad when he was only twelve, so soon after his own battle. If anyone could understand what Fiona was feeling—not what she was going through, because every experience was different—it was him.

He'd found it hard to see the big picture—why the cancer had struck him and why he would never have children because of it. Why he'd been deprived of a dad for most of his life.

So much time had passed since then, and he now understood that he'd had to go through those experiences to become the person he was today. He embraced what he'd been through.

Getting out his mobile phone, he sent Fiona a text. She'd get it when she was well enough.

You're stronger than anything you're afraid of. Take time to feel okay. We'll all still be here for you.

ᔕ

Carly rubbed her eyes and sat back down in the chair she had been dozing in before everyone had turned up. She shouldn't be tired, but the day had been so emotionally draining, she wanted to curl up and go to sleep.

'I'll sit here with her, while you go home and have a rest, Carly,' Jo offered.

'I know you would, Jo, thanks. But I don't want to leave her. I might lose her if I do.'

'You know I won't let that happen,' Scott said, his stethoscope in his hand, ready to check on Fiona.

'Yes, I do know that,' Carly said gratefully.

'But you need a rest, otherwise I'm going to have two patients to deal with.'

'How can I leave her?'

Scott raised his eyebrows. 'Do you really think I would suggest you have a sleep, in a bed, if I thought she was in any danger?'

Carly smiled and leaned her cheek against his arm. 'I'm sure you wouldn't.'

'Exactly. So let Jo sit here for a couple of hours while you have a shower and a sleep and begin to feel half human again. If there's any change, at least you'll be with the one person who is going to know first.'

'Is that right? And what makes you think I'm going to your place?' she said, trying to infuse some humour into the heavy atmosphere.

'I just do.' He winked at her, then leaned over and listened to Fiona's heartbeat before shifting the stethoscope to her stomach.

He looked at her chart and checked the drip going into her arm.

'She'll be a bit more awake tomorrow,' he said. 'Did you want me to ask the nurses to bring in a foldup bed for you when you come back?'

'That would be great,' Carly replied, getting up. 'Are you sure you'll be okay, Jo?'

Jo nodded, her hair falling around her face. 'I'll just sit and watch a bit of TV. If she wakes up, there's someone here, and if she doesn't, it won't matter.'

'Thank you.'

ᔕ

Jo waited until everyone had left the hospital before climbing onto the bed with Fiona. She put her arm over her stomach and snuggled against her body.

'I'm sorry,' she whispered.

The softly beeping monitor kept up its continuous noise, but there was no movement from Fiona.

Jo settled her open hand on her friend's stomach. 'How're you going in there, little one?' she asked. 'Don't you be coming out to meet us before you're supposed to. Arriving early is always a bit rude. Just like arriving late. On time is good.' She was rewarded with a tiny kick. Jo closed her eyes and smiled, then she grimaced.

Her shoulders were so sore and bruised. He'd tied her hands up over her head this time, to the bedhead. Not gently and with care as he'd done in the past, but tightly. After a while her shoulders had started to ache and pull and she'd asked him to undo her, but he hadn't.

Jo didn't think he'd even heard her. He'd been so intent on what he was doing; her voice hadn't filtered through to him.

About twenty minutes too late, he'd untied her. By then her arms were burning from being up for so long.

'What did you think you were doing?' she'd asked angrily.

She'd hated the lazy smile he'd given her. 'What I like.'

Chapter 32

'Could I please speak to Dave Burrows?' asked a female voice on the other end of the phone.

Jack adjusted the receiver and grabbed a pen, ready to write down a message. 'Sorry, he's out of the office at the moment. Can I help?'

'I don't know who you are.'

'Sorry, Jack Higgins. I work with Dave.'

'Are you a detective?'

'No, but I do a bit of the legwork and gather information for him.' He wondered where this was going. 'Can I have your name, please?'

There was a long silence and Jack speculated on whether she'd hung up. Then she said, 'Ros Willowby.'

'Okay, Ros, how can I help you?'

'I've got some information about Fiona Forrest that I think would be handy for you.'

Jack sat up straight. What he wouldn't do for some drum!

He'd just finished checking through Geoff's high school records and he hadn't found anything there. He was about to start on Fiona, then Leigh.

'I'd be happy to listen,' he offered.

'Well, see, now. The thing is, I'm hearing there've been some pretty nasty things happen to Fiona and I'd appreciate a little information in return.'

The light dawned. 'What paper do you work for?'

'Uh-uh!' With the tone she used, Jack could almost imagine her wagging her finger at him in a 'no-no' gesture. 'Don't hang up. You scratch my back and I'll scratch yours.'

'I can't do any deals. Give me your number and I'll have Dave call you.'

'Are you sure, Jack?' she purred. 'Wouldn't you like the notoriety of breaking a case? Especially one as emotional as this?'

Jack scratched his forehead nervously. Then his instincts kicked in. 'If you had good info, you'd be solving the crime yourself. Thanks for calling. Have a nice day.'

He waited a split second before taking the receiver away from his ear, in case she said something more.

'Hang on! Don't hang up.'

Jack nodded, pleased he'd read the situation correctly. 'I'm here.'

'Alright, I do have some information, but it doesn't involve Fiona Forrest. I'd like some information on her. Can you help me?'

'What does your intelligence revolve around?'

'A mine.'

'A mine? What sort of details do you have?'

'Nothing I'm going to give you. Unless you help me.' In the background, a dog started barking and Jack frowned, straining to pick up other noises he could identify. He could hear the hum of cars, then glanced at the number on the screen and realised it wasn't a mobile. Maybe she was calling from a public phone somewhere.

'Why do you want information on Fiona Forrest?'

'I'm not discussing that yet.'

'Give me your number and I'll call you back,' he hedged.

'Don't bother. I'll call you. When is Dave Burrows back in the office?'

'I'm not sure . . .' But he was talking to dead air.

Jack held the phone against his mouth, thinking hard. A mine? A mine . . . Ian Tonkin wanting to acquire land . . . But that was for a farming entity, not a mining one . . .

Opening his web browser, he googled 'mining in the mid-north of South Australia'. He quickly scanned down the page but nothing caught his attention.

'Mining magazines' was the next search. There were quite a few newsletters that seemed worth checking, so he flicked through the headlines. 'New case of Black Lung disease'.

'"Environmentally friendly" leaching agents contain cyanide'.

He raised his eyebrows at that one. 'Nice.'

'Rio Tinto to open new mine'. That piqued his curiosity, so he clicked on the link.

'Rio Tinto will resume . . .' Jack shut it down as quickly as he'd opened it. 'Resuming' wasn't what he was looking for. He thought he might be searching for a business that was opening a new mine here in the mid-north. He worried about whether he would find anything. Maybe there was nothing to be found. Did mining companies release that sort of information? It might be confidential until the land had been secured.

Googling BJL Holdings again, he tried to find out if they had any mining interests as well as agricultural ones, but as he'd told Dave previously, they seemed to fly under the radar.

Snatching up the phone, he rang Dave.

'I think I might have something—or a hunch at least.'

'Hit me with it. I'll take anything at this stage.'

He explained about the phone call. 'What if,' he said, 'what if a mining company, pretending to be BJL Holdings, wanted to buy Fiona's land? Then wanting to get her off the land would make sense.'

'That's a great hunch, Jack—brilliant, in fact, but I don't think it can be that.'

'Bugger.'

'I'll tell you why. You know how I've told you ninety-five per cent of murders are a crime of passion? Not love passion, but passion—fury, desire, anger, that type of thing?'

'Yeah.'

'A corporation that wants to buy land, no matter how badly, isn't going to take the ashes of somebody's loved one. Someone who knows Fiona is targeting her because they want her off the land, or . . .' His voice trailed off. When he came back on the line he sounded excited. 'Or they're trying to silence her because she knows something she shouldn't. They're exercising control over her.'

Jack could hear the tapping of Dave's fingers on the steering wheel. He grinned. That was a sure sign that he'd had an idea, or at least was thinking very deeply.

'I'm heading back to Booleroo. I want to talk to Fiona. But I'll be back in Barker tonight. Kim has already left to head home. If that woman rings again, see if you can set up a meeting with her.'

'Sure, no worries. I've finished checking through Geoff's background and I really can't find anything at all of interest there. And there was nothing on the SD card. A couple of birds flying by in the early morning and the usual cars—the ones that we know. I've checked all the numberplates Fiona gave us and there isn't a suspicious vehicle that I've seen. I'm about to start on Jo and Leigh.'

'But do any of them arrive at strange times? Just because they're numberplates we know, doesn't mean it's not who we're looking for.'

'Good point,' Jack said, scribbling a note on his pad. 'I'll check again, but nothing stands out.'

'Good-oh. I'll let you know what I find out from Fiona, if she's up to talking. Don't work too late. See you in the morning.'

Jack hung up with a short bark of laughter. He looked at his watch. It was already ten pm. 'Don't work too late,' he muttered, before bringing up the Instant Management System and typing in Leigh Bounter's name.

ɷ

The soft streetlight glow was too dim for Dave to see his way over to the hospital path, so he grabbed his torch and turned it on.

Flashing it around, he caught sight of Rob's ute. Briefly he wondered what he was doing back again.

The front-entrance door slid silently open to reveal the

darkened corridor of the hospital. The antiseptic smell hit Dave in the face and he wrinkled his nose. He hated hospitals. He realised how lucky he was not to be visiting Kim in one, then focused on seeing Fiona.

He found the nurses' station and asked if she was awake.

'She's been awake, but she's sleeping again. Rob's with her at the moment.'

Dave nodded. 'Can I go and sit with her for a while?'

'Sure, but don't put her under any stress. None at all,' the nurse instructed sternly.

'I won't.' He certainly hoped his question wouldn't do that.

Rob was sitting in the room with his back to the door, watching a late-night talk show.

'G'day again,' Dave said quietly as he entered the room.

Rob turned in surprise. 'Didn't think I'd see you again today.' His voice was low so he wouldn't wake Fiona.

'I could say the same thing about you.'

Rob shrugged. 'I sort of feel involved after being there this morning. I came back to check on her, and Jo needed a break. Carly hadn't come back, so I offered to sit with her until she did. I think we've started a tag team!'

'Have you talked to her?'

'Only briefly. She wasn't awake for long. I'm not sure if she's sedated or just sleeping because she doesn't want to face anything.'

'Our minds are powerful things,' Dave said.

'What's going on?' Fiona suddenly opened her eyes and looked blearily at both men.

Dave leaned forward. 'Hey there, nice to see you back with us.'

Fiona swallowed, blinked and licked her lips. 'Is there any water?' she croaked.

Rob got up and handed her a glass with a straw, keeping his hands around hers in case she dropped it.

'Thanks. Where's Meita?'

'I've got her in my kennels at the surgery,' Rob answered. 'She'll be well cared for until you're back on your feet. Don't worry about her at all.'

She cast him a grateful glance, before trying to pull herself into a sitting position. In the end, she relaxed onto her side, facing Dave.

'I remembered something last night,' she told him. 'I tried to find it, but I couldn't.'

Dave was immediately focused, listening intently to her faint voice.

'Charlie lent a gun to someone—I've only got vague recollections of it. Not sure if I overheard a phone call or something, but I know he lent a gun to someone. It'll be written in the notebooks in the office. I only went through one book last night, but there are five there.' The effort of talking seemed to exhaust her.

'Can I go out there and have a look at them?' Dave asked. Not that he thought it would fit the puzzle in any way, but at this point all intelligence was good intelligence.

Fiona nodded.

'Great, I'll call in on my way home. Where will I find a key?'

Fiona gave him a blank look. 'I don't know what happened about locking the house. But there's a key in Meita's kennel, right up the back in a plastic container.'

'No worries. Now, I need to ask you a question.'

She nodded again.

'Is someone blackmailing you to keep quiet about an important piece of information? Something that would help us find out who wants your land?'

Instantly Fiona said, 'No.'

Dave tried to work out if she'd reacted too quickly. She might have. 'Are you sure?' he persisted.

'No, nothing like that, Dave. I wouldn't put myself through it, I can promise you that.'

'Okay. You concentrate on getting better. Looks like you've got a good team behind you.' He nodded at Rob, got up and left.

ર

The next morning Dave pulled up at the police station and ran up the steps. Even with the little sleep he'd had he was jazzed.

Jack was snoring at his desk, but Dave didn't take any notice. 'Come on!' he banged on the desk to wake him up. 'Let's go. Get some coffee and wake up.'

Lifting his head groggily, Jack asked what he'd found.

'Nothing yet, but we will today. I can just feel it.'

He grabbed a pen and started to make notes and talk at the same time.

'Okay, we've got Ian Tokin wanting to buy land for BJL Holdings. My gut instinct is this is the key, but I can't work out how, because like I said to you yesterday, it's personal. This is a large company. Still, somehow it holds the main clue.'

'Hang on, let me make that coffee.'

'Be quick.' He continued to scribble and talk, but with his voice raised so Jack could hear him in the small kitchen next door.

'We've got a drone and a strange car hanging around Charona at night. Poisoned sheep, missing ashes, two dead men—and I'm not convinced it was accidental—a phone call giving us a hint about a mine. What did you find out last night?'

'Absolutely sweet fuck all. I can't link anyone to anyone.' Jack came back into the room, his eyes bloodshot. He rubbed his face, scratching at the overnight growth of stubble.

'We're missing something so obvious here, Jack. I promise you, it's staring us in the face. Call Ian Tonkin and ask who he is dealing with at BJL Holdings.'

'On it,' Jack said, before gulping his coffee.

Chapter 33

'I really need to know who you're dealing with at BJL Holdings,' Jack spoke sternly to Ian Tonkin.

'I don't think I'm at liberty to say,' he replied, his voice blurring as he expelled his breath heavily down the mobile phone line.

'If you don't answer the question, sir, I will get a warrant, and I'm sure your documentation will tell me what you're not.'

The heavy breathing continued and the silence lengthened.

'Leah Kent,' he finally relented.

'Thank you. Now, does she do the negotiating as well, or just sign the sale documents?' As he spoke he entered the woman's name into the IMS. She had a driving offence but that was all. He clicked on the *Persons* tab. This would give him information on every person she could be related to, criminally. There was no one.

They're bloody good at covering their tracks, Jack thought. *Unless we're wrong.*

'She does everything. I've dealt with her personally on the sale of all these farms.'

'And tell me, did she say up front that she wanted to buy Fiona Forrest's farm?'

'Not in those exact words,' Ian sounded unsure. 'I think she suggested that it would be a nice farm to get hold of.'

'Why do you think that would be, considering it hasn't got the rich black soils of the other type of farming land she's bought?'

'Mate, I don't know. What do you want me to do? Ring her and ask?'

'No, but I'd like you to give me her phone number.'

ᔕ

'I'd like to speak to Leah Kent, please.' Jack had the phone on speaker so Dave could hear the conversation.

'I'm sorry, she's in a meeting. Could I have her call you back?'

Jack looked at Dave for confirmation, but he shook his head. 'No, thanks, that's fine, I'll call back. When would be a good time?'

'If you'll hold for a moment, I'll check her calendar.' They listened to electronic chimes for a few seconds before the secretary came back on the line. 'If you could call back next Tuesday. She's out of the office for the next two days and won't be contactable.'

'Thank you for your help.' Jack punched savagely at the button. 'Damn!'

'Can't be helped, mate. We'll just keep trying to get hold of her. I reckon we should put together an application for a warrant so we can access her phone records. Can you start on that? If anything turns up on her that needs closer investigation, we'll go and see her personally.'

'Sure.'

'I'm going to finish reading these diaries of Charlie's to see what we get from them.'

The office fell silent as each man worked on his tasks. Dave was so engrossed in reading the entries that he didn't hear the phone ring, but he certainly felt the pen that Jack threw at him to get his attention.

'It's the woman who rang yesterday. Listen to the background noise. I'm sure she's not a journo—if she was there'd be chatter and phones ringing around her. I can only hear cars. There was a dog barking yesterday. And she's calling from a public phone—well, it's not a mobile anyway.'

Dave released the hold button. 'Burrows.'

'Ros Willowby,' she stated.

'Hello, Ms Willowby, or can I call you Ros? What can I do for you?'

She repeated everything Jack had told him about the call the previous day.

'I'm curious to know why Fiona Forrest interests you so much.' He let the question hang between them.

'Because I've been her.'

That made Dave sit up. *Because I've been her*, he repeated silently to himself. What the hell did that mean?

'Can you elaborate?'

There was a muffled sob down the line, then the line went dead.

Dave slammed it down in frustration. 'What the fuck is that supposed to mean?' he cursed. '"Because I've been her."'

Quickly, he summarised the facts for Jack.

'Okay, what's Fiona been? Pregnant, widow, farmer, suffering,' Jack threw the words out as quickly as they came to him.

'Search Ros Willowby's name in the IMS,' Dave instructed. 'That's if it's her real name. Try Roslyn or . . . What the hell is Ros short for?'

'Rose, Rosemary, Roseanne, Rosetta, Rosa, Rosalie . . . I could go on,' said Joan, coming in to drop some papers on Dave's desk.

'Damn!' Dave repeated. 'Anyway, anything hard is always worth it in the end. Let's go!'

'Nothing under Ros Willowby. Um . . .' Jack clicked at the keys on the keyboard, trying different combinations. 'Willowby, Willowby . . .'

'How are you spelling it?' Joan asked.

Jack began spelling it out for her. He hadn't finished before Joan started shaking her head.

'Try it like this.' She wrote it down and pushed the piece of paper across to Jack: Willoughby.

Dave was flicking through the pages of the diaries now, not reading, but scanning quickly.

This was a cryptic puzzle that Ros had put in front of them. She knew something really important. '"Because I've been her,"' he muttered.

He saw a notation dated six weeks prior to the accident with Eddie and stopped, flicking back.

Leant Leigh shotgun.

'"Because I've been her."'

'I'm going for a walk,' Dave snapped. 'Ring me.'

Jack didn't even look up. He was too busy trying different combinations of names.

Without realising it, Dave ended up at Kim's roadhouse. He'd walked over four kilometres to get there—but his head was a lot clearer than it had been before.

'Hey, sweetie.' Kim smiled at him from behind the counter, her face red.

He leaned across and kissed her. 'Been cooking chips?' he asked.

She patted her face. 'Is it that obvious?'

'Only to me. You look beautiful. I need a favour.'

'And here I was thinking you'd come to visit because you love me.'

'That, too. Can you get on Facebook and search something for me?'

'Sure, just let me put these chips in the warmer.'

A few minutes later she came out of the kitchen with two coffees, and her iPad under her arm. She opened the Facebook app and looked at him. 'What name?'

'Try Roslyn Willoughby.'

After a pause, she said, 'There're a few hits; do you know what she looks like?'

Dave rubbed his forehead. 'Is there one who lives in South Australia?'

Scrolling through, Kim shook her head. 'Not that I can see. There's one in Victoria and two in Queensland. Are you sure she lives in SA?'

That stopped Dave. 'Actually, there's no reason for her to be in South Australia,' he agreed. 'Can I have a look?'

Kim swung the iPad around and showed him how to open

each profile. 'But she could have shifted back here and not updated her "About Me" section,' said Kim. 'The information on Facebook isn't foolproof.'

'Good point.' He started to search through a couple of friends lists and didn't see any names that linked up to the ones they'd been talking about.

His phone rang. Looking at the screen, he saw it was Jack.

'What have you got?'

'I'm really not sure. I don't know how it links together, but there's a Roslin—it's spelled weird—Willoughby who was murdered earlier this year. She was a prostitute in Hindley Street and she was found in an alleyway. She'd been strangled.'

'Did they arrest anyone?'

'No. Not yet.'

'Who was her family? Did you pull the file?'

'I've just requested it.'

'Okay, good work, Jack. Just spell her name for me? And have you got her DOB there?'

Jack gave him the information and they both hung up.

'We're so close,' Dave muttered. 'I can feel it.'

'I spoke to Fiona today,' said Kim. 'She's much brighter.'

'Great,' Dave answered distractedly as he slowly typed Roslin's name into the Facebook search bar.

'You know, that Rob, he seems such a lovely bloke. I wonder if he's married.'

That got Dave's attention. He looked up. 'Now don't you go playing Cupid. That poor girl has so much on her plate; a romance shouldn't be on the cards.'

'Maybe not, but he's strong and stable. And gentle. I think that's exactly what Fiona needs. If it leads to something else, then . . .' She lifted her shoulders in a shrug and gave him a pouty smile.

'Her husband isn't cold in his grave!' Dave stared at her, astounded. 'She's going to have a baby!'

'Hey! I'm not saying anything other than he's lovely and she might appreciate a lovely friend about now.'

'You're incorrigible!' He pulled her close and kissed her, his lips lingering on hers. 'That's why I love you. Now go away, I have to look for something.' He tapped her affectionately on the bum as she walked back to the kitchen.

Turning his attention back to the screen, he looked at the profiles that had been brought up by his search.

He tapped on the first one and read the status. *Hanging for Brissy tonight, who's up for shots?*

He hit the return button and looked down the list of people there. The third one looked interesting—a girl with long black hair and dark, Gothic-looking makeup.

He noticed she hadn't written on her wall for a while, but other people had.

RIP, Ros. The first entry said.

Rossie, how'm I gonna cope without u? Miss u already xxx.

The next one made him sit back: *Rossie, my baby sister, how could this have happened? I'm devo with sadness, my love, my life. Fly with the angels.*

'Kim? How do I . . .'

'Huh?' She stuck her head back through the open doorway.

'I want to look at this girl. The one who wrote this. How do I do that?'

'Tap on her name. It should take you through to her page.'

He stabbed at it, wishing he could hear a click or something to make him know it had worked. As he watched and waited, the page finally opened.

She didn't have much on her wall either, but it said on the sidebar that her sister was Roslin Willoughby (dec). Dave's gut told him that it had to be this woman who had called.

Reading the page, he found a tab for 'About' so he clicked on that.

Checkout chick at Woolworths.

Likes movies.

Went to Salisbury Senior High school.

Chelsea Milton, thirty-two.

Because I've been her. What does that mean? He closed his eyes and thought.

ೞ

'Okay, I think I've found her,' Dave said without preamble. 'Do a search on Chelsea Milton. She's thirty-two and lives in Adelaide somewhere. I need to make a phone call.'

'Wait, how . . .' Jack looked at him, his mouth hanging open.

'Facebook.'

Getting out his notebook, he looked for Geoff's phone number and punched it into his phone.

After introducing himself, he asked Geoff the question that had been burning in his brain for the last few hours. 'Did you know anything about Charlie lending Leigh a gun?'

He answered slowly. 'Yeah, I reckon I do. I seem to remember it had something to do with him putting down a cow.' He paused. 'Like, you'd know, Leigh didn't have many guns, just the .22 for rabbits.'

'Okay, do you know when he gave it back?'

'Hell.'

Dave wanted to ask what, but he stayed silent.

'Reckon I heard a conversation on the back of the ute that night. Something about Leigh having brought a gun with him, so he could give it back to Charlie. Don't know if he was shooting with that gun or the shotgun Charlie had with him. Pretty sure he was shooting with that gun, too, 'cause Charlie had his big gun, the .303. I don't remember seeing a .22. Was there a .22 registered to Leigh?'

'There was.'

'Ah. Well, maybe I've got that wrong.'

Or maybe that was the decoy.

More questions burned in Dave's head. Why did Leigh borrow a gun when Eddie worked for him and he had guns?

Chapter 34

Jo came into the hospital room carrying a box of chocolates and two coffees. She moved slowly and it was clear that she was sore.

'Morning,' she said.

'Hello,' Fiona looked up, trying to work her mouth into a smile. It wasn't easy. She still didn't know who had Charlie's ashes, but she did know that her baby was safe. That was probably all that mattered at the moment. 'What are you doing here? I thought you'd be out in the paddocks working out how to kill insects!' She extended her arms. 'It's lovely to see you.'

Jo bent down to give her a hug, obviously stiff, despite her efforts to pretend otherwise.

'How are you feeling?' She put the chocolates on the table and sat on the edge of the bed, handed Fiona the takeaway cup and took a sip of her own.

'Exhausted. Drained, disappointed, sad. Empty. I don't know. All that.' She looked down and rubbed the edge of the sheet between two fingers.

'Where's your mum?'

'She's gone out to the farm to get me some clothes. Not sure why, none of them fit me. Guess I'd be better off buying some maternity ones now. Never thought I'd get to that stage. Even when I found out I was pregnant!' She watched her friend through tired eyes. 'What's up with you?'

Jo took another sip of coffee and avoided her stare.

'What?' The fear in Fiona's voice made Jo start.

She swallowed hard and then lifted her head. 'I've got something to tell you.'

Fiona froze.

Getting up to shut the door, she slowly took off her jumper and shirt, then turned around. Her back was covered in whip marks and bruises. She had rope burns on her wrists and there were finger marks on the skin of her upper arms.

Fiona couldn't say anything. She gasped and blinked, her eyes filling with tears.

'Oh my God, Jo, who did this to you? Will you tell me? Or at least promise me you won't go near him again.' Her voice was soft but intense.

'Leigh. It was Leigh.'

'Leigh? What?'

Jo gulped and put her shirt back on. 'I've been seeing him for about six months, hoping it was going to go somewhere. At first he was lovely, attentive and sweet. The way you see him in public. But, Fee, he has an awful side. It's almost like he has two personalities.' She touched her arm and pointed. 'When he first broached the subject of tying me up, I thought it would be a turn-on, you know?'

Fiona wanted to recoil, tell her she didn't see anything

arousing about it, but she kept her face neutral and listened.

'But it started to get more violent as time went on. And now this.' Tears started to stream down her face. 'And here you are, laid up in hospital and had all this appalling stuff happen to you and I'm crying over a few bruises.'

'Hey, hey, it doesn't matter. It's okay. We'll get this sorted.' Fiona reached out and tried to hug her friend, but Jo pulled away. 'Do you want to do anything about it? Report him?'

'I don't know. If I do, he might make things a lot worse for me. He did threaten that once. Said if I told anyone what he liked, he'd make sure that no one believed me. Look at him. He's the head of the community. Everyone loves him, respects him. He's the bloke you go to when you need help. And look how he's looked after you since Charlie died—always making sure you've had help when you needed it.'

'But if you've got the bruises . . . They take photos, he can't deny it.'

Jo let out a hard bark of laughter through her tears. 'Oh, Fee, I love you, but you are so naïve. Of course he can deny it. No one has seen him lay a finger on me. In fact, no one has seen him *with* me. It would only be my word against his. He'll make up some story about why I've got it in for him. He rejected my advances or something. That's the sort of bloke he actually is. Cold and calculating.' She sniffed and wiped her hand across her nose.

Fiona looked around for some tissues and handed them to her. 'Dave will help you, I'm sure,' she said softly. 'If that's what you want to do. How have you managed to keep this under wraps for so long? There are never any secrets in this town. Everyone knows everything about everyone.'

Jo shrugged. 'We were careful. I'd wait until after dark before I went to his place. He never came to mine. It's easier to hide things when you're on a farm than when you live in town.'

They were silent until the nurse walked in.

'Just need to check your obs, love,' she said, and wheeled the monitor over to Fiona. 'Finger?' She placed the clip on her finger to monitor the oxygen and strapped on the arm cuff. 'How's bub doing in there? Moving around a bit?'

'I think he's trying out for the Olympics,' Fiona said with a grimace. 'I never realised they moved so much.'

'Regular little Energizer bunnies,' the nurse said with a laugh.

Glancing over at Jo, Fiona asked, 'When is Scott due in?'

The nurse checked the watch hanging from her chest. 'I'd say in about fifteen minutes. He's usually here just before he has to open his surgery. He'll certainly be in to check on you. You gave us all a bit of a scare.'

'I gave myself one.'

The nurse looked down at her fondly. 'You're going to be fine.' She recorded the information. 'Anyway, you're all good. I'll let you get on with your visit.' She left the room, pushing the trolley in front of her.

'I want you to see Scott. To show him. At least then it's documented.'

'No!' Jo stood up and wrapped her arms around herself. 'No. I can't.'

'Jo, I'm not going to let you walk around being frightened of Leigh. Only bullies do this sort of shit to women. This is abuse. I'm sure it's loving in some people's eyes, but not mine, and you know it's not really. Please, please let Scott examine you.'

'Let Scott do what?' Scott asked as he entered the room.

Jo looked like a deer caught in the spotlight.

Scott narrowed his eyes. 'What's going on, ladies?' he asked in a firm tone.

'Please, Jo,' Fiona pleaded.

They waited and finally Jo raised the arm of her shirt and showed him her wrists.

'Okay, we'll get a room organised for you and you can tell me what happened,' Scott said, his face impassive. 'Wait there.' He turned and left quickly.

'Shit, shit, shit,' Jo muttered. 'What have I done?'

'The right thing,' Fiona said, trying to reassure her.

∽

Jack looked over at Dave with his mouth hanging open. 'Murdered. You think Eddie and Charlie were murdered? By who?'

'It's all circumstantial. But I think Leigh Bounter.'

Jack turned to examine the whiteboard. 'Leigh Bounter, Leigh Bounter.' He looked at his notes. 'Leigh Jake Bounter.' His head snapped up and he stared at Dave as the pieces began to fall into place. Loudly he said, 'Leigh Jake Bounter. Do you see it?' He stabbed at the whiteboard. Bounter Jake Leigh. BJL Holdings. That's what we've been missing. That's why it's personal.'

Dave stared at the board. 'Yeah,' he said slowly. 'Yeah!'

He jumped up and started writing on the board.

'Okay, Leigh uses Charlie's gun to somehow kill Eddie the night of the so-called accident. That in itself is going to be really hard to prove. And what's also going to be hard to prove, at this point, is the fact that he killed Charlie as well. I'm guessing he somehow got him into the car to make it look like suicide. Then he comforted Fiona, made sure she was where he wanted her, and started spreading rumours about the sale of the farm. He's the one who poisoned the sheep, stole the ashes. There's the personal aspect. But how does this company fit in? Why do they want to buy her land?'

'Now it goes back to what I was saying before. BJL Holdings wants to buy the land and on-sell it as soon as the mine starts sniffing around. He'll make a squillion on it.'

Dave nodded, pacing the floor. He turned and pointed a finger at Jack. 'But how did he know it was coming and why is Fiona's land so important? We've already established that it's good, but there's better land around.'

'He's the mayor. He'd know if there was a sniff of a mining company coming in, wouldn't he?'

'They keep those types of things under their hat until the land has been secured,' Dave answered. 'That's going to be the question—how did he know?' He rounded on Jack. 'Did you get that warrant organised for the phone numbers?'

'I've got it sitting here.' Jack tapped a piece of paper.

'Okay, you've got more to add to it. Let's see if we can find a link between this Leah Kent and Bounter. All we've got at the moment is a heap of hunches and a bit of circumstantial evidence. We're going to have to find more.'

ᔕ

When the phone rang in Barker Police Station, Joan picked it up, then practically ran into Dave's office.

'It's her. Ros Willoughby,' she said, breathless.

Dave shot up out of his seat. 'Trace that call. If you get a position, see if someone in Adelaide can swing by and pick her up,' he instructed Jack, who immediately grabbed the phone and called through to HQ to try to get a track.

'Ros, how are you?' Dave used his encouraging tone. 'I'm really pleased you've called back. How are you doing today?'

'Have you got anything for me on Fiona Forrest that I can put in my story?'

'Yeah, I do, but I'd really like to meet with you face-to-face, so I can give it to you. Can we meet?'

There was another silence. Dave took a chance.

'Chelsea, this is what you want, isn't it?' Dave lowered his voice. 'You want us to know what happened to your sister, don't you? We really want to help. Do you know something that will help us find your sister's killer?'

'I'm scared.'

'We can protect you. Tell me where you are and I'll send a car to pick you up.'

'No! He's too high up, he might be able to get someone to hurt me.'

'Chelsea, I promise, whoever it is, we won't let him hurt you. In fact, I'll come and get you myself. Where are you?'

The ticking of the clock seemed very loud while he waited for an answer.

'Hunter Street, in Salisbury,' she finally said.

'Chelsea, I'm going to give you my mobile phone number. Do you have a pen?' He indicated for Jack to get the car while he recited it. 'Can I have yours?'

In a hiccupping voice she gave her mobile number to him.

'We're coming to get you now.'

ග

Having bundled Chelsea safely into the car, Dave and Jack took her to HQ in Adelaide.

'My sister, she wasn't an angel, I know that. She lived around the place, always working the streets, then I finally convinced her to come home to Adelaide. I always said she could come and stay with me, that I'd look after her, but she wouldn't. She had a disability, you know? She was a bit simple, but she was beautiful. Men loved her.

'But one night, he picked her up. In a bar. I was there and I saw it happen. Sometimes I'd do that. Go to where she was working to make sure she was safe. I saw her go with him. And the next thing she was dead.

'I've searched for ages, trying to find him. I've hung out in bars and looked—I always knew I'd recognise him if I saw him again. His hands—they weren't the sort of hands you'd see on an office worker. They were thick and dry and on the night I saw him they had cuts on them.

'Then one night I found him. So I came on to him.' She hiccupped again. 'Oh, he was happy to have me. But he hurt me, too. I thought I was going to end up like my sister.'

With shaking hands, she wiped at her face. 'I decided that maybe it didn't matter. With Rossie gone, there wasn't much point in going on. I didn't have anyone left.'

'What did he do to you?' Dave asked.

'Tied me up, hit me. He's got a whole room full of stuff. Sadistic stuff.'

'Can you tell me when this was?'

'It was the fourth of April.'

Dave blinked. Fourth of April? Hang on, April was the fourth month. The fourth of the fourth . . . He looked over at Jack, who sat there impassively. He hadn't picked up on it.

'Do you want a coffee or something to eat, Chelsea?'

She shook her head.

'Why did you come to us? And what's Fiona got to do with it?'

'His phone rang while I was with him and I saw the name Albany Mason. I researched him and found out he was part of a mining company—Delany Mining. That's how I found out this bloke's name. Leigh Bounter. Albany Mason was talking to him about a mining venture and the names Charlie and Fiona Forrest were mentioned.'

Chapter 35

'It's not bloody circumstantial now,' Jack said, excitement in his voice. 'We've got a witness!'

'Not for anything to do with Fiona,' Dave cautioned. They drove back towards Barker, leaving Chelsea in the care of a kindly policewoman who would take her statement. 'Only for her sister and her. We need more—we need his foxhole to pin it on him properly. We know it's Leigh using the date-rape drugs and bashing women, but we need to bring it back to our investigation. Let the Adelaide boys deal with the other part of it, even though it's all linked.

'First things first, we need to get to his house and see if he's there.'

'Do we need backup?' Jack asked.

Dave looked out the window and watched the countryside flying by. He remembered Toe-cutter's threat and said, 'Let's get the STAR team up here. Just to be on the safe side.'

ᔕ

'His ute is in the shed and the engine is still warm,' Jack said as he put his hand on the bonnet. 'He's got to be here somewhere.'

They looked around the farmyard, then towards the house. In the distance, Dave could see a tractor spraying one paddock and a blip of white in another. He assumed Leigh's workmen were going about their daily business.

'Look.' Dave pointed to the front door, which was ajar. Getting out his gun, he knocked loudly on the door. It swung open further.

'Leigh? It's the police. Are you in there?'

No answer.

He motioned for Jack to go around the back, then crept into a small entry that led straight through to the kitchen. It was empty.

In his peripheral vision he realised there was a passage leading from the kitchen, further into the house. Keeping his back against the wall and his gun raised, he moved quietly towards it, all the while scanning his surrounds.

He saw a shadow pass by the window and froze, his senses on high alert, but breathed easily when he realised it was Jack's silhouette.

Stealthily, he advanced towards the middle of the house again. The silence was unnerving.

He pushed open the first door he came to, peering inside. Clinically clean and tidy. The bed covering even had hospital corners.

The next door revealed a sterile bathroom, but the following one opened onto what was obviously Leigh's bedroom.

At first glance, nothing stood out. Dave put gloves on and looked through the bedside table. Nothing.

Sliding open the cupboard door, he flicked on the lights and looked through the suits and work clothes. Something in the back caught his eye. Pushing through the clothes, he saw a pair of handcuffs hanging from a hook on the wall. Next to it, a coiled rope, nipple clamps and a blindfold. The gun cabinet Leigh had told him about was next to the 'toys'.

He got out his phone and snapped a few shots. As he was turning to go, he saw something silver glinting at the back of the pigeon holes. Dave pushed the jumpers out of the way and peered at it. He knew exactly what it was.

'Got you, you bastard,' he whispered as he snapped a picture of the urn in situ.

'Hey!' A voice from outside made Dave stop. 'Stop! Police.'

It was Jack. Dave, keeping low, moved to the window. Jack was running towards a shed.

Spinning around, Dave dashed into the passage and ran to the back door, where he could see Jack crouched next to the entrance to the shed, his gun drawn.

Dave bent low, his gun also drawn, and ran towards him.

'Bounter, you might as well give it up!' Jack yelled.

'Where?' Dave puffed as he arrived next to his colleague.

'Behind the tractor.' Jack pointed to a dark corner of the shed.

Looking around, Dave realised that if they used a pincer movement, they should be able to corner him.

He used hand signs to indicate his plan. Jack threw him the thumbs-up and nodded.

'It's Detective Dave Burrows, Bounter. Come out.'

Silence.

Dave moved towards the tractor.

'Bounter? This won't help you.'

A shower of dirt hit Dave's head and shoulders and he jumped, raising his gun towards the roof, where he could hear a squeaking noise. A rodent must have dislodged a willie wagtail's nest from a rafter. He turned his attention back to finding Bounter.

He glanced across at Jack to confirm he was in position. 'Now!'

Jack raced along one side of the tractor, yelling, 'Stop, Police!'

Dave did the same.

They met face to face at the bonnet.

'What?' Jack looked confused.

'Damn!'

They heard the scrabble of feet on gravel and looked around. Dave dropped to the ground and checked under the tractor. He saw boots heading for the shed door.

'He slid underneath and got out that way!' he yelled. 'Go, go, go!'

Jack slipped on the loose stones as he started to run after Leigh but Dave managed to get around him.

'Fuck!'

Squinting as he came out into the bright sunlight, he suddenly realised how exposed he was. He raised a hand to block out the sun and moved against the wall for cover, then looked around for Leigh.

On the verandah of the house.

Dave took off at a sprint, his instinct telling him Jack was behind him. 'House!' he called. 'Front!' He indicated that Jack should skirt around the shed and arrive at the front door.

Dave stopped abruptly on the front verandah, breathing heavily as he saw Leigh standing in the doorway, his gun raised.

'Nice of you boys to visit.' His eyes didn't stray from Dave's face. 'Where's your mate Jack?'

'Now, Leigh, is there any need for this?' Dave raised his hands in a conciliatory gesture. 'We've just got some questions for you.'

'Ah, I don't think there's any need for that, do you? After all, you wouldn't be here unless you knew what I'd done. Shall we just get it over with? Jack!' he called out loudly. 'Would you care to join us?'

Dave realised they were dealing with a psychopath and that he would have to be very careful.

'Get what over with? Did you want to tell me everything?'

Jack came slowly around the side of the house, his gun holstered.

'Nice to see you again, Jack. Why don't we continue this discussion inside?' Leigh directed them into the lounge before turning his attention back to Dave, his eyes narrowed. The gun didn't waver. 'Think you can take me in? I don't think so. But,' he continued in a conversational tone, 'I'll tell you about Charlie. I felt bad about Charlie. And Fee's a sweet girl, if boring. She probably deserves to know.'

'Go ahead,' Dave said. 'I'll have to caution you though.' Watching Leigh closely, he tried to work out how they could disarm him. He hoped that Jack was doing the same. He started reciting the police caution while Leigh stood there impassively.

'Did you want to sit down?' Dave asked after he'd finished. 'Your arms will get sore holding up the gun. In fact, I'd be happy to take it from you.'

Leigh smirked but didn't change his stance.

'I wanted to make millions, you see,' he started. 'My mate Albany Mason was in mining and he came to me. Said they'd found a deposit of copper underneath Charona and he wanted me to get it for him. I said I would. At any cost, he told me.

'Charlie wouldn't sell. I asked and asked, but he just wouldn't. Shame, really. I always felt a connection with Charlie. Neither of us had any parents—mine died and his—well, his just abandoned him. We were two men alone in the world. Then Fiona came along and I was still alone and he wasn't.' Leigh sighed. 'Of course, he was good to me when I was hurt,' he acknowledged. 'So I really didn't want to kill him. Then when all of this happened, I saw a way to make it happen.'

'You killed him?' Dave asked.

'And made it look like suicide. He'd asked me to go down for a drink that evening. He wanted to talk, ask some questions. He'd picked up on this missing gun, you see. We had a couple of drinks, I slipped him a pill and the rest, as they say, is history. Funnily enough, he fought me a little bit, even after I drugged him, which was surprising. But he didn't fight enough for me to stop. Got a few cuts and scratches on his hands. I was amazed no one ever mentioned it.

'You see, I'd had to stop him from topping himself once before.

'About three weeks earlier, I'd turned up at the shed just after he'd thrown a rope over the rafter. I talked him down and convinced him to see a counsellor. It didn't work. He was still depressed.

'In the end I'm sure Charlie would have been glad I did what I did. He was in pain and by the time I'd finished he wasn't.'

'Interesting you should bring up that missing gun,' Dave

commented, still holding eye contact with Leigh. 'The investigation shows we're missing a gun. A .22. Do you know anything about it?'

'Charlie's gun. I do. I dumped it. I took it that night when I ran to get help. But you don't need to know where I dumped it. There's a history to that gun and it's safe where it is.' Leigh raised his gun, which had begun to dip. He swung it between the two men. Jack took a step backwards.

'So you're telling me this missing .22 isn't anything to do with this case?'

'You are smart. I can see why they made you a detective. Unlike that idiot who turned up on the night.' He shook his head slightly. 'No, nothing to do with this. I needed a clean gun, borrowed Charlie's with every intention of returning it, but all this happened. Thought it was easier to get rid of it than it turn up while you lot were asking questions.'

'Want to tell me what it was used in?'

Leigh snorted. 'Not really.'

'He wasn't wearing any shoes, Leigh,' Dave said, changing tack quickly. He hoped it might unsettle Leigh and get him to admit to something else.

'No.' Leigh mused. 'I decided to take them. I like mementoes, you see. I have quite a collection.

'It was all going well until you turned up and interfered.' Leigh levelled the gun at Dave's head. 'Then I thought I'd be able to scare Fiona into selling. Turned out she wasn't as pliable as she seemed, which was unfortunate, too. I certainly hadn't planned on hurting her too much, what with the baby and all. I'd commandeered Jo to help me get at Fiona, but she wasn't much use either. It's all been so very disappointing.'

'So what are you going to do now?' Dave asked. 'We're here. You've just admitted to murder. And we've got a few other little things on you. Maybe you should tell us everything. Like, what is so significant about the number four?'

Leigh blinked. 'Oh, you've put that together, have you? Very clever. It started a long time ago.

'There was a little boy with a dream of becoming an AFL player. He had a coach he loved and trusted, and this coach promised, if this young boy would "cooperate", he would help him make it to the highest level.' Leigh's eyes didn't leave Dave's. 'But then he broke his promise by moving away and leaving the boy feeling isolated, filthy and powerless. I never wanted to feel like that again. So, the fourth of April was when I became mayor, someone everyone looked up to. I felt powerful for the first time. And that's the day I like to celebrate.'

'You celebrate by raping and beating women?' Jack asked, the disgust plain in his voice.

'Don't be so quick to judge, mate. Give it a go, you might find you like it. But it's not just that.' He frowned at Jack. 'It's about authority and supremacy. Reminding myself that's exactly what I am—*power*.' The muscles in his arms clenched as he spoke.

'I don't quite understand how Eddie came into this.' Dave tried to get the conversation back on track.

'He caught me out. Knew about my secret life. Came to me and told me he knew about my dirty little secret. Blackmailed me to keep me quiet. That was okay for a while—I supplied him with all the prostitutes he wanted, but he began to want more.

'So I waited. The opportunity came up that night.' He shrugged. 'When the ute started to tip, I was holding Charlie's shotgun. I aimed and shot Eddie. And in all the confusion, I managed to get Charlie's hands back on the gun so that his prints were on it. Genius, really, wouldn't you say?'

'So the dead sheep, all the little things that have been going wrong at Charona?'

'Oh yes, all me.' Leigh stopped. 'You're very good,' he said to Dave. 'I didn't plan on telling you all that. How did you manage to get me to?'

'I think you wanted to brag,' Dave answered.

There was a noise outside and Leigh turned.

Dave launched himself at Leigh as the STAR team barged into the room, yelling, 'Get down, get down, get down! Police! Get down!'

'Get the fuck off me,' Leigh tried to yell, but his voice was muffled as Dave shoved his head onto the floor and yanked his hands behind his back.

'I don't think so,' he leaned over and whispered in his ear. 'Maybe you'll find out what it's like to be the one who's hurt. I won't be responsible for the blokes who take you to Adelaide and lock you up.' He clicked the handcuffs together and stood up, yanking Leigh to his feet.

'Great job, Dave.' Steve walked in, his bulletproof vest on the outside of his uniform. 'You, too, Jack.'

'Thank you, sir,' Jack replied as he re-holstered his gun.

'We got it all on tape. Bloody good thing you cautioned him, otherwise none of it would be admissible. And, Dave, you did it without being a one-man band.' He clapped Dave on the shoulder and walked out.

Epilogue

'That's it, one more push,' Scott said.

Fiona, sweaty and tired, wanted to hit him. 'I can't,' she said through gritted teeth.

Carly grabbed hold of her hand. 'You can, you've got this, just one more.'

'Oh, look at that, here he comes, here he comes.' There was true emotion in Scott's voice as the baby slipped into his hands. 'It's the boy you've been waiting for, Fee.' He placed him straight on her stomach and smiled at Carly, who had tears rolling down her cheeks.

'Hello, Hamish,' Fiona whispered. 'I've been waiting for you.'

The little face screwed up and the cry of a newborn filled the air. After a few moments, he quietened and nestled into Fiona's chest. She ran her finger down his face and examined his features, looking for Charlie. He was there in her baby's eyes. She watched as Hamish opened his mouth and gave another loud scream. 'Shh, shh,' she whispered.

As quickly as he'd started, he stopped screaming and a familiar expression passed over his face.

Goosebumps rose all over Fiona as she leaned closer to him. That was Charlie's expression when he told her he loved her.

'Can we tell the others?' Carly whispered, running her hand over her new grandson's head.

'Yes. Yes, please.'

'Here, I'll get him wrapped up and then you can feed him,' Scott said in a soft tone.

'It's a boy!' Carly yelled from the doorway.

Fiona laughed as she heard the cheer go up.

Jo and Kim would be out there, along with all of Carly's friends. And Rob. Rob would be there, too.

Kind and gentle Rob, who had been at her side constantly since that day. He was a good friend. A friend who might become something more when the time was right.

But at this moment in time, it was her and Hamish, her and her little Charlie. And together they would face everything that life threw their way.

Acknowledgements

My clan—the best one in the world! Cal and Aaron, Em and Pete, Heather, Jan and Pete, Robyn, Tiffany, Scottish.

Rochelle and Hayden—my everythings.

Mum and Dad, Nicholas and Susan and the rest of my family. Always at the end of the phone, still loving me despite the challenges I bring!

Dave Byrne. Book 8! Thank you so much for your wisdom and advice, your knowledge and help.

My agent, Gaby Naher. Your knowledge, support and kindness is so much appreciated. My publisher, Louise Thurtell—again, thanks for these wonderful opportunities and support (and patience!). My editors, Sarah Baker and Alex Nahlous, thanks so much for your help in whipping a grotty manuscript into a shiny piece of work!

All you wonderful readers! Thank you for being alongside me as I keep writing. Without you guys, I wouldn't be where I am.

Please feel free to get in contact. I love hearing from you all and I do my best to respond to everyone!

Facebook: https://www.facebook.com/FleurMcDonaldAuthor/?ref=bookmarks
Twitter: @fleurmcdonald
Website: www.fleurmcdonald.com